The Raptor Zone

On the foggy coast of Oregon, where the precipitous mountains drop into the Pacific, the tiny community of Sundown perches between a wild ocean and a wilder hinterland. In this seeming wilderness live a group of cultured people, who have evolved an urbane lifestyle that encompasses both gourmet food and a passion for the natural world. Not for them the worry over violence and substance abuse suffered by city dwellers. The only crime in Sundown is that of exploitation, as the local logging industry destroys the habitat of the spotted owl.

Living in this civilised enclave are several authors, most notably Lois Keller, the successful crime writer and, more regrettably her husband Andy, a rather less successful screenwriter. And there is Boligard Sykes, the Hemingway lookalike who hasn't published anything – yet – and the shadowy Gideon d'Eath, who is reputedly kind and ordinary but who produces weird adult comics that leave his sole distributor laughing all the way to the bank.

Then Andy Keller introduces his 'assistant' Gayleen, a girl with the looks of a Mexican beauty queen whose doll-like face conceals a personality of an altogether different nature. An introduction which demonstrates superbly Keller's ability to put the cat among the pigeons. And his perverse sense of humour makes him attach a bumper sticker to his wife's car: I LOVE SPOTTED OWLS. ROASTED.

When Miss Pink arrives in Sundown on the heels of Andy and Gayleen she finds a volatile situation, barely contained by good manners. And some people have decided to take matters into their own hands. Raptors have begun to operate in the canyons between Cape Deception and Fin Whale Head, and not all of them are feathered.

by the same author

LADY WITH A COOL EYE
DEVIANT DEATH
THE CORPSE ROAD
MISS PINK AT THE EDGE OF THE WORLD
HARD OPTION
OVER THE SEA TO DEATH
A SHORT TIME TO LIVE
PERSONS UNKNOWN
THE BUCKSKIN GIRL
DIE LIKE A DOG
LAST CHANCE COUNTRY
GRIZZLY TRAIL
SNARE
THE STONE HAWK
RAGE

non-fiction

SPACE BELOW MY FEET
TWO STAR RED
ON MY HOME GROUND
SURVIVAL COUNT
HARD ROAD WEST
THE STORM SEEKERS

The Raptor Zone
Gwen Moffat

MACMILLAN
LONDON

First published in 1990 by
MACMILLAN LONDON LIMITED
4 Little Essex Street London WC2R 3LF
and Basingstoke

Associated companies in Auckland, Delhi, Dublin, Gaborone, Hamburg,
Harare, Hong Kong, Johannesburg, Kuala Lumpur, Lagos, Manzini,
Melbourne, Mexico City, Nairobi, New York, Singapore and Tokyo

ISBN 0-333-54580-X

A CIP catalogue record for this book is available from the British Library

Typeset by Macmillan Production Limited

Printed and bound in Great Britain by Billing and Sons Ltd, Worcester

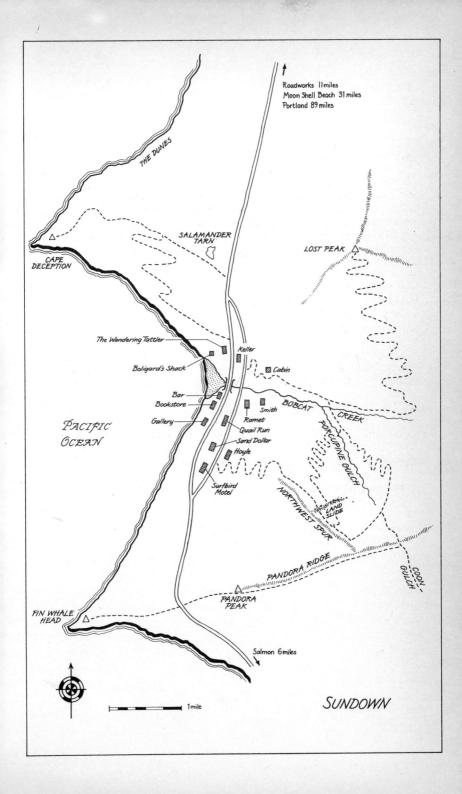

Roadworks 11 miles
Moon Shell Beach 31 miles
Portland 89 miles

THE DUNES

SALAMANDER
TARN

LOST PEAK

CAPE
DECEPTION

The Wandering Tattler

Keller

Boligard's Shack

Cabin

Bar

BOBCAT   CREEK

Bookstore

Smith

Gallery

Ramet

PACIFIC
OCEAN

Quail Run

PORCUPINE GULCH

Sand Dollar

Hoyle

LAND
SLIDE

Surfbird
Motel

NORTHWEST SPUR

PANDORA RIDGE

COON
GULCH

FIN WHALE
HEAD

PANDORA
PEAK

Salmon 6 miles

1 mile

SUNDOWN

Chapter 1

Two people sat on Cape Deception in the fog. 'I'm frightened,' the woman said. 'I don't know where I am.'

'Fog never bothered you before.'

'That's not what I meant.'

The man made no immediate response and they lapsed into a silence that held an element of tension. After a time he said quietly and without heat, 'You should leave him.'

'Be reasonable, Chester; it's my home. My father built it.'

'Then make him go.'

'How?'

'He's away now; don't take him back.'

'What do I do: change the locks? Don't crowd me, man.'

'You raised the subject.'

He glanced sideways. Her face, which he thought was beautiful, appeared relaxed in profile but when she turned towards him her eyes were filled with tears.

'This has to be an early menopause,' she said helplessly. 'These last few days I've felt drained, bereft, as if someone died. I even cry when I'm alone.'

'Oh no, not you!' He was shocked.

She shrugged and turned back to the white space below the headland, then she gasped. 'Oh, look! Look, Chester!'

The fog had swayed and parted like a cosmic curtain, revealing a stretch of shadowed water across which a line of pelicans flapped with lazy wingbeats.

'About time too,' said Chester Hoyle, relieved at the diversion. 'It's unusual for the fog to persist so long in August. The sun should burn it off by mid-morning.'

'We've affected the whole global weather system: drought

7

in Africa, floods in India, destruction of the rain forest, the greenhouse syndrome, earthquakes.'

'Not earthquakes.' He smiled indulgently. 'We're not responsible for earthquakes.'

'How do you know that?' Her face softened, her eyes dwelt on his gentle mouth. 'Of course not,' she conceded. 'I love you, Chester; you keep my feet on the ground.' She paused. 'You keep me sane,' she added.

He looked down at the water and his mouth twitched as if at a spasm of pain. The fog was melting away like steam. She glanced southward at the rollers creaming past the sea stacks to break and spread along the pale sand. A few figures were down there in the cove below the village and they could hear faint calls. A dog barked. From the cliffs under their perch the sea lions could be heard: females crying dolefully, the males growling.

'I'd hate to be a sea lion,' she mused. 'Imagine: swimming in deep water, and knowing the great whites are about. How could you live like that: a hungry carnivore lurking out there on the fringe of your world?'

'There must be a hundred times as many people killed on this highway as are taken by sharks.'

'Sharks on the highway?'

They giggled and leaned towards each other. They might have been husband and wife, not long married; they were both in middle-age, although separated by a decade, both spare, neither of them particularly striking but nor were they nondescript in appearance. Lois Keller was forty today, a woman of average height but muscular. She had short curling hair: chestnut-brown but not shaped nor tinted. She wore no make-up. Her features were regular, the mouth wide and full, the teeth uncapped, the eyes expressive under dark brows. She wore shabby hiking boots, faded jeans and a T-shirt with pumas and the exhortation to Protect California Mountain Lions. She looked like – and was – a backwoods traveller, a person who, if she did get lost, would very soon find her way again.

Chester Hoyle was lean and fit for his age. He wore spectacles, he looked bookish, clever, concerned. He was concerned with her; she was concerned with herself, at least, with her family problems. Chester was careful about his appearance: he wore a grey chamois shirt, laundered Levis, oiled boots. Lois didn't bother about appearances except where the environment was concerned.

'This is a dreadful coast,' she said now, observing intermittent splashes of surf where no rock was visible. 'Look at that submerged reef! And if you were in a boat trying to get out from shore into deep water you'd run on to the Spine.'

They considered the rocks they called the Devil's Spine some two miles offshore. 'It's all right if you don't sail,' he pointed out. 'It's great scenically. You love the Oregon coast.'

'It's like the sharks: fascinating to see the fin cruising above the surface but no way would you want to be out there.'

He frowned. 'You're in a very negative mood this afternoon. Did something happen you haven't told me about? Has he called?'

'No, he didn't phone. And he hasn't written. I wouldn't expect him to. He'll come back when he's tired of whoever it is, whatever it was, took him to the city. I think I've got the autumnal disease or condition or whatever. I'm always like this at the end of summer, and I guess I'm becoming more perceptive with age. Everything's dying.'

'Oh, come on! Look around you— '

'Most of the birds have left. The young have flown, the swallows will soon be gone, the vine maple's turning red— '

'There are buds; there are catkins on the alders.'

'So – you talked me out of it – "and if winter comes, can spring be far behind?" Who said that? Problem: how do we get through the winter?'

'The same as every other winter, except that this one you've got me besides your other friends. And that reminds me, shouldn't we be getting back?'

'What would I do without you?'

They stood up, she gracefully, he with the incipient stiffness of his years. They didn't start back immediately but stood for a moment surveying the ocean with keen eyes.

'No whales,' she said. 'Too early for the greys but there's always the chance of a blue whale.' Her gaze passed over the long southern cliffs, timbered to their wild summits. Inland conifers friezed the spiky skyline unevenly and draped the canyons, hiding contours, crags and waterfalls: a wall of green fur that was bright in the sun but with folded shadows in the depths. At the foot of this bastion of the coastal range the roofs of the village showed above thick brush, appearing, from their tiny scale, vulnerable to all the elements: fire and water, earth and air. Rain brought landslides, drought and lightning produced forest fires; with the winter came the gales. Permanency here lay in the ocean and the forest, and both were dangerous.

'Yes,' Lois Keller said quietly, as they strolled across the scorched grass, 'this place suits me.'

'You're a chameleon. You can be happy anywhere, providing the circumstances are congenial.'

'That's the point.' She stopped and stared at him. 'I never told you this but you remember the little girl went missing recently from the campground on the Rogue River?'

'Of course I do.'

'Before he left this time he told me to keep quiet that he was in San Francisco that weekend.'

'So?' His tone was loaded.

'So on that Monday he came up the coast and he spent Monday night in the same campground, the one the child was at, the night she disappeared.'

'Are you telling me— ' He couldn't go on but shook his head savagely.

Her shoulders slumped. 'I'm telling you what he told me, Chester; he was at that camp the night the kid was taken and he told me to keep quiet about it. If anyone asked I was to say he was in Portland that weekend: the opposite direction.'

'He's crazy.' They resumed walking, Chester a pace ahead, his back stiff. After a few steps he swung round on her. 'He's trying it on: pushing it, riling you, tormenting. It's his form of humour; it's obscene.'

'Bad taste,' she said weakly. 'All the same— '

'All the same, what?' All gentleness had gone and he was so furious that he didn't realise she was getting the fall-out from his anger.

'Grace thinks like you, and she says he was nowhere near the Rogue River, except possibly to stay in a motel at Gold Beach that night. She says that doesn't mean he's not attracted by the kind of situation. And he is attracted or he'd never have appropriated the crime, as it were.' He was silent. She went on defiantly, 'Well, Grace left home; she's safe.' Her hand went to her mouth as if to repudiate that but he was still silent and this

10

seemed to provoke her. 'Small thanks to me, you think? Hell, Chester, you don't know what a man's nature is when you marry him. It's not like us; we've known each other for over a year, we have the same interests, we discuss things – and there's no sex to get in the way' – he flinched at this but, watching the trail, she missed the movement – 'that was the problem with Andy and me. It was a long time since Grace's father died and – well, OK, I made a mistake when I married Andy, but let's be thankful for small mercies: we didn't have any children. And Grace took no harm.'

'She hates him.'

'No, she's – contemptuous.'

'Lois!' They were at the first bend in the trail and they halted on the elbow. 'How can you live with a guy who's so neurotic, so' – he had to search for the words – 'so rabidly exhibitionist he's compelled to – demonstrate to his own wife that he's a pervert and a killer, a man who makes passes – who tries to seduce his own step-daughter— '

'No, no!' Lois laughed.

'Don't *laugh*!'

She shook her head. 'I have to, what else can I do? He didn't try to seduce Grace; he said she tried to seduce him.'

'That's worse. That's sick. So why— '

'That's why, Chester.' She was suddenly serious.

'You're sorry for him.' All the heat was gone. They had both quietened. It was an old and familiar argument and now they fell into a kind of shorthand where there was no necessity to fill the gaps.

'Other women have loved rogues,' she said.

'He knows you backwards.'

'You have a strong sense of responsibility too.'

'There are limits.'

'Grace is all right.'

'You put him first.'

'She stands on her own feet. He can't.'

'That's over the top, my dear.'

She didn't respond, and the trail, narrowing as it zigzagged down from the back of the headland, forced them into silence. She led now, he followed, and both watched their footing.

From here there was no view but the great firs were so

11

widely spaced that vegetation covered the slopes, chequered by light and soaking wet from the fog. Drops of moisture flashed with tiny rainbows, scarlet gilia hung frail lamps against the gloom, a woodpecker hammered a rotten stump. The walkers were oblivious, lost in thought.

A hundred feet above the cove they emerged from the trees to ground which, although brushy, allowed them glimpses of the village. Close below them, at the foot of a crumbling brown cliff, the sea stacks, white with guano, rose ragged but majestic from water that was navy above rock, jade above the sand. The tide was full and most of the visitors had left rather than sit on weedy rocks which were all that remained at high water. For this reason Sundown was not a popular resort for family holidays; in fact it was not a resort at all, merely a scatter of cottages on the coast highway.

The village had grown by chance. There had been a small farm here – no one could call it a ranch when the grazing amounted to no more than a few acres cleared from the brush – and in the twenties the owner had sold the land in lots. People built cottages and a few wealthy latecomers cleared trees and carved ledges out of the mountain to build places so secluded that they showed only a gleam of glass here and there, or a trail of smoke from a chimney. No one farmed in Sundown any more and no one was a native but then, as the residents would point out, who *was* native in these United States? Even the Indians came from Asia by way of the Bering land bridge. People in Sundown were touchy, feeling that outsiders might regard them as a community of retired folk, of middle-aged drifters, second-rate artists and others out to make a fast buck from the summer visitors.

'Not much money about,' Lois observed now, looking over the blackberry bushes to the cove. 'Jason's closed the store. There he is: sitting on a log at the mouth of the creek. What d'you think he's reading? Louis l'Amour, I'll be bound. He should be running to Fin Whale Head; he's getting very fat.'

'It can't be helped when Mabel Sykes stuffs her menfolk like steers in a feed-lot, but he's a clever boy; you're the one says he has a good brain.'

'That boy is thirty-five if he's a day. He's clever but he's got no application. And he doesn't care. He's got no ambition, he's not the slightest bit vain; look at him now: no shirt on. How can anyone expose all that flab to the public?'

'He's conditioned. He probably thinks we're anorexic.'

'Boligard's not fat. He's paunchy just.'

'Boligard doesn't count. Jason's Momma's boy.'

Lois looked at him sharply. 'You're getting very perceptive. Perception's my department.'

'There are times when I wonder if you are all that perceptive.' She gaped at him. He went on easily, 'It stands out a mile; they don't laugh at him but they do indulge him, and what can you expect? The cap, the trimmed white beard, the pale, piercing eyes: you see them all down the coast and round the Gulf: Hemingway lookalikes. If Boligard had the money he'd be out there big game fishing – if he had the skill. Because Hemingway did.'

'Did Boligard upset you?'

'Not particularly.'

They dawdled, eating the luscious blackberries. Ahead of them the dust on the trail turned to mud where a spring trickled down the slope. She laid a hand on his arm and his eyes widened as her fingers squeezed.

'A garter,' she whispered.

Coiled in the luminous shade of some showy asters was a small snake.

'It shouldn't be here,' she said loudly, and the snake lifted its head, tasting the air.

'Shouldn't be here?' he repeated, bewildered.

'It's obvious to anyone coming down the trail.' The garter started to weave backwards carefully, crimson spots on its sides catching points of sunlight. 'Beautiful,' she said, peering close. 'Each spot is only four or five scales.'

'Watch it,' he warned as the snake feinted delicately. 'Maybe they bite.'

'Pugnacious little beast.' She straightened. 'They bite. I saw one catch a lizard: like a cat pouncing on a chipmunk. This one can't go until we back off; it needs to turn round.'

They moved away and the garter slid like water into the undergrowth. 'Now he's safe,' Lois said with a small sigh. 'Safe from men who think every snake is the devil incarnate.'

He made to speak and checked.

'What?' she asked.

13

'I was going to say: you do get involved.'

'Someone has to be involved. They can't look after themselves; they have no defence against people. Man is a *vicious* predator, nothing else is. A fox gets in a chicken run, he don't kill for fun; he kills out of panic. Nothing else kills for *fun*.' She spat it out. 'Sport,' she said. 'Recreation. Re-creation. You re-create yourself by killing? I was reading about some hit-man in Texas – Alabama, one of those places. The book – quite well written actually – said this guy's recreation was killing rattlesnakes.'

He sighed and looked away.

She regarded the back of his head, a well-shaped head with thinning grey hair. 'That's your strength,' she said thoughtfully. 'You can ignore it.'

'Not exactly, but it tears you apart: compassion, empathy; it takes all your energy.' He turned and held her eye. 'Did it never occur to you that you have the same attitude towards your husband that you might have for a rattlesnake?'

'I have?' She was startled, then she gave a snort of amusement. 'He's not dangerous. You got the wrong simile. He's more like an abandoned dog – no, a stray cat: amoral, no feelings, but in need of a home, you know?'

'Cats don't have malice.'

'No, but they get bored, they walk out, leave you for weeks at a time.' She smiled wryly. 'Cats don't have loyalty either.'

They had resumed their slow progress down the trail but now she paused, studying the dust. 'Grace was here. That's right, she said she'd make a blackberry fool for dessert.'

'That's Grace's shoe?'

'Of course. A Vasque Clarion, size seven. I gave them to her for her birthday, remember? And she turns her right toe in slightly since she broke her leg skiing.'

'You're an amazing woman.'

'Oh, come on, Chester! You can tell the difference between warblers' songs.'

'Not all of them – why, look who's here. Hi, Miriam!'

A schnauzer came trotting round a bend followed by a brown woman in shorts and T-shirt and running shoes. She was a tiny woman and although her hair was black, virtually jet-black, her face was scored with the tiny lines that old women collect when they have lived a long time in a hot dry country. She

14

was, in fact, in her mid-seventies, stringy as a bean but with powerful legs. Now she raised an inquiring eyebrow and eyed them suspiciously.

'I take it Grace is making all the preparations for the party.'

'Why not?' Lois was cool. 'It's my party.'

'Oh, sure. Many happy returns. How does it feel?'

'It feels good. It's only men who die a little death at forty – present company excepted.'

'Is that so?' Miriam Ramet turned to Chester. 'You never minded being forty?'

'I never minded being anything. Serenity comes with age.'

'You could have fooled me. Did Andy remember your birthday, Lois?'

'Probably. We've been out since noon.'

'What did you say he was doing now? My memory! It has to be Alzheimer's.'

'A screenplay,' Lois told her. 'Based on *Fool's Gold*. I always wanted a movie made out of it.'

'Oh, of all your books, dear. So he's in Hollywood?'

'He could be anywhere, chasing producers, directors, you name it. You know Andy.'

'We all do,' Miriam said sweetly, and started a careful jog up the easy gradient of the trail.

'Miaou,' Lois murmured as they continued downhill. 'What do you think it was like: married to Miriam?'

'For my money, fine, if you go for the type. She's a good cook and when she accepts a man as her superior— '

'As her *what*? Miriam?'

' —then she'd be a dutiful wife: housewife, hostess, perhaps even companion.'

'You think she had that kind of relationship with her husband?'

'Definitely. That's why she's so bossy now, and catty. Bossy because she's getting her own back for decades of being in a subordinate position, and catty because she envies you. You have a beautiful and successful daughter, you have youth yourself, and beauty, and you have men dancing attendance. Of course she's envious; Miriam hates being old. It's not fear of death but vanity. Her beauty didn't last; she doesn't have good bones. You, on the other hand, have everything.' His tone had dropped and softened to a caress.

15

'Chester! You never talked like this before. What's come over you?'

'Just because I don't talk doesn't mean I don't have thoughts – about the neighbours.'

'So why do you suddenly become articulate about them?'

'Only in your presence. Because you're forty today? You joined the club.' He was smiling. She returned the smile, but absently. 'I love you dearly,' he said.

She grinned as if reassured. 'But of course. I love you too. My, what a lot of reassurance we need. And what a pretty evening it is.' Without a change of tone she switched subjects, regarding the cove and the hinterland with sparkling eyes. 'I never noticed before how the houses creep up into the forest like little animals.' She looked down to where an arc of wet sand showed. The tide had turned. 'Those old logs,' she said, 'like bones of long-dead whales.' She turned to him and her face was radiant. She took his hand. 'Your mood's infectious; I caught it too.'

'You could do worse,' he said, and they went on, laughing.

Chapter 2

The Keller place was one of the higher houses in the village, backing on to a long loop road that had been carved out of the slope and which provided access for vehicles. People wanting to go to the shore on foot used steep little paths through the chaparral between their gardens and the highway.

The Keller house was built of red cedar, walled and shingled, but the west wall was mostly glass so that the occupants looked out through the plumes of hemlocks to the cove and the stacks and the sea where, at the start of this bright still evening, the fog bank lurked some three miles out beyond the Devil's Spine.

At the kitchen end of the huge open-plan room Grace Ferguson swore as she dropped an anchovy fillet.

'Still working,' chided her mother, coming in from the deck. 'Go and change. I'll do that.'

'I'm finished. Lovejoy! Here, food! How was your hike?'

A black and white cat stalked across the parquet, sniffed at the anchovy and turned away.

'The cape was fun,' Lois said. 'Were there any messages?'

'Leo and Sadie may be a little late; something about trying to identify an owl over in Coon Gulch?'

'A hiker reckons he saw a spotted last week.'

'Isn't that where they're threatening to clear-cut? So if it's a spotted, you got a problem. I hope you're not going to spike trees again.'

'I never did.'

'That's your story. Who put sugar in the loggers' gas tanks?'

'Yes, well . . . Did anyone else call?'

'Oliver Harper came by, offering to help. I sent him on his way.'

'He seems to have taken a shine to you.'

17

'He'd better watch it then or Miriam will be giving him his marching orders. What was the term you used?'

'Gigolo. We met Miriam on the trail. She wasn't in a good mood.'

'No wonder. Oliver was supposed to go running with her. He said he's sprained his Achilles tendon.'

'Don't let it slip to Miriam that he was up here.'

'Mom! You don't owe Miriam anything, and so what if her boyfriend calls on a neighbour – is she that possessive she'll make an issue of it?'

'Yes, she is, and I have to live with her.'

'You could thumb your nose at her.' Grace opened the refrigerator and pushed a plate of canapés into the crammed interior. She slammed the door and wiped her hands on her apron. 'You're a rich successful lady,' she said. 'You did it all yourself, you don't owe *anybody* anything.' The emphasis was studied.

She met her mother's eye and Lois turned away, saying over her shoulder as she made for the staircase at the end of the room, 'So, no one else called?'

'No.' Grace stared after her, frowning, the little girl showing in the jutting lower lip, the angry eyes that loved her mother and deplored her behaviour: begging to know if her husband had remembered to call on her birthday.

As Chester Hoyle said, Grace was a beautiful girl. The long red hair, straight but of an unbelievable colour that was wholly natural, was caught back in a bow of blue ribbon but tendrils had escaped and clung to her damp neck. Her eyes were grey-green like Cumbrian slate, and her high cheekbones had only the faintest suggestion of a tan. Like all redheads she had to be careful of the sun. She was taller than her mother and on the thin side of slim: a model's body, her friends told her, but there was muscle too. She was a stylish skier, unlike Lois who would career down the steepest slopes, ragged and fast, juddering on the turns, giving it everything she'd got.

The old longcase clock started to strike. Grace threw it a startled glance and dashed for the stairs. Behind her Lovejoy came in from the deck to see if anything had been left out, forgotten in the excitement. Parties for Lovejoy were treasure-trove. There was nothing on the tables now except silver and china and glasses; there would be pickings as soon as the people came, and

18

talked, and turned their backs on canapés on low side tables. From upstairs came the sound of showers, and an occasional shout between open doors. Lovejoy found the patch of sunshine on the corner of the Bokhara under the piano and settled down to wait.

Chester came first, appearing without sound on the deck. 'Hi, there,' he called and walked in carrying a gift package. He wore a cream silk shirt, a scarlet cravat and black slacks. His hair was still damp and he looked neat and distinguished. Lois, running down the stairs in a white and gold caftan, smiled happily. 'I meant to tell you not to wear a tie,' she said. 'You look just right.'

'Many happy returns.' He kissed her cheek and gave her the package. It was a book.

'You found it! Oh, Chester, how can I ever thank you? It's a classic.'

'What is it?' Grace floated down the staircase in a cloud of Charlie and red chiffon. 'Hi, Ches, you do look nice.'

'You're a vision,' he said with sincerity. 'I should have worn a tie.'

'No sweat, it's ladies' night. And who else owns a tie in this neck of the woods anyway? Apart from Leo.' She held out her hand for the book.

'No, sweetie.' Lois was firm. 'It's forensic medicine. Nasty pictures. Coloured.'

'One of those? Yuk.' She glanced at Chester and smiled. 'Something you wanted, Mom?' It was a cue.

'More than anything.' The doorbell rang. 'Would you let them in, Chester?' She slipped the book among others on a shelf and put on a party smile to welcome the guests while Grace started to unload the refrigerator.

When the party had been in swing for an hour Lovejoy stood up, stretched, and sniffed a flake of pastry which had just landed on the parquet. It smelled of fish. He moved forward and reared bonelessly to push his head past a fold of rosy tussore and closed large jaws on the remains of a lobster puff. Above him Miriam Ramet enthused about New Guinea. 'Still very uncivilised,' she was saying. 'In the back country there are tribes who practise cannibalism yet. They say if you know where to go you can buy a shrunken head.'

19

'Did you?' Chester asked.

'Of course not. What would I want with a shrunken head?'

'A trophy?' Grace suggested, approaching. 'Have a lobster puff.'

'I have one.' Miriam turned to her plate, and frowned.

'What else did you do in New Guinea?' Chester asked politely.

'I had only a couple of days in Port Moresby then I flew to New Zealand.' Her tone lightened. 'And there I met Oliver.' She sparkled at the approach of a lean young man in designer denim. 'Get me another glass of champagne, sweetie. It's over there on the sideboard. Charming boy,' she told Chester. 'Very talented, you know? Screenplays.'

'Oh yes. Like Andy.'

'No, not quite.'

Oliver returned with a brimming glass and looked round the room. Miriam drank absently and watched him. Chester said, 'I have to speak to Sadie,' and crossed to a sofa and a fragile elderly woman with an anxious expression. She brightened visibly at his arrival and patted the seat beside her.

'Leo's collecting the goodies,' she said. 'I feel a little pooped after Coon Gulch.'

'Did you see the owl?'

'We heard a great horned several times but we don't think there can be a spotted on that side of the ridge. It's been logged and you know how they like old-growth. I hope there isn't a spotted. It's too soon to have another fight with the loggers. They're so vicious.'

'Who's vicious?' A tough brown person with grey hair, cut uncompromisingly short, was planted in front of them. She held two overflowing plates.

'Loggers,' Sadie said. 'You brought me too much. You always do that.'

'I'll eat what you can't. Hold these while I go back for the bubbly.' She strode off, a purposeful little figure in a white pants suit and black shirt, a turquoise bolo at her neck.

Chester regarded the straight back and said, 'Anyone'd take Leo for a boy.'

'She's fifty-nine,' Sadie said proudly. 'She'll still look like that when she's eighty. You should have seen her driving in those spikes— ' She stopped and stared at him wide-eyed.

He took the plates from her and put them on a coffee table. 'It's all right, Sadie; everyone knows who spiked the trees on Lame Dog Creek, but no one's about to talk.'

'Well, you wouldn't, Chester.'

Leo Brant returned with three glasses of champagne. 'Had to drink most of mine,' she told them. 'Couldn't carry three. I told Jason to come over with refills.' She handed them their drinks, sat down and regarded the canapés thoughtfully. 'Caviar, oysters, lobster – and that's just for starters. Right, let's get stuck in.'

'With your energy you can,' Sadie said fondly. 'You'll burn it off tomorrow without even trying.'

Leo checked with an oyster puff halfway to her mouth. 'You feeling OK? Eat a little. Try one of those crab sandwiches. You like crab.'

Chester observed them indulgently, thinking that they were like an old married couple, except that married couples were seldom so considerate of each other. Lovejoy's whiskers appeared at a corner of the sofa. 'Here's that bloody cat!' Leo exclaimed. 'Did you hear about our Audubon's warbler, Chester? This bugger got the male.'

'He doesn't travel that far,' Sadie said. 'I think it had to be the marsh hawk.'

'Rubbish. We don't have marsh hawks.'

'I saw one that day, a female— '

'On passage. Goin' through. This cat took our Audubon's.'

'He did?' Lois stood before them, smiling, attentive.

'I reckon so.' Leo capitulated, but only fractionally.

'I'm sorry. What can I do? Would you want me to have him put down?'

"Course not. Natural for a cat to kill birds.' Leo was surly as a child.

'Like pumas taking deer,' Lois said. 'Let me get you some more champagne.' She moved away.

'That's some lady,' Leo said. 'Did she hear from Andy, Chester?'

Sadie frowned and jerked her elbow. Leo's eyebrows shot up.

'Not that I know of,' Chester said.

Sadie broke in breathlessly as a newcomer approached: 'You're looking very colourful this evening, Jason.' Which was an understatement in view of the fat man's fern-green pants and garnet

21

turtle neck. The plump face was ingenuous, the eyes naïve behind thick spectacles. He carried champagne and napkins.

'What were you reading this afternoon, Jason?' Chester asked.

'This afternoon?' He blinked. 'Where was I?'

'Sitting at the mouth of Bobcat.'

'So I was. I was reading *Dark Canyon* by Louis l'Amour. Why?'

'We were guessing. We were on Deception.'

'Who's we?'

'Lois and me.'

'Oh yes, of course.' He filled their glasses with a steady hand. 'I like Louis l'Amour,' he confided. 'I know what he's about.' He caught the drips deftly with a napkin. 'I can't understand Lois; she's too clever for me.'

'She's – intricate,' Leo conceded. 'But once you know how her mind works you can understand her.'

'You figure you know how her mind works?' Chester registered astonishment and Leo fell for it.

'I mean,' she turned to Sadie, 'we usually guess, don't we? We know who the murderer is before the last chapter, and we're getting better at it.'

'I think she's becoming more simple,' Sadie said. 'She's pruning out the deadwood and bringing up the essentials.'

Leo stared at her. 'What on earth makes you say that?'

Sadie giggled. 'Two glasses of bubbly. I'm just at the right stage of perceptiveness.'

'Huh. Good job you're not driving.'

'Why, hello you guys! Why aren't you circulating?'

They looked up: three of them in a row, like children admonished by teacher – or the nurse that Mabel Sykes had been and could never forget. She was large and heavy, her face beaming with good humour above a double chin, her body encased in yards of yellow cotton, vaguely ethnic. 'Great party,' she said. 'Yummy food, champagne flowing like water' – she held her empty glass out to her son – 'everyone's having a super time.' She surveyed the room with the eye of the practised entertainer. 'And here's Eve and Carl at last.' Another plump old lady, this one in cream slacks and a sequinned top, was on the deck, accompanied by an elderly man, ramrod-straight, in neat khaki. 'Better late than never,' Mabel said comfortably. 'Eve's got a new necklace. What *is* that? Can't be turquoise, that size.'

22

'Did you hear about the crushed turquoise on the market?' Sadie asked eagerly. 'It's ground up and then kinda cemented together and sold as the genuine article, only much cheaper.'

'Really,' Mabel breathed, staring with amusement at the pendant on Eve Linquist's shelving bosom. 'Myself, I'd sooner have something real, and inexpensive.' She was wearing a rather fine string of chunky amber which everyone knew had been anything but inexpensive.

Eve Linquist approached smiling politely but her eyes scanning every corner, noting who was there and what they were wearing. Her husband drifted away to the kitchen alcove. Mabel sighed. 'Just like country dances in the boondocks,' she remarked as Eve came up. 'Men in one corner, girls in another.'

'Oh, I don't know.' Eve tucked her arm through Jason's. 'We have the most handsome men in the room with us. Why bother about husbands?'

'Let me get you a glass,' Jason said, and bolted away, blushing.

'Cradle-robber,' Mabel said lightly.

'You got the wrong old lady, dear.' Eve looked across the room to where handsome Oliver Harper was laughing with Lois. Mabel's smile was fixed. By the piano Miriam's eyes narrowed as she looked to see who was making her escort laugh rather too loudly.

'Folk shouldn't have birthdays after they're thirty-nine,' Mabel said to Eve. 'It reminds other people how ancient they are.'

'Not ancient, dear; we're seniors, senior citizens; it's a term of respect.'

Chester stood up. 'I want a word with Fleur.'

'Scared him off,' Leo said, not bothering to lower her voice as he moved away. 'This corner's too bloody feminine.'

Mabel stared at her, Eve's lips thinned, Jason, arriving at that moment, gave a smothered giggle, caught his mother's eye and busied himself with the drinks.

Chester paused beside a slim woman in a naval jacket with gold trim. 'That's an amusing outfit,' he said with interest. 'You belong on a millionaire's yacht in Bermuda.' He was patently sincere.

Fleur Sanborn smiled her appreciation. She was dark with magnificent eyes and thick hair worn daringly loose – daringly because she was in her forties, but she had the presence to carry off loose hair above the parody of a commodore's jacket and a striped T-shirt in navy and gold.

'Amazing,' Chester said, studying the ensemble.

'Pretentious for Sundown.' She had a clear Eastern accent. 'Grace brought it from her boutique. I made a mistake wearing it tonight.'

'Nonsense. Lois will accept it as a compliment to her party. How's the gallery doing?'

'We've had a good season. Winding down now, of course, end of August. And we got the timing wrong. Gideon's new book is due out any time. But we can catch the Thanksgiving trade, and Christmas. Don't sneer, Chester; Gideon and I laugh all the way to the bank.'

'I'm not sneering.' He was hurt. 'I admire you, Fleur. And people who come in to browse among Gideon's atrocities will buy one of your paintings occasionally.'

'Naturally. I sell what people want.'

'How do you account for folk who buy perceptive water-colours *and* Gideon's puerile output?'

'I can't, unless it's husbands buy one thing and wives the other.'

'Which?'

'Now, Chester.' The deep eyes glowed with something that could be anger. 'Gideon's a fine draughtsman.'

'Oh yes, he can draw, I'll grant you that, but his content's something else: obscene worms with a head at each end, naked women, gorillas in full suits of armour – every rivet correct.' He giggled, shaking his head in wonder.

'It sells. I supply a demand.'

'You're corrupting the masses.'

'The masses watch *The Living Dead* and *Alien*, they rent snuff movies.' Her eyes were blazing now. 'Gideon's stuff is no more pernicious than Lois's murder stories – less so, in fact. Gideon is fantasy, Lois is reality; on occasions she comes very close to home.' He was silent. She softened and laid long fingers on his wrist. 'I was retaliating, Chester. I don't like people poking fun at Gideon. He's by way of being my financial mainstay, and I'm immensely grateful to him. And if you can't take *that* seriously – ' Her eyes implored him to see it her way.

'How can you— ' he began, and then he got the message. 'I'm sorry, my dear. And who am I to judge? You sell good

24

art and comics; I made war planes, or was instrumental in their manufacture. I was patronising. Forgive me, and let me get you a drink.'

'Good God!'

'What?' He looked to see what had startled her.

'Andy,' she breathed. 'It can't be! I didn't even know he was home.'

'No one did,' he said absently. 'Who's that with him?'

'How would I know? He can't have brought her. She *is* with him. Chester, what's he up to? Where's Lois?'

Lois was on the other side of the room and had been among the first to notice her husband on the deck, not least because the evening chill had driven people indoors. As the sun set, the fog had rolled in, embracing the stacks and creeping up through the village until the rail of the deck was merely a silhouette against matte space. Out there the new arrivals looked vaguely menacing although a certain incongruity was quickly apparent. Andy Keller wore a Stetson; his companion, as tall as he, was in stilt-like heels and a mini-skirt; both Stetson and mini were bizarre in this company.

Lois's husband was a gangling fellow whose legs seemed too long for his torso. He was ill at ease and as he stepped over the threshold he tilted his hat nervously, revealing restless eyes. His nose seemed to have been recently broken and had healed crookedly, giving him the air of an ageing fighter. His mouth was thin, his skin like brown crêpe. He moved without grace and emitted a faint odour of whisky.

The girl was blonde with a bush of ruffle-permed hair, and the almond eyes, plump cheeks and pretty mouth of a Mexican beauty queen: a doll-like face above a fabulous body. Her dress was so deeply cleft that her breasts showed with her movements. The dress itself was a puzzle: made of dull cheap material, but there was something about the grubby black flounces above the golden thighs that heightened the effect of sensuousness. Among these women who had dressed with care and who were aware of the slightest nuance in behaviour her presence was an insult, a threat to their lifestyle.

That lifestyle included good manners. By the time Andy reached his wife (the girl crowding his elbow as if they were crossing a field of cows) conversation, which had faltered momentarily,

25

was moving again: not flowing as it had before their arrival, but people were talking with apparent nonchalance even as their eyes remained riveted on a scene that promised drama.

But Lois was smiling, her brows raised in polite inquiry, looking at the girl. Andy neither kissed his wife nor removed his hat. He said without contrition: 'Shoot, I forgot your fortieth birthday! Still, we made it in time, just. This is my new assistant, Gayleen.'

'How do you do, Gayleen.' Lois held out her hand. She turned. Jason was at her elbow, staring. 'Jason, give Gayleen a drink.' She said to her husband, 'And you'll have a Scotch,' but he was already moving towards a table that held the hard liquor, ignoring the company, the hat on the back of his head. Jason handed Gayleen a glass of champagne and Lois asked him if he could find some food. She turned back to the girl who was licking her lips.

'Nice,' she said, indicating her drink. 'The soda pop. Flavoured with something?' Her voice carried. Heads turned slowly.

'Did you have a good trip?' Lois asked. Seeing the other's hesitation she rephrased that: 'Did you come far today?'

'Just from Portland. Oh, wow!' Jason was back with a plate of canapés. She took it from him and regarded it helplessly, the other hand occupied with her glass.

'Let me take the plate,' Lois said, and stood patiently while the girl started to eat as if she'd been a long time without food.

'This is neat,' she exclaimed, looking round the room, then returning to her pastry: 'What's this?'

'Caviar.'

'Pardon?'

'Fish's roe. Fish eggs.'

'Yuk, I can do without that.' She replaced the barquette and considered another with a shrimp on top. 'Would I like that?'

Grace came up. 'You go and circulate,' she told her mother. 'I'll take over here.'

'Hi,' the girl said. 'I'm Gayleen.'

'Were you born with that name?'

'I were christened Marilyn but that's no good if you're in movies.'

'You're in movies?' Grace's eyes strayed to the décolletage.

26

'You think this is over the top?' Gayleen asked anxiously. 'He told me to wear it. Andy. It's wrong, isn't it?'

'Oh, I don't know. People on the coast dress according to individual taste; so far as that goes you're conforming. Where do you come from?'

'You mean today? Portland. She asked me that. Andy's wife, ex-wife, whatever.'

Grace gasped and caught herself quickly. 'So how do you assist him?' she asked conversationally.

But Jason had arrived. 'Oh, yeah, I'll have some more.' Gayleen held her glass for him to fill. 'Why, it's champagne,' she cried, catching sight of the label. 'I thought it were some posh kind of soda pop with all that fizz. Great! I never had champagne before.'

'You're Andy's assistant?' Grace reminded her.

'So – I do anything he wants. I mean, anything needs doing, like answering the phone, running errands; you know: groceries and stuff.'

Jason hadn't moved away. Now he said, 'I wouldn't drink it so fast if you haven't had it before. It's stronger than you think.'

Gayleen gave him all her attention. 'You live here? What do you do – I mean, for kicks? I didn't even see a bar.' She looked past him and caught Andy's eye where he lounged at the kitchen sink. He raised his glass to her and winked. 'Who's he talking to?' she asked carelessly. 'I guess I ought to get to know folk.' The champagne was obviously having an effect.

'He's with my dad,' Jason said. 'He's by way of being – ' He faltered, at a loss. 'Shall I introduce you to people?'

'Leave it to me.' There was a warning in Grace's tone and he nodded, uncomprehending but obedient as a well-trained dog. 'Does Andy wear his hat in the office?' Grace asked.

'We don't have no office; he works in the motel.'

'Which motel?'

'Why, the one where we – he lives: the Fountain, out on the north side. His hat? He just bought it.'

'You said you were in movies. Would you be on your way to Hollywood?' It sounded silly but one could be literally going to Hollywood from Portland by way of the Oregon coast.

'Not today,' Gayleen said, without any awareness of inanity.

27

'He just came – that is, Andy drove down to get his stuff. I come along for the ride.'

'His stuff?'

'His possessions and that.'

'I see. He's leaving?'

'Was he ever here? And she won't take him back, will she?' Gayleen gestured with her empty glass to Lois who stood by the piano, talking to Miriam, her back turned. 'She seems a nice enough lady,' she said casually.

'Why shouldn't she be?'

'Well, you know: men and stuff, at her age! I'm sorry for Andy. He's been treated something shameful.'

'I suppose— ' Grace checked, blinked and started again. 'I know: his wife doesn't want him, got tired of him? Goes to other men, threw him out, humiliated him? And now she wants a divorce. Then he's going to marry you. He knows people in the movie business, right? You're going to be in one of his films?'

'Look, I hope I haven't started anything.' Gayleen was anxious. 'You sound rather sweet on him yourself.'

Grace, knowing where she was now, was nodding, then, catching this last statement, shook her head abruptly.

Gayleen went on, relieved, 'Most of what you said was right except he's a screen-writer just, but he does know directors and that.'

'Let me tell you something,' Grace said . . .

'Where did you find her, Andy?' Oliver Harper asked. 'And where did she find that dress?'

'Like some of it, would you, my man?' Andy grinned loosely. 'She's not for sale – yet.'

Oliver's eyes narrowed. 'For rent perhaps? Gone into the pimping business, have we, Andy? Watch it' – as the other man moved – 'I know how that nose got broken.'

But Andy Keller wouldn't hit a hard man here nor anywhere else. Oliver knew that, and Andy knew he knew. Now Andy appeared to relax. 'I know what a gigolo is, dear,' he said, 'but what's the term for the old lady who keeps a gigolo?'

Oliver's lips stretched. 'A benefactor, dear.'

* * *

28

'Mind yer back,' Leo growled as someone spilled her wine. They had finished the champagne and were now on the Yugoslav riesling. 'Oh, it's you, Andy,' she muttered grudgingly, and froze as she saw his flushed face and the bottle of Scotch in one hand, uncapped.

He swayed and grinned. 'The top of the marnin' to ye, sir! How's the wife?'

He lurched away. Beside her Fleur said softly, 'And unfortunately he's so drunk if you could think of something withering it would go right past him. Feel like wasting him? So do I.'

Leo exhaled with a deep sigh. 'He got to you too?'

'It doesn't matter. He discovers one's delicate areas – emotionally – and probes. He's a sadist. Now he's reached the stage where he's just gross. I see Eve and Carl are on their way. The party's breaking up. And a good thing too.'

'Bloody shame,' Leo said. 'It's ruined her birthday.'

'Maybe it'll bring things to a head. If Barbie Doll there will hang on to him long enough for Lois to sue for divorce, if she *would* divorce, maybe we could be rid of him for good. Now he's cornered Boligard – and there goes Mabel to the rescue.'

'Only a third-rate talent,' Andy was saying, slurring his consonants. 'Slapdash and precious at the same time; gay writers always are.'

'That man had more masculinity in his little finger than— '

Andy roared with laughter.

'What's the joke?' asked Mabel with ominous good humour.

'He says Hemingway was homosexual!' Boligard was livid.

'Takes one to know one,' Mabel said equably, her hand on her husband's arm. Andy opened his mouth to retaliate but at that moment Lois turned away from the door where she had been speeding her guests and looked at him. He lifted the whisky bottle and drank. Lois blinked once but for the rest, her thoughts might have been a world away.

'No,' she said. 'Not in any circumstances. How can you suggest it? It's outrageous.'

'Rubbish. Here are four people and two bedrooms. It's the most civilised arrangement— '

'*Civilised?*'

'Either I stay here, or you and Grace bunk together and

29

Gayleen an' me'll have Grace's bed. You can't turn your husband out, not to speak of a guest. Where are your manners? And I have a prior right: conjugal, it's called.'

'You can't claim conjugal rights and propose to sleep with your mistress under the same roof.'

'Which would you prefer?'

'I don't believe this.'

'I asked you a question.'

There was a knock on the bedroom door and Grace's voice: 'Can I come in, Mom?'

'Yes, sweetie.'

The door opened. Grace saw her mother at her dressing-table, her step-father sprawled on the quilt in his boots and still wearing his hat.

'What do I do with Gayleen?' Grace asked.

Andy sat up. 'Gayleen,' he repeated thoughtfully. 'What happened to her?'

'She's downstairs.' Grace pushed the door wide, like a hint.

He got off the bed. 'We'll go to the cabin. Plenty of bedding, is there? Mattress, blankets, pillows? We'll be down for breakfast. Gayleen likes bacon and eggs and sausages. I'll have waffles and maple syrup, and we'll both drink mocha coffee. I'll see you around eleven, twelve. Better make that brunch.'

Chapter 3

By nine o'clock next morning the telephone was busy as people called Lois to thank her for the party and put into operation the strategy they had agreed on last night – excitedly phoning each other a moment they got home. The aim was to find out how long Andy Keller and Gayleen were staying, because no one was going to return Lois's hospitality until they were gone. So they were asking Lois what her plans were for today, might one join her for a hike or a trip to town?

She said gently that she was tied up for the day and would call back when Grace returned to Portland. She was scheduled to leave today. Ah, people thought, then maybe the others will leave today too, but no one mentioned their names. Even Chester, ringing with his thanks for the evening, waited to see if she would introduce the subject but when she didn't, he said, 'I must spend some time in the yard today, so I'll be around if you feel like company,' meaning he was accessible should she need help.

She thanked him and replaced the receiver. Grace had not come down yet and there was no sign of Andy and Gayleen. She went outside to look at her Chevrolet. The cabin was inaccessible for vehicles; people came and went to it by a trail that zigzagged up through the conifers to this tiny one-roomed structure that Lois's father had built partly for amusement but mostly because at fourteen she was already writing. She maintained that the house was too noisy for concentration. Now the cabin was used as a guest room and visitors thought it quaint. Honeymoon couples loved it.

The Chevrolet had scrapes down one side. It would have to be resprayed. She glanced inside. There was no luggage, only crushed styrofoam beakers, candy wrappers, the new road atlas, ragged and stained. The boot was unlocked and empty. She closed it and caught sight of a bumper sticker. It said:

I ♥ SPOTTED OWLS. ROASTED.

'Hi, Mom.' Grace came along the deck, barefoot in slacks and T-shirt.

'You're dressed,' Lois said inanely.

'I would hardly come down *undressed* this morning.' The tone was loaded. 'What's that?' She came closer and gasped. 'Jesus!'

For a moment they stared at each other, then Lois turned deliberately to the view. 'Going to be another hot day,' she said brightly, although no blue showed above the fog. There was silence from behind her. She turned. 'What are you doing? No, Grace!'

The girl straightened from the bumper where she'd been scraping at the sticker. 'What?' She was flushed with rage.

'Leave it.' Lois was smiling but her eyes were like flint.

'Oh.' Again they exchanged long looks. 'Of course,' Grace murmured. 'Clever Mom.'

They went indoors to breakfast.

'"I'm a rhinestone cowboy,"' Jason sang happily, aligning his books, tut-tutting at a Science Fiction which someone had carelessly replaced among the Westerns. A shadow darkened his store and he glanced out of the window to see a large person studying the titles he'd arranged below the coloured poster of Monument Valley. She wore a blue shirt like a Big Mack, but even against the light he could see that was no workman's shirt – and if those were Levis, not designer denim, she'd shopped around to find a pair that fitted her solid hips without emphasising them. Her hair hadn't been cut by a village hairdresser either, and that gleam of gold on her wrist was too subdued to be anything else but the real thing. Jason was immature in some respects but he was perceptive in his own field and he knew this was a good customer. He saw money, he sensed appreciation: of beauty, and of capital crime. She stepped down into the store.

'That poster of Monument Valley certainly compels attention,' she said, startling him out of his wits with an English accent. It was something she would be accustomed to because she went on easily, giving him time to recover, 'I must take *Skinwalkers*; I haven't read it, and I'd like some extra copies to send home. Do you have other Hillermans?' She looked round the store with interest.

Jason said quickly, 'Not right now. I have a selection on

order; 'fact, they're due any time, possibly this afternoon. He's so popular I sell out faster than Agatha Christie.'

'Perhaps you should order more.'

'Of course; I should at that.'

She moved away to the shelves. 'There must be a demand for Westerns too, Mr – ?'

'Jason. Jason Sykes, ma'am. I'm a Western fan. I've got a lot of Louis l'Amours there.' His voice rose hopefully but she was moving out of sight, disregarding the Westerns.

Leo Brant appeared in the doorway. 'God, what a party!' she exclaimed, not seeing the customer who was hidden by shelving. 'The man's unbalanced, Jason, and as for that gruesome— ' She stopped, puzzled by his frantic gestures. Catching sight of a third person she glared, trying to compose herself, and asked heavily, 'So – did the McClures come?'

'Not yet.'

'And my Audubon Guide you got on order: *Pacific Coast*. Don't tell me there's no sign of it *yet*!'

'I reordered, Leo.'

'I need it. I'm doing this piece for *Continental*. They pay the earth! I gotta deadline, Jason.'

'I'll call the distributor again.'

'Hell! It's not in the libraries, the Forest office don't have it. You'd think, wouldn't you' – turning to the other customer who was approaching the counter, appealing to her – 'wouldn't you think the definitive work on the Pacific coast would be carried by every stockist *on* the Pacific coast?'

'Indeed yes. It sounds interesting. You write about the coast?'

'I'm not really the writer. We do it together: my friend and me. I do the research, she brings it all together. She taught English. I was Physical Education. In our old age we're naturalists, that's our thing.' She thrust out a brown hand. 'Leo Brant.'

'I'm Melinda Pink.'

'Nice to meet you. Staying in Sundown?'

'As a matter of fact I'd like to take a cottage for a week or so. I stayed at the Surfbird motel last night. I walked along the shore this morning and was on my way to the realtor when I saw the poster for *Skinwalkers*. Who can pass up any bookstore, let alone one with Monument Valley in the window?'

She paid for her purchases and amid Jason's invitations to

step by again, the Hillermans might be here this afternoon, and Leo's demands that he call his distributor, they stepped out into the sunshine just as a brown Chevrolet swept into the miniature mall and pulled up outside the bar.

'Damn cowboy,' grunted Leo. 'Thinks he owns the road. What's that on his sticker? Cheek, it's not even his car.'

They peered at the Chevrolet as they passed behind it.

'What the hell – ' Leo hissed.

'What does it mean?' Miss Pink was frowning. 'Is there some ulterior implication?'

'It means just what it says.' Leo was vicious.

Andy Keller got out from under the wheel of the car. On the passenger side long brown legs appeared and Gayleen stood up on her spiky heels. They went into the bar.

'The implication?' Leo turned to Miss Pink. 'The implication is that here is a man with a self-destruct button. The loggers use that sticker but no logger'd dare stop in Sundown with it on his bumper.'

'The spotted owl is rare? You'll have to forgive me' – as Leo's eyes widened in amazement – 'I'm a stranger to Oregon. Logging destroys habitat, is that it?'

'Spotted owls,' Leo said heavily, 'need three thousand acres of old-growth timber for territory. Old-growth provides valuable lumber. This forest cuts twenty million dollars' worth of timber annually. I don't know if anyone worked out what three thousand acres of old-growth is worth as against the value of a pair of owls. And once we defeat them in one area, they threaten to cut some place else. We just won a fight with 'em over to Lame Dog Creek; we – people were spiking trees: you know, driving in spikes at night so's the saws would break when they came to drop the trees? And they put sugar in tanks – I don't mean us' – she glared at Miss Pink – 'I mean the Sierra Club, Audubon's Society, like that.'

'I see. So this man' – Miss Pink indicated the car – 'is asking to have his tyres slashed?'

'Not exactly.' Leo was thoughtful. 'It's his wife's car and no one will damage Lois Keller's property.' She smiled and Miss Pink realised that the leathery features were amazingly attractive. Considering this face which she had thought heavy and masculine she scarcely registered the words: 'But a husband's

34

hardly property, is he?' Then Leo changed tack. 'You're looking for the realtor. Don't call him that to his face. Boligard's a bit sensitive about having to earn a living like ordinary folk. You'll find him behind the Tattler.' She pointed: 'You go down the side of the restaurant past that bank of petunias and there's a path will take you to a tacky old shack, if it hasn't fallen into the ocean, which it's going to do any time . . .'

The Wandering Tattler was a long low structure built of white clapboard with sash windows and a hanging sign, like those on English inns, depicting a plump wading bird with yellow legs. As she followed directions past the vivid petunias Miss Pink became aware of gulls' calls and the susurration of the sea. The land behind the restaurant was unfenced and a narrow path took her through undergrowth to a decrepit shack with wooden steps at the side and a rusted flue emerging from a roof of tarred sheeting. The door was open and from the interior came the sound of typing.

'Why,' she exclaimed, peering in, 'I didn't realise . . . you're Mr Sykes, from the motel.'

Boligard coughed. 'Yes, this is my – sanctum, I guess you'd call it. For privacy, you know; too much going on at the motel.'

'Of course. I must have misunderstood Mrs Sykes. I'm really looking for accommodation – '

'Ah, well, yes. I do act as an agent for a local realtor, just as a favour.' Then, in a burst of confidence: 'Writers aren't exactly well paid; outrageous when you think about it: a book costs less than a meal in a restaurant. Are you aware of that?'

Miss Pink made appropriate noises of surprise and sympathy but she was absorbing the room, such as it was, even as he expounded on the greed of publishers, the arrogance of agents, the stupidity of readers: 'None of them will look at a book unless it's by an established author. It's a bad time for writers with talent, people who don't care to write blockbusters.'

On the shabby planking were photographs of heeling sailboats, dead fish hoisted on hooks, riders whirling lariats from the backs of galloping horses. There was a much younger Boligard on one knee, rifle in hand, holding an antelope's head by one horn.

'You've had an adventurous life,' she commented, implying that she thought he was the subject in all the photographs. He gave her a shy but practised grin, acknowledging the adulation.

35

With his trimmed white beard and weathered skin, the pale eyes, even the swelling paunch, Miss Pink needed no one to tell her that Boligard was not his own man but a model of Papa Hemingway. Now she had listened for long enough – and she was the customer.

'I'm looking for a small place for a week or so,' she said pleasantly. 'With all conveniences, of course; a bath and shower, adequately furnished . . . '

She took the second place he showed her (the first had a landslip in front of it and looked as if, with the next high tide, a few more yards would slide into the sea, taking the house with it). But then he took her up the hill to a light and airy little cottage on the loop road above the village. It was on such a steep slope that although all on one floor and approached by a flight of steps at the side, the façade, which faced slightly north of west, was on stilts. A wall of sliding glass opened from the living-room to a balcony or deck on which were chairs and an iron table. Below the house the ground dropped away and she looked over a rioting jungle of fuchsias and huge fruiting blackberries, past glimpses of roofs to the cove, the stacks and the open sea. She absorbed the view and then she turned to Boligard and started to haggle. He had been expecting this and they settled amiably to an activity at which each felt he was competent. She knew that the seventy-five dollars a week which they agreed on was half what she would have to pay for a comparable place in Britain, and what was comparable to this stretch of the Oregon coast? She glanced towards the forested slopes that, southwards, plunged to the shore. 'I understand there are spotted owls in the woods,' she said.

'Oh yes, we have spotted owls, great horned owls, deer, bears – not to worry you, of course; you'll see the deer, you won't see bears.' He had a single-track mind and was still trying to sell her the cottage although they'd agreed on a price.

'You're all naturalists in Sundown,' she murmured, and in the face of his blank stare: 'I met Miss Brant. Leo, is it?'

'Oh, Leo's an expert; so is Sadie, her friend – both writers.' He frowned and winced. 'In fact,' he continued brightly, 'we're all interested in the ecology since we immigrated to Sundown. Can't help being drawn back to the wilderness' – his eyes shone – 'finding our roots. The forest is a place of eternal magic, you'll discover that for yourself.'

36

'It attracts interesting people, this fusion of trees and ocean: wild, pristine— '

'It's a terrible place to write.'

'Terrible, Mr Sykes?'

'There's far too much happening. The social life is hectic. A big do last night – and now everyone's waiting to return the hospitality. Etiquette can go too far. No life for a creative person. You have to shut yourself off – and you can't. You'll get drawn into it as a matter of course, but that's all right: you're not an author.'

'But not everyone is a naturalist.'

'What was that, ma'am?'

'I said not everyone here is a naturalist. I saw a car in the parking lot with a bumper sticker: "I Love Spotted Owls. Roasted."' He gaped at her. 'A man in a Stetson with a tall blonde in a black mini-skirt and high red heels.'

'That's Andy Keller. And the girl he— He put *that* on his bumper? Andy? He *dared*?'

'They're a local couple?' She was the picture of innocent surprise, although she couldn't hold that expression long in the face of his own amazement; but now he was thinking, which was something that didn't come easily to Boligard, at least in these circumstances.

'His wife,' he muttered, almost to himself, 'is a dedicated conservationist, and Grace feels the same way . . . 'course, he's only her step-father and often there's resentment, isn't there? They tell me Bill Ferguson was a regular guy, pity he got himself drowned. Fine sailor, they say.' He shot her a glance. 'This guy with the bumper sticker's married to Ferguson's widow.' But Miss Pink looked bewildered and he made an attempt to change the subject. 'Gossip,' he said firmly. 'Place like this, all we got to do is gossip about the neighbours. You'll meet them all; Lois Keller is a fine woman, she's a published author, writes crime novels, murder mysteries and stuff, makes a good living too. The blonde – lady – in the short skirt is her husband's assistant. Keller writes screenplays.' He regarded her steadily. This was fact, he implied, not gossip.

She smiled. 'I see why your social life is hectic.'

He nodded but she had the impression he wasn't listening. 'There's a restaurant here but no food store,' he told her. 'We mostly shop in Salmon, ten miles south. You can get everything you need there.'

'I came through Salmon on my way here. What is the food like at the restaurant?'

'It's gourmet food,' he said, his thoughts still elsewhere.

He wasn't far out in his judgment of the Tattler's cuisine. If the rest of the menu proved as good as the bowl of clam chowder she had for lunch – and the portions as generous – she was faced with the familiar problem of balancing intake with a vast expenditure of energy. In her sixties she felt that, at a time when one might be excused for hoping to take life easily, it was most unfair that burning off fat should have become such a strenuous chore. She sighed as the waiter asked her what she would like to follow, declined his suggestion of various pies and ices, and asked if he were the son of the house.

He beamed at her. 'No, ma'am, I'm merely helping out.'

'You live here?'

'I'm staying with a friend. What part of England are you— '

He stopped as the couple from the brown Chevrolet came in. Miss Pink regarded them benignly, wondering if the man – Andy Keller – had alopecia or some other condition that might account for his not liking to remove his hat indoors, wondering why his assistant was dressed so unsuitably for the seaside. There was a clatter as the waiter dropped a knife and fork and, straightening, backed into a chair. As he made his way to the kitchen the couple watched him, the girl smiling, Keller with a look of contempt.

Miss Pink sipped her coffee and contemplated the highway beyond the dining-room windows. After a minute or two an elderly man came in from the back quarters; his face and bearing: close-cropped hair, bristling moustache and rigid stance, reminiscent of the old soldier but this impression marred by a large plastic apron. He stopped at the other table.

Keller looked at him with amusement. 'Charming,' he announced in a ridiculous falsetto. 'Quite charming.'

'I work in a kitchen,' the old fellow said. 'Grease sticks. Like all dirt.' He held the other's eye.

'You're the cook?' the girl asked in amazement.

'Yes, ma'am. *Cordon bleu*.'

'You speak French too.' Keller's eyes widened.

The chef sagged a little, like an old horse resting a leg. He didn't look at Miss Pink. 'I'll take your order, Andy,' he said calmly.

'You haven't given us the menu.'

'I can tell you what we have— '

'Bring a menu for my lady here.'

'No, that's OK; you can tell us.' In contrast with her flamboyant appearance the girl had a shy breathless little voice and she was obviously ill at ease in this place with its linen tablecloths and real flowers, its one other customer minding her own business. The chef disregarded the protest anyway and brought menus from a sideboard. As Keller studied his the old fellow regarded the Stetson thoughtfully, then shot a glance at Miss Pink, surprising her own vague stare.

They ordered crab and cheese sandwiches. The chef retired and after a moment a plump woman emerged from the kitchen and advanced on Miss Pink with the bill. She asked if everything had been satisfactory.

'Delicious.' Miss Pink smiled. 'Too good, but I shall come back. I've taken the cottage called Quail Run.'

'I know. We shall be glad to see you. We like our food at the Tattler. My husband trained in Paris, and he's worked at the Dorchester and the Ritz.'

'You wouldn't get clam chowder like that in London.'

'Well, they don't have the ingredients. You might get it in New England however, providing they had my husband to prepare it.' She smiled serenely and moved away, pausing at the other table to remark pleasantly, 'A splendid hat, Andy, but you need tooled boots and spurs to go with it. Even a horse. Or a car.'

'He's got the car,' the girl said, going along with the joke.

'Oh, has he, dear?' The woman looked puzzled and nodded towards the windows. 'Not the Chevrolet. That belongs to *Mrs* Keller.'

The kitchen door swung to behind her broad back. Keller swallowed as his eyes came back to the girl. Miss Pink rose and walked out. In the open air she paused and exhaled, and realised that she had been holding her breath.

She returned to her cottage to find a small man busily engaged in cutting back the brambles from her parking space. A schnauzer rushed round the corner of the house barking, chased by a tiny woman making grabs at his collar. Dark and sharp-eyed as a chipmunk, she wore fine pink cotton marked with sap stains.

'I'm your neighbour,' she said, extending her free hand. 'Miriam Ramet. My place is along the road, on the creek. I'm a friend of your landlord and I look after things when he's away. If we'd known you were taking the cottage we'd have cleared the yard before you arrived.' Her tone implied disapproval of the lack of notice.

Miss Pink murmured something about not bothering with it, and paused to be introduced to the man who, however, continued to slash at the brambles.

'That's Willard.' Miriam acknowledged the pause carelessly. 'And this monster is Oscar. He doesn't bite.' She released the terrier which ran straight to Miss Pink's car to urinate on a wheel. 'Establishing territory,' explained his owner.

'Won't you come inside?' Miss Pink asked politely, and Miriam entered the cottage without so much as a glance at Willard.

This, the first guest at Quail Run, had no small talk but was concerned to discover a person's background and intentions as quickly as possible. In a very short time she had elicited the information that Miss Pink lived in Cornwall with a housekeeper, two cats and a large garden, that she was travelling up the coast to British Columbia, that her hobby was birding and she had an interest in food – and that gave Miss Pink an opening.

'I lunched at the Wandering Tattler,' she said. 'The clam chowder was superb.'

'Too rich for me. Carl Linquist uses cream in everything. I mean, look at his wife! I eat sensibly and I run four miles every day. I'm ten years older than Eve Linquist.'

'Really. And who is the boy?'

'What boy?'

'Waiting on table. Is he a student?'

'What's he look like?' Miriam was bristling with an emotion that was too intense for curiosity.

'A handsome lad, quick and deft . . . shortish hair, wearing a T-shirt with a killer whale on the front. He said he was staying with a friend, just helping out at the restaurant.'

'Did he now. That's Oliver. He is, in fact, staying with me.' The tone was acid. 'No doubt he got tired of my tuna on cracked wheat for lunch. I can think of no reason other than food that

40

could take Oliver down to Eve Linquist's place. Of course, she's a very *comfortable* person.'

Miss Pink refused to confirm or deny this. Instead she said idly, 'They were quiet at lunchtime; I suppose most tourists will picnic on the shore. There were only two customers besides myself. A man' – she smiled wryly – 'who wore his Stetson in the dining-room, and a very striking blonde.'

'Oh yes.' Miriam's eyes shifted. She studied the ocean. 'You see how the fog lays out there, just offshore? Like an animal, I always think, waiting to come back in the night.'

'It's a wild coast. I'm not surprised that you should see no boats out on the water.' They stared at the stacks. 'Is Willard your gardener?' Miss Pink asked.

Miriam took a deep breath. 'He's the gardener, handyman, dog-sitter when I go abroad. When my husband died I built a little house on my land and Willard lives in that and looks after things for me. You feel more secure with a man around.'

'Surely there's no crime in Sundown?'

'Not among the locals, but you never know who's about in the summer. Hikers stop at the bar, and you see some very peculiar people on the road. After all, if you wanted to get to San Francisco from Portland and avoid the highway patrols, you'd come down the coast instead of taking the interstate. And there are some nice homes in Sundown; a criminal would expect to find some good jewellery lying around.' She glanced at the large ruby guarding her wedding ring. 'And most of us aren't into guard dogs and guns in the night table. Except perhaps Carl Linquist. A gun, I mean; they don't keep a dog.'

'He's fond of guns?'

'Carl's a redneck. So is Eve. Perhaps redneck is too strong; it implies low-class people. Let's say the Linquists are a trifle reactionary in their attitudes.'

'He made it obvious that he disapproved of the man in the Stetson.'

'Did he say anything?'

'His wife did. She made some remark about his needing a horse to complete the outfit, even a car, and seemed to be telling the girl that the Chevrolet outside belonged to – a Mrs Keller?'

'And I bet she smiled when she said it.'

'Well, I was on my way to the door— '

41

'And I have to finish clearing up your yard— '

'Please don't trouble— '

'No trouble. It's Willard's job . . . '

Voicing amicable platitudes they parted, and Miss Pink drove to town to stock her larder and refrigerator.

The coast was gorgeous but she paid it little attention, thinking as she drove about that little community on the edge of the Pacific with the towering forests behind the village and the fog in front, lying on the water, waiting to come back in the night. The people seemed a little off-beat but not so much as might be expected: living in an ambience of potential violence, albeit elemental, not human. A good place to pause for a week and watch nature play out her dramas, she thought contentedly and, returning to basics, focused her attention on road signs and traffic as she entered the town of Salmon at the mouth of the Sockeye River.

Chapter 4

Before dark the fog came back to Sundown and that evening Miss Pink basked in the cosy atmosphere of her temporary home. She lit the fire in the wood-burning stove, pulled the curtains, switched on a couple of lamps and stood back to approve the result.

Her living-room was predominantly white, the carpet and curtains a flat grey. Colour was disposed carefully about the space: lampshades in old rose, gentian cushions on grey chairs and sofa, glass floats in lemon and bottle-green on white shelves. A television set was hidden in a white wood cabinet. She didn't switch it on. Quail Run was a seaside cottage that smelled of salt and weed; it seemed appropriate that the only sound to penetrate its walls should be that of the fog horn. In such surroundings it was like the call of a friendly water beast. That thought was less fantastic than a curious book which she found on the shelves: a well-produced comic that was a mish-mash of popular science fiction and ancient myths. There were mermaids and mermen and beautiful naked female bipeds writhing in the gauntlets of monsters in armour – armour perfect down to the last ring of chain-mail. There were worms, fat and oozy with a head at each end. The commentary was a form of prose-poetry. She found the whole thing silly and rather nasty but she appreciated that it would have considerable appeal for people nourished on juvenile comics. She replaced it on its shelf and turned to the map she had bought in Salmon.

This was a Forest production and, since the Forest Department's boundary reached the shore on either side of Sundown, it covered the area from the ocean to far back in the hinterland, although not in detail. She sighed for Ordnance Survey maps where even the walls of fields might be delineated – but there was one peculiar advantage to a map with a scale of two miles to the inch, and no contour lines: it held surprises. The map was crude. On a vast plane of green (forest, not lowland) a trail left the loop road north of Bobcat Creek and zigzagged past a black dot that could be a house but was most probably a cabin because there was no road to it. There was no indication of gradient other than the zigzags, and the fact that beyond the black dot the trail ran straight to Bobcat Creek, which it crossed to follow a stream up Porcupine Gulch. The stream headed in Pandora Ridge, which was an arc of a great rim of high ground that enclosed the basin at the back of Sundown and which was drained by Bobcat Creek.

Other routes were marked to Pandora Ridge, one starting only a few hundred yards from Quail Run, and starting with close zigzags, indicating a steep slope. Another, between that and the trail up Porcupine Gulch, was too short to be anything else but precipitous. She folded the map contentedly; tomorrow she would go up Porcupine – the route would be no more than nine miles if she descended directly to her cottage; moreover it would be feasible in poor weather: a pleasant woodland walk.

The trail started easily, more like a path through a Devon wood than one in the coastal range of Oregon. Opposite a drive with a post and the name Keller burned in a slab of driftwood, was a narrow earthen trail and a Forest sign that said 'Coon Gulch 5m, Pandora Ridge 4m, Porcupine Gulch 1.5m'. The introduction seemed a trifle pedestrian, even more so when, having strolled slowly up the graded zigzags to give her knees the chance to absorb the feel of a slope again, she came to a cabin with Navajo blankets thrown over the rail and a pair of chukka boots on the porch. The door was closed and the fly screen obscured the side window so she couldn't tell if it were open. There was no sound from inside as she walked past, treading carefully on the pine needles. She glanced at her watch. It was ten thirty.

The fog showed no signs of clearing and she had gone only a short distance beyond the cabin before it was out of sight. Now she was surrounded by the trunks of trees: insubstantial pillars that disappeared in a cotton-grey ceiling with no hint of how far above her head were their crowns. From the size of their trunks she calculated that the trees, mostly Douglas firs, were probably well over a hundred feet tall. Nothing moved, no bird called; the loudest sound was that of a leaf brushing the twigs of a myrtle as it fell. The leaf was scarlet and had come from a vine maple. She frowned; there was something intimidating about a country where leaves changed colour in August.

The trail was damp, the dust laid by the fog, and in the silty surface were the marks of shoes and cleated soles. For over a mile the gradient was so gentle that it was almost level although she traversed a steep slope. This section of the forest had been logged a long time ago; among old but massive stumps there was an under-storey of shrubs and huge ferns that must have been all of six feet tall, and there were mounds so covered with mosses that it was impossible to see whether the base was rock or rotting wood. Once she heard a squirrel scolding in the fog, and when it stopped she was aware of water close at hand. She had come to the creek. The big trees stopped on the lip of the eroded bank and some had fallen to jam the stream. There were alders here, and maples, and among them small warblers with flashes of yellow flitted through the foliage.

She crossed the creek at a point where a tributary came down the far slope and started up the course of Porcupine Gulch. After a short distance the trail left the water to rise in sharp zigzags, the drop increasing rapidly. For over two miles she had seen no grass to speak of, and no trace of cows; indeed, in the upper reaches of the timbered depression it was obvious that no cow would be able to keep its footing off the trail. This coast range was a world away from the Rocky Mountains where, despite the altitude and the alpine grandeur, there were flowery meadows and marshy lakes where cows grazed and riders could gallop through the forest to plunge down slopes and splash through creeks, jump fallen logs and never bother about a trail. Here – she looked around – you could only pray that your horse didn't put one foot off the trail; in fact she had a sudden terrifying thought: if a *walker* left the trail, in a dozen places he would fall, and almost anywhere he would be lost.

Her pace slackened. She was aware, not only of the profound silence but that, apart from the squirrel, the water and the occasional falling leaf, there had been no sound for over an hour. The fog muffled noises, of course (she hadn't heard the horn since she left the village) and it could be that it was the fog itself that was responsible for a sensation that she related, not to the absence of sound, but to the presence of something animate. Her quiet

45

progress became that much quieter and where it had been idle it became wary. She was not alone in this place. Bears, she thought; there's a bear about, but she had seen no tracks.

The path bore right and there was a lifting of the atmosphere, a feeling with which she was familiar; she looked up and saw the fog move, but there was no blue sky. A breath of air came down the slope and grey wraiths wafted through the canopy, lifting long strands of lichen that looked like Spanish moss.

She came to a signpost indicating that a left branch of the trail crossed the spine of Pandora to Coon Gulch. The right fork appeared to contour the slope below the crest towards a subsidiary spur that descended in the direction of the village, although she could see nothing below because the basin and the cove to seaward were under the cloud. Above her too there was cloud: a dismal grey nimbus. There was moisture in the air that could be the start of drizzle. She sighed. At that moment there rose out of the well of fog a rending noise that mounted in a terrible crescendo to a thump like an abbreviated explosion. Something gave a creaking yell and she whirled to see a bird, big and black as a crow but with a flaming scarlet head plunge from a tree to jink wildly as it caught sight of her and blunder back to cover.

Her mouth was dry as cardboard. She took off her pack and extracted a flask of lemonade. So, she had seen her first pileated woodpecker – but what was the *other*? Not an aircraft flying supersonically because there was that tearing sound in advance, a sound which she recognised, the sound of a tree falling, but no one was logging here. There had been no whine of a chainsaw, no thock of an axe. Once, a while back, she had fancied she'd heard voices but she'd dismissed them as imagination, probably voices in the stream. If that had been a tree falling on its own, weakened by disease or storm, it was a sobering thought that any of these giants could come down at any time. She looked at the towering conifers with fresh eyes and then sat down to think about it, to eat her lunch, and hope against hope that the woodpecker might come back. But the bird had been too startled to return while she was in the vicinity and after a quarter of an hour she packed up and continued across the slope and round a corner to a depression that was full of magnificent hemlocks and sitka spruce. This was old-growth forest but, although she was on the alert for spotted

46

owls, the only raptor she heard was a red-tailed hawk that kept up a constant complaint from the depths below.

There was one other sound which momentarily she thought was a second tree falling but then she heard following crashes and identified this as a rockfall. And where she might have thought it curious that rock should fall in a timbered depression, she remembered the angle of the slopes, particularly in the upper reaches; in a place where everything was unfamiliar – climate, geology, terrain – what she thought curious could be quite normal. Perhaps even the fact that the steepest ground was high and the rockfall came from below would be explicable to a native.

She came to a fork and a confusing signpost. It read 'Sundown 3.5m' (pointing right) and 'Sundown 3m' (to the left). She would have thought that her chosen route, to the left, would have been the longer because less steep, but when she looked at the map she saw that the right fork, although plunging straight down the slope below her, was longer because it didn't go directly to the village but to Bobcat Creek. She had passed the bottom of it when she started up Porcupine Gulch; she must have missed the sign in the fog.

Her path descended the spur, running through timber so that for long periods there was no outlook, but then she came to an unexpected clearing. The side of the spur was laced by springs and the runnels of water courses, the latter choked by ferns, but in this place heavy rains – perhaps coinciding with an earth tremor– had stressed the slope beyond its capacity to hold, and the surface layer had slipped, taking timber, rocks and soil, and leaving a gash that wasn't terribly wide but it was long. It faced away from the ocean which was why she hadn't seen it from the village. She must have passed quite close to it this morning because Porcupine Gulch was below, and then she recalled the fog and the trees and the fact that her trail had been on the far side of the stream. Below her, the red-tailed hawk floated into view, silent now – if it was the same one that had been calling earlier.

The fog had disappeared completely but the outlook was bewildering. The village and the ocean were hidden by the closer trees and the only feature she could identify was Porcupine Gulch. She couldn't see the trail down there; indeed, she couldn't see much of the landslip, but she guessed that in this place of streams and side streams and hidden crags, there could be some nasty drops below.

The light was failing yet it was only afternoon; the cloud ceiling must have dropped. A low soughing filled the air and zephyrs wandered up the gully, cool one moment, muggy the next. By the time she came to the end of the ridge the rain had started: sudden and heavy. She quickened her pace but the trail turned slick, and silty water cascaded through the slime. The wind was strong, bending and cracking the pines; where the forest had been tranquil a few hours before now it was full of motion and noise. She slithered down the last mile to the loop road and hurried to the haven of her house.

As she closed the front door the telephone started to ring. It was Miriam Ramet complaining that she had been trying to get her neighbour for hours. Did she have any leaks? She should look around, make sure she hadn't and then would she like to join Miriam and the painter, Fleur Sanborn, for dinner at the Tattler?

The Tattler had a sun-room on the south-west corner of the building. There was a bar and there was, fortunately, heating. Miss Pink followed the sound of voices and paused in astonishment as she stepped over the sill. The large windows of the sun-room looked out on a wild sea where all the stacks were spouting spray; a moment later they were obscured by a slash of rain that made her flinch. With the warmth, the furniture upholstered in pale striped tweed, with the flowers and glass and polished wood, the Tattler was like a bathysphere in a dream world.

Miriam was at the bar talking to Boligard Sykes who, unshaven and rumpled, looked as if he had just come from work. Miriam, on the other hand, was resplendent in a silk blouson with a blue and silver dragon rioting across the back. Eve presided behind the bar, colourful in fuchsia, her white hair braided, and secured with tortoiseshell. Miss Pink advanced firmly, well aware of eyes inspecting her Calvin Klein jeans and piqué shirt. She remarked that it was a wild night for August.

'Where were you?' Miriam asked. 'I was worried. I kept calling.'

'I was hiking.' She considered asking where Oliver was but rejected it. She had to live in the same village as Miriam for a week. Instead she told them where she had walked, but before she could elaborate an imposing woman arrived and was introduced as Fleur Sanborn. Miss Pink studied her with interest. She towered over the voluble Miriam, listening but looking at the view, her eyes lighting up when a lull in the gusts revealed the stacks below: ghostly spires with spume like geysers on their windward faces.

'Were you painting today?' Boligard asked, following the direction of her gaze.

'I was on the cape until the light faded.'

'You were painting in the fog?'

She hesitated. 'Trees,' she murmured: 'tree trunks on the edge of the cliff, very softly silhouetted. There was a feel of this tremendous abyss below. The problem was to get the feeling with paint, otherwise it was just tree trunks against fog and could have been level ground below, no space. I wanted that' – she gestured with big hands – 'that delirious plunge.'

'Did you succeed?' Miriam asked carelessly.

'I don't know. You'll have to tell me.'

'Oh, my dear! I'm no judge.'

'That never stopped you trying,' Eve Linquist put in drily and then, as Miriam turned on her: 'What happened to Oliver?'

'He had to go to Portland.'

'He was here yesterday.'

'He had a phone call. Something to do with his work. I don't ask questions.' The remark was pointed.

'Did he go with Andy?' Fleur looked inquiringly at Miriam who seemed at a loss.

It was Eve who responded. 'Andy left? When?'

Fleur sketched a shrug. 'This afternoon, after the rain started. They passed me as I was coming down from the cape. They waved.'

'Oliver left yesterday.' Miriam had found her voice but now she appeared to be angry.

'I just thought he could have been in the back of the Chevy.' Fleur eyed her curiously. 'You can't tell with those smoked windows. Gayleen and Andy were in the front. What I meant was: did Oliver go with them, because he had to go with someone, didn't he? He doesn't have a car. Unless you gave him a lift. But obviously he didn't go with Andy – if he left yesterday.' Miriam was staring at her. 'It's of no importance,' Fleur protested.

Boligard rubbed his hands. 'Great! Now we can all get back to normal.' His face fell. 'Or were they just going a short trip, coming back this evening?'

49

'How do I know?' Fleur was annoyed. 'I assumed they were leaving. They were heading north and in one hell of a hurry, trying to make the roadworks before they closed.'

'Poetic justice if he hit a bulldozer,' Boligard said.

'That girl had a marvellous figure.' The statement from Fleur silenced them until Boligard saw a connection.

'You don't paint people.' It sounded like an accusation.

'I don't have to in order to appreciate good bones.' She shuddered. 'I'd hate to think of that body in an accident.'

Eve raised an eyebrow. 'But you wouldn't be bothered about Andy.'

'No one,' Miriam said acidly, 'would be bothered about Andy Keller.'

'Except— ' Eve stopped and regarded Miss Pink. 'Are English villages like this, ma'am: all living in each other's pockets?'

'Oh, far worse.' Miss Pink was cheerful. 'It's the same all over the world, and no one minds the stranger: ships that pass in the night, you know? I shall never come this way again – and the visitor minds her own business.'

'Discretion is the better part of valour.' Boligard was portentous. 'I have to fit action to the word and go home. I'm in deep trouble as it is for stopping in the Tattler without changing my clothes first.' He nodded to Eve and left in a flurry of knowing laughter that stopped with the closing of the front door.

'Was Hemingway frightened of his wife?' Miriam asked.

'Probably.' Fleur put her empty glass on the bar. 'Is anyone else as hungry as I am?'

'Boligard,' Miriam said to Miss Pink as they moved into the dining-room, 'was drawing our attention to the fact that he'd been incarcerated in his shack all day working on an epic. He's like Pavlov's dogs: conditioned to forcing us to acknowledge him as an author. Force,' she concluded meaningly, 'being the operative word.'

'Everyone has to start some time,' Fleur murmured, smiling at Eve who was placing bowls of soup before them. 'And Jason says that second-rate writers are openly producing books in the style of popular people who are dead. Someone published a book recently that Raymond Chandler began; someone else is imitating Ian Fleming. Boligard may surprise us yet with a blockbuster in the style of Papa.'

'He's trying,' Eve was standing back, watching their faces, 'if the hours he spends in that old shed are any indication.'

'This is delicious,' Miss Pink said, tasting her soup. 'Avocado?'

'Cream of avocado.' Fleur sighed. She wasn't fat but it was clear that the only person in this room who didn't have a weight problem was Miriam, and perhaps she had too. 'If Carl observed modern principles of nutrition,' Fleur told Eve, 'you'd go out of business.'

'And we like money,' Eve said.

'Don't we all.'

'And how *is* Gideon d'Eath?' asked Miriam.

'Fine. The next book's due out very shortly.'

Miss Pink frowned, recognising a familiar ring to the name.

'How you can . . . ' Miriam protested, letting it hang.

'Like Eve said: money.' Fleur was cool. She addressed Miss Pink. 'A few years ago I bought my clothes at thrift stores. This' – she gestured to her ensemble of velour pants and top in orange and pink – 'this is Neiman Marcus. Gideon d'Eath pays for my clothes now – and most everything else.'

'Not her lover,' Miriam explained. 'A comic strip illustrator.'

Fleur's eyes moved as Eve reappeared with a loaded tray. Miss Pink realised they were dining *table d'hôte* and had no qualms.

'*Coquilles St Jacques*?' Eve was simulating concern at her elbow.

Miss Pink beamed. 'My favourite!'

'And did you decide on the burgundy or the moselle?'

'I forgot to ask,' Miriam said crossly, glancing towards Miss Pink who suggested that a white burgundy would be nice, and had visions of its being held under the cold tap.

Fleur guessed the thought. 'Carl will have both at the right temperature,' she said. 'How about that? We'll have both: the burgundy first.'

'Fleur,' said Miriam, 'likes her wine.'

'Tell me about Gideon d'Eath,' Miss Pink demanded as they started on their scallops and she realised that Carl Linquist was living up to his reputation of cream with everything. Eve returned with the wine and poured a little in Miriam's glass. Miriam tasted it with an affectation of boredom, watched by Fleur with amusement and the expressionless Eve. Miss Pink applied herself to her food.

'Fine,' Miriam announced coldly, and Eve served Miss Pink.

'Gideon produces fairy tales,' Fleur was telling her. 'They're not to everyone's taste; you wouldn't care for them, but they sell like hot biscuits. On the other hand I love to paint, but although I run a gallery, no way could I make a living on what I used to sell before Gideon came on the scene. He provides me with my income – or rather my commission does – and the leisure to do my own thing, which is to close the gallery whenever I feel like it and walk out my door and paint trees in the fog on Cape Deception. And that's more than most people can say.' She permitted herself a glint of triumph in Miriam's direction.

'It sounds a very satisfactory lifestyle,' Miss Pink acknowledged. 'There's one of his books in my cottage.'

'What did you think of it?' Miriam asked.

'He's an excellent draughtsman but I didn't think much of the content. It reminds me of modern cult religions: a bit of everything, unoriginal. I understand its appeal but it's not for me.'

'Not for any of us here.' Fleur was unconcerned. 'Jason Sykes tells me he thinks Gideon is "too good" and he prefers Westerns. Jason finds anthropoid monsters disturbing.'

'I thought they were humanoid,' Miriam put in.

Fleur grinned. 'Like Miss Pink says: they're a bit of everything provided it's horrid.'

Miss Pink asked if Gideon d'Eath was a local man and Fleur said he lived in LA.

'She guards his anonymity,' Miriam said. 'And small wonder. She's his sole outlet. You ask me,' she added darkly, 'there's something going on between those two.'

'You're only jealous.' Fleur's smile was engaging.

'I'm jealous because you have a— ' Miriam bit her lip. 'Because you shop at Neiman Marcus?'

'Miriam!' Fleur was horrified. 'Are we going to argue over the relative merits of dress shops? I adore your dragon. Escada, isn't it? Well, look who's here! Hi, Chester!'

The outer door had opened to admit a man in a sou'wester and a yellow slicker. Chester Hoyle bowed politely as he was introduced to Miss Pink. Miriam invited him to join them but he declined and, leaving them to finish their meal, he went to the bar.

'Did Grace leave?' Miriam asked in a low voice.

'She went yesterday,' Fleur said. 'So maybe Lois will be down.'

She turned to Miss Pink. 'Lois Keller is our local celebrity; she writes mysteries. Grace is her daughter and she has a boutique in Portland.' She stopped and glanced at Miriam.

'I passed the house this morning,' Miss Pink said, and checked herself, but less abruptly.

The silence stretched until Miriam said, 'Lois had a big party at the weekend, for her fortieth birthday. Everyone came.'

'That would be her husband,' Miss Pink mused, 'in here at lunchtime yesterday?'

'That was him.' Eve had approached soundlessly. 'With his assistant.'

'They've left,' Fleur told Miss Pink, somewhat superfluously. 'So you won't be meeting them.'

A stiffness had descended on the party but that could have been the result of the rich food and wine; between them they had drunk the burgundy and most of the moselle. Deciding against dessert they returned to the sun-room where lamps glowed cheerfully, and curtains had been drawn against the outer gloom. Chester Hoyle joined them for brandy and coffee and they discussed the storm.

Miss Pink found Chester interesting despite his plain appearance. She learned that he was an engineer, had been with Boeing, was now retired, widowed and childless, but absorbed in the kind of activities that might occupy a man in similar circumstances in an English village. He tended his garden, looked after his house and was interested in natural history. He voiced the same complaint as that of the elderly Englishman: 'I'm busier now than before I retired,' but he smiled as he said it.

The main reason for his contentment became apparent with the arrival of Lois Keller: a slim brown woman in a cotton shirt and jeans. After she was introduced she sank into a squashy chair exuding fatigue and an odour of bath talc. She beamed at them but her eyelids drooped. At the bar Eve Linquist poured brandy.

'I worked out that chapter,' Lois said to Chester as if he were the only person present, then she glanced at Fleur: 'You know how it feels.'

'I know how it feels to get a painting right,' Fleur said. 'Were you having problems?'

'It's all over; I don't want to talk about it. Ah, brandy, you're an angel, Eve. I was in such a fog when I finished I haven't had a drink yet.' She drank, sighed and focused on the stranger. 'You must think me crazy. I write mysteries and I've been bothered for days with a difficulty in the plot. Today I got it right. I'm winding down now; I'll be normal after another brandy.'

'I guessed,' Chester said. 'You wouldn't answer the phone.'

'I never heard it ring!' She continued to address Miss Pink: 'I keep my phone inside a sleeping-bag in another room.'

'You should have an answering machine.' Miriam was heavy with disapproval.

'Answering machines are rude.'

Fleur giggled and Chester's eyes gleamed, then the gleam faded and Miss Pink, watching him, saw the softness of his expression and knew that the business of cultivating his garden and watching wildlife were only gloss on his retirement. Chester was in love.

Miriam fiddled with the straw in her margarita. 'What time did Andy and his assistant leave?' she asked.

'Before four. I was at work by then.' Lois grinned. 'Well – work; I mean I was in my study at four; it took me a while to get the continuity again. After all, I'd done no work for four days!' Her voice rose as if she'd only just realised the fact.

'And you never got to keep your Chevy,' Miriam said nastily.

'Oh, Miriam, it's five years old. Who cares? I'm not possessive.'

'You can say that again.' There was a load of meaning in the cliché. Lois stared and the little woman avoided her eye.

Fleur leapt to the breach: 'I saw them leave; Andy was going like the clappers to make the roadworks.'

'Really?' Lois was vague. 'They don't close till six.'

'What are these roadworks?' Miss Pink asked. 'People keep mentioning them.'

'There was a landslip on the coast road north of Sundown,' Chester told her. 'The Highways people repaired the damage but now it appears the slope isn't safe and they're stabilising it. Seems to be taking longer than the original repairs.'

'They've been at it for weeks,' Miriam complained. 'They go home at six and they don't start work again until eight in the morning, so the road's closed all night and they put those great earth-moving machines across so there's no way you can get by.'

'They're afraid of people going over the edge,' Fleur pointed out. 'But it can be a nuisance; it means if you have business north of the roadworks you have to come home before six. And you can't go to Portland for the evening.'

'Unless you stay the night there,' Chester amended. 'But it doesn't really affect us, not in summertime. Concerts and such don't start until the fall, and who wants to dine in Portland? We've got everything we need here.'

Fleur looked round and saw that Carl Linquist was behind the bar. 'Come and join us,' she called. 'Bring a drink.'

'Eve's watching television,' he said as he joined them and, turning to Lois, 'So it's back to normal, is it? After all the excitement.' She nodded; it didn't need a response. 'I passed them,' he continued. 'Andy lifted his hand' – his lip curled – 'Gayleen waved.'

There was a charged silence, broken by Lois. 'Actually,' she said, 'if I had her legs I would wear a mini-skirt and high red heels.' She looked wistful. 'I've always hankered after a pair of shoes like that – and every time I come out of the shoe store with yet another pair of moccasins or kilties.'

'Oh, come on, Lois!' Fleur pretended to be shocked. 'She was— ' She checked and blinked.

'No better than she should be,' Carl completed for her, then thought he'd gone too far. 'Assistant or whatever,' he muttered with a bothered glance at Lois.

'I like her,' she said brightly. 'She spent the day at the house and she told me quite a lot about herself.' She looked round their circle. 'That child's had a hard time; she was a change girl in Las Vegas, whatever that is— '

'Worked in a casino,' Chester supplied. 'Carried change for customers.'

'So – she's been everything: short order cook, gas pump attendant; she even auditioned for a showgirl but couldn't make the grade. She never stays in a job for longer than a few weeks. She's only eighteen and very immature. I'm sorry for her. I'm afraid she's not a survivor.'

'That was obvious,' Carl said.

Miriam had been thinking. 'What was Andy doing while you were having this *tête à tête*?' she asked. 'I can't see him joining in a girlish conversation.'

'No, hardly.' Lois smiled. 'He went for a hike.'

'Would he have been looking for spotted owls?' Fleur asked coldly.

'How he dared!' Miriam exclaimed. 'On your car too!'

Lois shrugged. 'It's black humour, Miriam; there's no malice behind it. Andy puts spiders out of the house, and he adores Lovejoy.'

'I didn't think the malice was directed towards animals,' Miriam said, looking hard at her.

Lois smiled and refused to rise to the bait. She turned to Miss Pink. 'Are you interested in the local wildlife? Did they tell you about our spotted owls?'

Chapter 5

By dawn the storm had blown itself out and there was merely a stiff onshore breeze. Above the strand there was a haze made up of spray and salt and vapour from damp vegetation; through this the sun shone with a soft brilliance and cast black shadows. It was muggy and chill at the same time. Humidity was high.

The breakers rolled shorewards: huge, regular, hypnotic. Miss Pink, walking south towards Fin Whale Head along the fringe of foam bubbles, was reminded of her childhood. The sand was clean and beautiful, matte round her boot as her weight pressed out the moisture, and among the rocks there were pools full of sea anemones and shrimps, while offshore the stacks stood up like benign sentinels. Below Sundown people were beachcombing after the storm, looking for Japanese fishing floats in the weed. The houses behind them resembled toy houses – and where the land started to rise towards the big cliffs of the headland there were caves and arches. Inland the spired conifers deepened the nostalgia: Hans Andersen trees fronting a magical ocean. A string of pelicans came beating past, checked, circled and, one by one, started to fish, plunging like gannets into the heaving sea.

Miss Pink walked to a dry rock, removed her socks and boots, rolled up her jeans and returned to wade through the spent waves.

Within two miles the sand ran into jumbled rocks where the cliffs were crumbling into the sea. She turned back then to find a flock of sanderlings feeding on the ebb, their tiny legs twinkling as they rushed after receding water, to turn and scamper back ahead of the next breaker. The sanderlings were about the only familiar feature of this wild coast, for the feeling that it shared a similarity with the Devon of childhood was, on reflection, ridiculous: she had been misled by the salt spray that permeated everything, and which would be the same the world over: Sundown or Maine or the Isles of Scilly.

Ahead of her one figure stood out from the distant beach-combers, looming large, something else breaking away to one side. The sound of yapping came clearly on the breeze. Oliver Harper was trotting towards her, the schnauzer beside him, racing back and forth in a vain attempt to catch birds. Oliver came up and stopped: young and splendid in skimpy shorts, his chest heaving gently with the exertion.

'I've heard all about you now, ma'am,' he announced, smiling, knowing he looked marvellous, 'Miriam filled me in. Enjoying your hike?'

She enthused about the morning, admired the terrier which was waxing hysterical over the behaviour of the sanderlings, and left him to his run. He trotted to the rocks and came back, waving gaily as he passed, shouting something about seeing her this evening. She regarded his brown back with approval and wondered why Miriam wasn't running with him. Oliver had been to Portland, she recalled, so had Lois's daughter, Grace – and Lois's husband and his pretty assistant 'or whatever', as Carl Linquist had put it. Portland was, of course, the lodestone for this coast; there was probably nothing curious about all the youngsters – well, Andy Keller wasn't young, but the other three – all being in the city at the same time. No doubt there was a simple explanation, if it were not a coincidence. Miss Pink liked to know the answers to questions that arose, however idly, in her mind, and it didn't occur to her at this moment that there were questions of which she was unaware.

Oliver's remark about seeing her this evening, and Miriam's absence from the morning's run, were explained when the lady herself called with an invitation to dine at her house that night; she was cooking, she explained, neatly pre-empting any speculation as to whether she could keep up with Oliver's pace. Miss Pink had scarcely replaced the receiver before Leo Brant was on the line, asking if she would eat with them the following evening. It would appear that, with the embarrassing Andy Keller out of the way, people were hurrying to return Lois's hospitality of the previous weekend. No doubt eating out was one of their ways of having fun – and small wonder if the food in private houses rivalled that of the Tattler.

Over the next few days she made the rounds of Sundown society and found the experience interesting and, occasionally, informative. She dined with Miriam in her old and slightly shabby redwood ranchhouse but where the carpets came from Aleppo and the smoked salmon from the Spey. Oliver was present but Willard Smith did not appear. She wouldn't have been surprised at this anyway but Sadie Locke, whom she had thought of initially as a gentle person, called her attention to Oliver with some remark concerning his youth. Miss Pink, not troubling to mince her words with this ingenuous old soul, had asked what was his position in the household – a distant relative perhaps?

'He's the handyman,' Sadie told her.

Miss Pink said she thought Willard Smith was the handyman.

'Oliver,' said Sadie, 'is the *new* handyman.' And Miss Pink turned to find the old lady regarding her with a gleam of amusement.

The other guests at Miriam's house were Lois and Chester, and Fleur Sanborn. These, forming a kind of inner circle of Sundown society, trooped round to each other's houses. It was understood that the Linquists were unable to leave the restaurant, and the Sykeses had to attend to their motel, although Jason appeared from time to time, like a cross between a well-trained retriever and a peripatetic butler: opening wine, handing canapés, getting up from the table to turn down the oven or bring fresh butter.

Dinner at Sand Dollar – Leo's and Sadie's place – started with a tension that no one appeared to notice other than Miss Pink. Sadie was a nervous cook but after a while she emerged from the kitchen, sparkling and talkative.

'Leo allows her one martini after the guests arrive,' Fleur explained to Miss Pink, 'and shortly before we sit down. But you notice Leo is distrait. I guess there's something on the stove which has to be attended to. She'll send Sadie back in a minute. Sadie can't hold her liquor. Not *and* cook.'

But the main dish was crayfish as good as any Miss Pink had enjoyed in the Jura. They ate off Portmeirion ware and drank from Dartington crystal. It was evident that Leo and Sadie didn't have much money to spare but what they had they used well. Their little clapboard house was carefully maintained (they did everything themselves, Fleur said; Leo had even rewired the place); the furniture was old but good and the rooms looked as if they were vacuumed daily.

Chester didn't cook and his entertaining was done at the Tattler. Miss Pink enjoyed four excellent dinners in a row and had it not been that she starved herself during the day, and went for long tramps, by the following weekend she would have felt like a Strasbourg goose, but each morning saw her setting out diligently to burn off the previous evening's excess. After Miriam's party she walked with Lois and Chester from Fin Whale Head to Porcupine Gulch by way of Pandora Ridge. They utilised two cars for that and they saw the pileated woodpecker and three Roosevelt elk.

After the party given by Sadie and Leo she did a dull but strenuous plod to the summit of Lost Peak on her own. This was the culminating point of the ridge on the north side of Bobcat Creek. It was approached by interminable zigzags, hidden in the timber, and there was no view. That evening she grumbled a little as they ate Chester's dinner in the Tattler, and Fleur said immediately that the following morning they should go to the dunes north of Cape Deception.

The day was a little like a dull summer's day in England except for the fog which, having retreated by mid-morning, lay in a solid bank a few miles offshore. The sky was cloudy and the air quite cool. The dunes beyond the cape were separated from the highway by a belt of conifers interspersed with myrtle and other hardwoods. Freshwater pools stood in marshy depressions and the grass was alive with frogs and little garter snakes splotched with red.

When they reached the dunes Miss Pink was surprised to find them almost covered with vegetation that was so high and tangled, so impervious to human penetration that it had been necessary to erect posts to mark the trail. 'You'd be lost without them,' Fleur said. 'In fact, people get lost *with* them – in the fog, at night.'

Miss Pink shivered. They were in a dip and she could see no posts anywhere. Narrow trails made by raccoons or skunks looked no different from the one they should follow. 'Yes,' Fleur said, guessing the thought, 'this is the place gave Gideon the idea for his first book, *The Walking Dune*.'

'You're making it worse. Does Gideon do anything else besides these books?'

'He doesn't need to.'

'I meant, he draws so well— ' but Fleur had stopped and was squinting northwards. 'Do you hear something?' she asked.

'Only breakers – or is there a train? No, there's no railway here.'

They resumed walking and shortly they emerged from the scrub to the open strand. There was no one about other than themselves and visibility was about a mile. The tide was nearly at the full, the wet sand dark and hard. Higher up it was the colour of crab shells. Black turnstones were feeding on the edge of the foam and the long, low breakers came rolling in: inexorable, infinitely exciting.

'There *is* something,' Fleur insisted. 'Can't you hear it?'

'I heard it before but it still sounds like a train to me, an engine anyway.'

'I know! It's something at the roadworks – but they're all of ten miles away.'

It wasn't earth-moving machinery; it was a helicopter. It came along the shore, flying low. They looked up at it without surprise; there were a dozen reasons why a chopper should be here: the Coastguard on call or patrolling, the Highways Department, the Forest Service, a private machine chartered by a professional photographer – but it was none of these. They walked for miles along the strand and went home to discover that the close-knit community was seething with speculation. The helicopter had brought policemen. Lois's car had been involved in an accident and the driver had run away.

'Naturally,' said Lois, 'they thought it was me driving so they flew down here to take me back to Portland in shackles.'

They were all gathered in the sun-room at the Tattler, this being the evening that Miss Pink had taken it on herself to be the host.

'I can't think why they sent detectives at all,' Jason said. 'Just for a little hit-and-run, and no one got hurt.'

'It was the run bit,' Fleur told him. 'The running away: it looks suspicious.'

'They were nice guys though' – he hadn't heard her – 'came in the store and chatted, bought some Louis l'Amours; they stayed a while, told me all about detective work in the city.'

'What did you tell them?' Oliver asked.

Jason blinked owlishly and said he couldn't remember, and what sort of things did Oliver mean?

61

'He means, dear,' Lois said kindly, 'that they're checking on me with other people because it was a woman driving.'

Fleur said, 'But you don't wear mini-skirts and frequent Portland's red-light district.'

Lois giggled. 'The police don't know that.'

The accident itself had been minor. A van driver had emerged carelessly from a side street and rammed the Chevrolet. The person in the Chevy had tried to extricate her car by reversing, only to find the bumpers of both vehicles locked. She had then jumped out and run – this despite the fact that she was the innocent party, at least as far as that incident was concerned. This had happened two evenings ago, in the dark, but there had been witnesses. They said the driver of the Chevy was tall and was wearing a mini-skirt and white sandals. The area was one frequented by prostitutes.

'It had to be Gayleen,' Fleur said now. 'But why should she run? Is the Chevy insured only for you and Andy?'

'The police asked that,' Lois said, 'but it's just ordinary insurance, anyone can drive it.'

'Oh dear,' came Sadie's gentle voice, and Leo confirmed the thought: 'So Gayleen's got something to hide; couldn't face the fuzz.'

Oliver said, 'Could she have left Andy and taken the car?'

Lois said firmly, 'Obviously it wasn't Andy driving so' – she spread her hands – 'I just left it to the police, sort of opted out, you know? As Jason said, they were charmers. The younger one even has a cat like— '

Mabel Sykes interrupted, smiling unpleasantly: 'But if Gayleen stole the Chevy, why didn't Andy report it stolen?'

Lois blinked. 'Has he had time?' she asked uncertainly, then more firmly: 'He wouldn't want to cause trouble for her. Anyway, why should she have stolen it? It could be she was just shopping, using the car; she got a bump and couldn't face the police.'

'Because – ?' Mabel's smile was now a grin.

Miss Pink said, 'Perhaps her licence has been suspended. It could be some small infringement, not something criminal.' She glanced at Eve who was advancing with a cocktail shaker and changed the subject: 'I'm sure everyone could do with a second martini . . . ' Out of the corner of her eye she saw that Leo was framing a question and heard Sadie's clear response: 'They have to eat somewhere; you can ask them when they come.'

They could be referring to the police, who seemed to have their own problems. Either the helicopter had been needed elsewhere in a hurry, or they'd allowed it to go, thinking to hire a car, but there were no cars for hire in Sundown and now they were stranded and running up a terrific telephone bill apparently trying to find a car or a chopper to pick them up tomorrow morning. Meanwhile they had booked a room at the Surfbird and Boligard remained up there putting through their telephone calls.

The detectives walked into the dining-room after Miss Pink's party had sat down to dinner. Eve had anticipated their arrival and put as much distance as possible between the tables, but it wasn't a large room and no conversation could be private if conducted in normal tones. There was an air of restraint at the big table emphasised by a somewhat noisy gaiety, and an avoidance of any subject that related to cars or crime or the police. With varying degrees of fervour they concentrated on spotted owls, storms, whale-watching: anything that was innocent, and all the time they were uncomfortably aware of this *presence* at the side of the room.

The detectives, on the other hand, were making the most of their enforced sojourn in the backwoods. They ordered chablis with their lobster thermidor (they had to eat the same food as the main party; as usual Carl had prepared only one dish) and they listened attentively to Oliver who had been pressed into service as their waiter, leaving Eve free to attend to the other table.

Oliver was getting on splendidly with them, at least with the one Lois said was the senior partner: Laddow. He was talkative and ebullient but not vulgar. He had expressive eyes and a wide mouth, and hair that reached his collar but otherwise was cut so short that his head appeared to be framed in a dark halo. His face was extraordinarily mobile; whether he was asking questions or just listening, all his features, even his nose, twisted like soft rubber, reflecting his emotions or the emotions he sought to display, while his hands: broad, with stubby fingers, were never still. He was a large man, a little overweight under the tan suit and silk polo shirt, but not flabby.

His companion, who was called Hammett, was a different kettle of fish. Seemingly some ten years younger (Laddow was about forty), he was prematurely bald but with a lot of hair at the back of his polished skull that gave him the look of an egg-head in a slippery toupee. His large eyes were accentuated by wire-rimmed spectacles and his mouth was small and prim. He wore a modish shirt striped in rust and cream, and beige slacks. He said little; Laddow did most of the talking.

Miss Pink, deceptively bland, brought her attention back to the table and noted that her guests were losing their inhibitions. Unobtrusively she checked the levels in glasses and bottles, looked to see that everyone was eating well, and wondered how many of them could manage Carl's peach compote, even without the cream. The meal wound down gently and, at a sign from Miss Pink, Lois rose and led the way to the sunroom.

When they were settled in front of the windows with coffee and liqueurs, pointedly concentrating on the sunset – which, behind a partially cloudy sky, was fiery – there was a sudden lull as if a curtain were about to rise. At that point the police entered, smiled – Laddow smiled – and waited. Lois introduced them: Eddy Laddow and Mort Hammett.

As Lois went round the company naming people the decision whether to ask the detectives to sit down was taken out of Miss Pink's hands by the beaming Laddow who absent-mindedly turned a chair to face the ocean and subsided into it. Hammett went to the bar. Laddow appeared to notice the sky for the first time and gasped. 'It's like an explosion!' he exclaimed, and the villagers regarded him indulgently.

'Don't you ever go to the ocean?' Leo asked.

'I see it occasionally, ma'am, but I never saw a view like this, with those rocks and the cape there. Ah, thank you, my boy.' He took a whisky from the expressionless Hammett. 'Get a chair, get a chair.' He was fussing; Miss Pink felt sure he was putting on an act, that he was preparing for something. She looked at the others, saw that they too were aware that something was toward and she felt their frisson of alarm.

'You'll have the number of your husband's office,' Laddow stated conversationally, addressing Lois.

'He didn't have an office,' she responded weakly.

'His apartment then?' He sipped his whisky, not watching her, but Hammett did.

She glanced helplessly round the company. 'I – the name of it escapes me. Did anyone hear it?' People shook their heads like marionettes.

'Why?' Leo asked, sounding belligerent and then, at a movement from Sadie: 'You must have taken his phone number when he reported the theft of the car.'

'He didn't report it.' Laddow looked at Leo with interest. She was chic and boyish tonight in a lemon shirt with an agate bolo. 'Why do we need to see Mr Keller?' he asked, and answered his own question: 'Because we got a report on the car, on Mrs Keller's Chevy.' He turned to Lois. 'What happened to the trunk, ma'am?'

Miss Pink was puzzled and then remembered that the trunk was the boot of the car.

'The trunk?' Lois repeated, her voice rising. Then, aware of her own stridency, her shoulders dropped and she relaxed visibly. 'I didn't know anything happened to it.'

'It's been forced.'

They stared at him and after a moment Chester said slowly, 'If the car was stolen, without the keys – hot-wired – but the trunk was locked, it would have to be forced to get inside.' His voice strengthened as he envisaged the situation: 'The thief would want to see if there was luggage in the trunk.'

Hammett said, 'You can get into a trunk by taking out the rear seat.'

'Not on the Chevy,' Lois said absently. 'That back seat is jammed, something to do with the ratchet.' She frowned. 'What makes it important: the trunk being forced?'

'When did you last look inside it?'

Her eyes glazed. 'I remember looking inside; I was wondering if Andy – my husband – had brought his laundry, so that must have been shortly after he arrived.' She was bothered but she went on raggedly, 'The party – it was the Sunday . . . I would have looked in the trunk next morning.'

'Was it locked?'

'No.'

'Did you notice anything odd about the interior, anything there that shouldn't be?'

Her eyes sharpened, and now some of the others had caught on: drugs, they were thinking, and one or two of them: so what, it was *Andy* using the car. 'No,' Lois said firmly. 'I didn't see anything. Should I have done?'

'A smell, for instance?'

Eyes widened. Several people sniffed.

'No,' Lois said. 'I don't remember anything. Why?'

'Because a body's been carried in that trunk,' Laddow said.

Chapter 6

It was a long time before anyone spoke. No one wanted to be the first, and the police did nothing to ease the situation. Hammett had remained standing, a tumbler in his hand, but he wasn't drinking. Then Miss Pink remembered that it was her party, that she was still the host. She turned to Laddow, remarked in the voice she used to call to order meetings of the Women's Institute: 'Perhaps you would elaborate, Mr Laddow,' and had the satisfaction of making that rubbery face go completely blank for a moment. She sensed resentment; he would have liked to ask her where her own interests lay, but he didn't. Hammett, alert as a hawk, would be wondering that too, but he had to leave the initiative to his superior.

Laddow looked from her to Lois. 'We have to find your husband, ma'am.' Emotion had returned: his intensity justified by an appearance of anxious distress.

Lois had recovered from the initial shock of learning that her car had been used to transport a body. She had had time to think, to work things out. 'Of course it was stolen,' she said quietly, addressing no one in particular, 'and there's an obvious reason why Andy didn't report it.' She looked at Laddow. 'He was working on the screenplay of one of my books and a Burbank studio was interested. What happened, what must have happened, is he left the car in the airport parking lot in Portland and flew to LA. It was stolen from the airport and he doesn't know about it yet.'

'Or Gayleen drove him to the airport,' Sadie put in, 'and the Chevy was stolen from her, or— ' She stopped in consternation, seeing where that was leading.

Hammett said, making a question of it, 'It would be helpful if someone could remember where Mr Keller was staying?' He looked round the group and stopped at Jason who was staring at him open-mouthed. 'Yes, sir?'

'Grace!' Jason exclaimed. 'Grace was trying to find out where. She'd know. I heard Gayleen say something about a motel, but I didn't catch the name.'

'Would you like me to call my daughter?' Lois asked politely.

'If you would, ma'am.' Laddow responded in kind.

She left the room and the others shifted awkwardly, avoiding each other's eyes except for Leo who tackled Laddow bluntly: 'You knew about this all along; that's why you stayed. You sent the chopper away deliberately.'

'No, no!' He was shocked. 'There was this smell, you see.' Now he was apologetic. 'Unpleasant. So the car was with the Forensic people. They called us this evening with the results— '

'Like I said— '

'A woman,' he went on. 'It was the body of a woman.'

'Well, that knocks my theory on the head,' Jason announced. They stared at him.

'What was your theory, sir?' Laddow asked with interest.

Jason nodded as if acknowledging a tribute. 'Why, they picked up a hitch-hiker and the guy killed them both and stole the car. I wouldn't have said that with Lois here, of course; too distressing for her. But if it was a woman in the trunk, I mean a female body, what happened to Andy's body?'

'He could have been alone when he picked up the hitch-hiker,' Hammett said reasonably, as if this were an academic discussion between equals.

'No.' Jason was confident. 'He left with Gayleen.'

'So you figure they picked up a hitch-hiker on Tuesday afternoon,' Laddow said, and Miss Pink noted that he had the times off pat.

'When did you say the accident occurred?' Chester asked. 'When the driver ran away from the Chevy?'

'Late Thursday evening, two nights ago.'

'So where— '

Lois came in slowly as if uncertain of her reception. Everyone regarded her expectantly. 'He was staying at a motel called the Fountain,' she told them. 'On the north side of the city.'

'Did you call the motel?' Laddow asked sharply.

'No, I— ' She bit her lip. There was a flicker of fear in

her eyes, quickly suppressed. Chester looked concerned.

'If you'll excuse us one moment.' Laddow rose and left the room with Hammett.

Now they did stare at each other: questioning, appalled. Chester leaned towards Lois and said quietly, 'It was a *woman's* body in the trunk.' She stared at him blankly. 'Of course the car was stolen,' he added.

'Of course it was.'

'Oh, it had to be,' Fleur put in, but the tone lacked warmth.

'What are they doing?' Sadie gestured towards the door.

Leo scowled. 'Calling the motel.'

Eve approached from the bar. 'Oliver will find out,' she said. 'They heard everything: him and Carl; the door to the kitchen wasn't closed.'

'Who needs to know?' Mabel asked, her eyes glinting.

'I want to.' Lois was coldly angry. 'If Andy's mixed up in anything— ' She stopped, then went on stiffly, 'This concerns my family.' She stared at the door and again Miss Pink caught that suggestion of fear. 'I think Laddow will tell us what he finds out. He's a gentleman,' she added with a kind of desperation.

'Well, he's putting on a good act,' Miriam said. Since they left the dining-room she had sat unobtrusively to one side, merely a part of the audience that was a background to the principal performers.

'They're a competent team,' Miss Pink murmured.

'What's your base-line?' Leo asked, and then elaborated: 'I mean, what do you base your judgment on? You don't know American police.'

'Or do you?' Chester eyed her keenly. When she had been walking with him and Lois, she had confessed that she wrote gothics for magazines, and the odd travel book, but she'd said nothing about her activities involving crime. Now, before their combined attention, she shifted uncomfortably.

'I've had a little to do with them,' she admitted, and was immediately plied with questions. Laddow and Hammett, appearing in the doorway, paused and listened. The group in the window was excited and obviously relieved to have the subject changed – or at least to have the location shifted away from home. Homicide was now something that had concerned Miss Pink in Montana and Utah and California, not one of themselves.

69

Miriam wasn't giving undivided attention to Miss Pink's reminiscences; she seemed jumpy, glancing towards the kitchen and the dining-room, so it was she who saw the police and said loudly, '*Now* maybe we'll have an explanation.' The tone was a warning.

Talk stopped as if a switch had been thrown. Laddow came and sat down. 'Yes,' he said heavily, as if he were continuing a conversation, taking them into his confidence, 'they're worried at the motel. They haven't been seen since last Sunday morning.'

'They?' Jason repeated stupidly.

'Sorry.' Laddow widened doggy eyes at his own sloppy speech. 'Gayleen and Andy haven't been back to their room for just on a week.'

No one dared to speak, mutely deferring to Lois. She ignored the less important implication and said without expression, 'So they didn't go back to the motel after they left here . . . Maybe they didn't go back to Portland at all, but went south from here: down to LA.'

'But— '

'The car— '

Fleur and Laddow spoke together. Charmingly he gestured to her to continue. She said, 'They were driving north when I saw them.'

'And Carl,' Eve put in. 'Carl passed them north of here.'

'And the car turns up in Portland,' Laddow mused. 'It's not conclusive but it does look as if they went back to Portland.'

Jason started to say something, glanced at Lois and his mouth snapped shut, but she had seen. 'What were you going to say, Jason?'

He licked his lips. 'It was nothing.'

She stared at him and he flushed. She looked at the others, at Laddow, her eyes stricken. 'You think— ' She couldn't go on.

Laddow stood up. 'What I think, ma'am, is we should stop speculating. We don't know what happened yet but' – he looked round the circle – 'you all in Sundown are safe; Mrs Keller's daughter's unharmed in Portland, you got nothing to worry about. I suggest we all go home and get a good night's sleep.' His features twisted lugubriously. 'I'm being subjective there; personally I'm ready for my bed.'

'Shamming,' Miss Pink said, addressing Fleur as they heard the outer door close.

'He can't fool you.' Was there a hint of sarcasm there?

'Well,' Miss Pink began, and frowned. 'Not on this occasion. He's gone back to the Surfbird to use the telephone. Boligard's going to be up late tonight.'

'Listening in?'

'Quite, but d'you think Laddow and Hammett aren't aware of that?'

'Talk of eavesdropping, here's Oliver.'

He and Carl Linquist had come in from the kitchen, Oliver making an obvious but vain attempt to conceal his excitement, Carl making a similar effort but succeeding only in looking angry.

'Oliver!' Miriam's tone was a command. 'Come here. Did you hear the call to Portland?'

'We did.' He came and perched on the arm of her chair. 'But there was nothing sinister about it. Of course we only heard his end of the conversation – the jolly one, Laddow, isn't it? He asked if they' – he paused at the pronoun but recovered easily – 'were staying there, and then he asked when they'd left and when they were expected back, and if they'd taken their stuff. Then they went into a huddle: Laddow and his side-kick, and I couldn't hear any more.'

'They knew you were listening,' Miriam said.

'Undoubtedly.'

'What I want to know,' Carl put in angrily, 'is what's it got to do with us?'

'Nothing, dear.' Eve was reassuring. 'It's just the car – isn't it, Miss Pink?'

Thus appealed to she pulled herself together; she had been thinking, like Laddow, of bed. 'They'll be tracing the car's movements,' she suggested. 'First confirming the ownership – they'd have got that from the registration' – she glanced at Lois who raised her eyebrows a fraction; she was plainly exhausted – 'now they're concerned about what happened to the car between here and Portland. The implication is that the inquiries will shift away from Sundown to the highway. We may have seen the last of Messrs Laddow and Hammett.'

For a moment, next morning, the opposite seemed to be the case when two cars arrived at the Surfbird and large men in civilian clothes were directed to the Tattler where Laddow and

71

Hammett were eating breakfast. The Sykeses and the Linquists monitored the activity as closely as possible and it transpired that, far from being reinforcements, the newcomers were merely delivering a car to the erstwhile stranded detectives. The strangers drove back north in the second vehicle, and Sundown braced itself for a resumption of the inquiries, only to experience an anti-climax when Laddow and Hammett checked out of the Surfbird, got in their transport and took off themselves, northwards. There were people who thought this smacked of rudeness: 'After all,' Jason said petulantly to Miss Pink who had stepped into his store to chat, 'they might have said goodbye, at least.'

'It wasn't a social visit.'

'No, but – talking like that, last night, it was sorta *intimate*, and then to take off without speaking to anyone. It was offhand.'

'They could be coming back.'

'What for?'

She sighed. 'I don't know. But they have to find Andy Keller – and Gayleen, of course – and this was Andy's home, and where he was last seen— '

'That's ridiculous! I'm sorry, I didn't mean to be rude; I mean, hundreds of people must have seen him – them – after they left here; well, dozens.'

'The police work forward, Jason. This is the last place where someone is *known* to have seen them. Fleur, then Carl, saw them on the road. Now the detectives have to find the next person who saw them. For my money the reason why Laddow and Hammett have gone north is because they're making inquiries along the highway, trying to discover if Andy stopped for gas, a meal, whatever.'

'What happens if they don't find the next person?'

'Then they'll concentrate on the last person who says he saw them, and that's Carl, and that's what will bring them back to Sundown. Who did they telephone last night after they left the Tattler?'

'They just called their office to finalise transportation for this morning. They didn't make private calls from the motel.'

She looked at him sharply. 'Where did they make them from?'

'The call-box outside the bar. It was Laddow did the talking with Hammett standing by, making sure no one could get near enough to hear.'

'How do you know this?'

'Several people saw them; they didn't make a secret of it.' He regarded her in surprise. 'They're not going to make private calls from the motel, are they, with my dad and mom listening?'

'So they're making private calls but they're not concerned that people know it. I suppose you could say that they're conditioned to secrecy.'

'What else could you say?'

She raised her eyebrows. 'That they're trying to intimidate us?'

That 'us' was not a slip; she felt herself involved – and she was in an irritable mood this morning. She had come to enjoy the company of the local residents and, although she was only a visitor, relationships had been forged; she felt a sense of loyalty. She would have liked to go for a walk but it seemed ill-mannered to leave them, and yet when she considered which one she might ask to go with her, she fancied her company could be an embarrassment. When she made an effort to analyse this presentiment, she guessed that they would all be discussing the events of last evening among themselves: Sadie and Leo, Miriam and Oliver, the Linquists, the Sykeses, Lois and Chester. That left only Fleur, who had walked with her yesterday but hadn't phoned this morning to suggest a meeting.

Miss Pink compromised. Leaving Jason's store she took a short walk along the strand towards Fin Whale Head. There was no sign of Oliver this morning and she saw no one else whom she knew. She returned to the village by way of a path that traced the edge of old and overgrown grazing land above the shore. The path emerged on the highway close to Fleur's gallery – which was the reason that she'd taken it.

The gallery was an old whaler's cabin, built of wood with plank walls and a shingled roof. The planks had shrunk and the shingles curled up at the edges; everything was grey, weathered to the colour of rock. Inside, that same drabness became a foil for colour where brilliant pieces of stained glass, from window panes to goblets and lamps, had been set strategically to catch the light.

Fleur sold a variety of objects, from fused glass to wind chimes and books. The emphasis, of course, was on Gideon d'Eath but Miss Pink, who initially had been overwhelmed by kitsch, had discovered Fleur's own water-colours among the junk.

She found them enchanting for their feeling for rock and sand, in smudges of colour that implied the dense blanket of forest rather than delineating it, in the sense of space westward to a horizon beyond the fog.

This morning Fleur was standing in the middle of the cabin, smoking, and watching the highway through the window. 'They just passed,' she said without preamble. 'I'm wondering where they went.'

'They?' But Miss Pink knew the answer.

'The police. At least, it was the car Laddow and Hammett were driving when they left after breakfast. They must have gone to the motel; there's no one else lives south of here.'

'There are houses on the loop road.'

'Then they'd have taken that road before they reached the village.'

'Not necessarily; it's dirt, it's smoother to come through the village, turn back . . . '

They stared at each other, jumpy as cats, arguing about nothing.

'Why did they come back?' Fleur asked. Miss Pink didn't reply. Fleur drew on her cigarette. She noticed Miss Pink move back a step and apologised. 'I smoke only when I'm under stress. It doesn't happen often. Tell me, what do *you* think is the explanation? The Chevy was stolen? So who was the girl ran away? Not Gayleen, surely, because if it was Gayleen, who was it in the trunk?'

'There would be fingerprints on the car,' Miss Pink mused. 'She didn't have time to wipe them off.' She paused, then continued, 'The police checked out from the motel, according to Jason, so since they've returned then they've discovered something new, something that concerns Sundown.'

It was indeed Laddow and Hammett who had returned, checking in again at the Surfbird, but whatever they had discovered, initially they were seeking information. When, after half an hour, their car didn't appear on the highway, Fleur rang Jason. The bookstore was only a few yards from the gallery but they could see that he had customers. When he answered she asked him quietly what was going on.

'I'll tell you,' he said meaningly.

'Come over for a coffee when you're free.'

His customers left and he emerged from the store to shamble

quickly along to the gallery. He was obviously excited. 'Did you see the police?' he asked, without even looking to see if they were alone.

'That's why we told you to come over.' Fleur was impatient. 'What happened?'

'Mom says they're asking what Gayleen was wearing.'

'*What*!' Fleur was flabbergasted. Miss Pink said nothing.

'It was a black skirt,' he went on, 'a mini with' – his hands scalloped the air – 'sorta frills— '

'Flounces,' Fleur murmured. 'A flounced skirt: shabby, like *old* black. Red heels.'

He nodded eagerly. 'Yeah, red shoes; Mom told them that and, she said, a ruffle perm.'

'Very low-cut dress,' Fleur told Miss Pink, forgetting she'd seen Gayleen. 'Striking, most unsuitable; vulgar, in fact. An awful lot of make-up, like painted on.' She turned on Jason. 'Why did they want to know all this?'

'They didn't say.'

'Oh, come on, Jase! They had to say something.'

'Not that Laddow guy. Mom says not, anyways. Now they've taken the loop road.'

'Where? Who did they go to?'

'They didn't tell Mom.'

'Well, now – ' She ticked them off: 'There's Chester, and Sadie and Leo, and you' – to Miss Pink – 'and Miriam and, of course, Lois.'

Miss Pink said she would go home but when she reached the highway she didn't take the steep little path to Quail Run but walked down the road a short distance until she was below Sand Dollar where another path climbed the slope. She emerged on a terraced rockery and went up wooden steps to the deck. French windows were open in the living-room but when she called there was no answer.

People converged on the entrance to Sand Dollar's drive. As Miss Pink came up from the house Leo was raking gravel while Sadie touched up their gate with white paint. A car crept along the road and stopped. 'Good afternoon, ladies.' Laddow beamed from the passenger seat. 'It's turned warm.'

Sadie twittered at him like a bird. 'Indeed yes, Mr Laddow, quite warm even for August. May we offer you a glass of lemonade?'

Such hospitality verged on the familiar given the circumstances, but perhaps Laddow attributed it to approaching senility, perhaps he'd been intending to call on them anyway. Hammett parked the car and they all trooped down the drive. 'Great,' Leo muttered to Miss Pink. 'We'll have a party. What the hell do they want with us, d'you know?' Miss Pink shook her head in denial as they went round to the deck.

'You'll be wanting to know why we came back,' Laddow told them when they were settled with glasses of lemonade. He glanced at Miss Pink who said easily that she understood they were asking for a description of Gayleen. Leo glared at her but Sadie regarded Laddow with childlike expectancy. The detectives regarded the view, which from this point, framed by shore pines, was magnificent.

'Forensics found something relating to Gayleen's clothes in the Chevrolet?' Miss Pink prodded.

Laddow withdrew his gaze reluctantly. 'I've never worked on a case in such neat surroundings,' he said, and Miss Pink flinched. 'No, ma'am; we found a body.'

'What – oh, the body in the trunk!' Sadie amended that: 'The body that had been in the trunk. Where did you find it?'

Leo was squirming with frustration, wanting to order her friend to keep quiet, and not daring to do so.

'On a vacant lot,' Laddow said. 'In Portland. She was fully clothed. That's why we needed to know what Gayleen was wearing.'

'Is it Gayleen?' Sadie asked.

'The clothes fit, ma'am, and the hair. They're getting her landlady to identify her: the woman at the motel. We should know any time.'

Sadie and Leo were staring at each other in consternation. 'How did she die?' Miss Pink asked.

'There was a gunshot wound in the back of the head.'

As if they were one person, the eyes of Sadie and Leo were suddenly unfocused and Miss Pink, her own cool gaze passing from them to the detectives, knew that the three of them were aware of the question in the minds of the other two: who owned a gun?

Chapter 7

'Who owns a firearm?' Laddow asked.

Sadie and Leo were embarrassed; even in normal circumstances this was an indelicate question in Sundown, particularly among naturalists. 'Private matter?' His expression was sympathetic. 'Awkward subject?'

'Not at all.' Leo was indignant. 'I have a pistol. It's my daddy's old Colt. Want to see it?'

'Please. A forty-five?' He turned to Hammett. 'Did you ever handle one of those?'

Hammett shook his head. Miss Pink remained expressionless. Did Laddow think these women so unworldly they would believe a detective had never handled an old Colt?

Leo came back with the pistol. Laddow hefted it and ejected the clip. He sniffed the barrel, peered down it and handed it to Hammett. 'Beautiful piece of work,' he commented. 'Who else owns a firearm?' It was incisive and he was apologising for nothing.

Sadie stared at him vacantly. Leo's face darkened. She said stiffly, 'No way do we discuss our neighbours' business.'

'You may have to.'

'Really?' Sadie looked interested. 'How is that?'

He studied her face. 'A murder has been committed, ma'am.'

'What does it have to do with us?'

His face cleared. 'Well, I'll tell you.' He exuded bonhomie. 'Mrs Keller's got a pistol too; that is, she had one until now. It's disappeared.'

The schnauzer barked as Miss Pink approached Quail Run. Miriam, sitting on the steps, slapped the dog's nose and he yelped in surprise. She looked drawn.

'The police are at Sand Dollar,' she said accusingly, as if Miss Pink were at fault.

She nodded. 'Come in; I'm going to make tea. I've just come from Sand Dollar.'

Miriam couldn't wait. As the kettle was being filled she was saying, 'I saw their car outside. You were there? What's going on?'

Miss Pink took mugs from their hooks and apologised for not providing cups and saucers. 'Haven't you heard anything?' she asked. 'Surely you knew the police came back?'

'We were hiking: Oliver and me. Willard said he'd seen them go towards Lois's place so I called her and Chester answered, but he was close-mouthed: admitted the police had been there but he wouldn't tell me anything. I didn't speak to Lois. There was no answer from Sadie and Leo, nor from you; Fleur said you'd gone home, and she didn't know what the police were doing. So I went along our road here, trying to find someone, anyone, saw the police car outside Sand Dollar, and I came back here to see if you'd turned up. What do you know?'

'A body's been found that seems to be Gayleen's, and she was shot. They're asking who owns guns.'

The kettle started to whistle. With a grimace Miss Pink fumbled with the tea-bags that she loathed, and hung them in the mugs.

'What makes them think it's someone from here?' Miriam asked, but the silence had stretched too far. 'She left here; both Fleur and Carl saw them on the road.'

'There's a gun missing.'

'Whose?'

'Lois's.'

'So' – they went into the living-room and Miriam collapsed on the sofa as if she were worn out – 'so it's Andy that they're – they're looking for?'

'I hadn't thought about that angle, and they didn't say.'

Miriam squeezed lemon into her tea. 'And now it's gone too far to ask Lois,' she mused. 'There's Chester though.' Her tone sharpened. 'That's ridiculous! Why should Andy kill her? I mean, he's not exactly a passionate man, Andy – and look at what he has to lose. He's a screen-writer, he's got contacts in Hollywood; Andy's going places. I don't believe it.'

'No one said it was Andy.' Miss Pink's tone was mild.

Miriam's eyes were like obsidian. 'Who else could get hold of her gun? You're not suggesting Grace – or Chester? Or one of us . . . this is utterly bizarre . . . Motive, that's what we need: motive; who *had* to kill Gayleen? Why do people kill? There's greed, lust, terror, jealousy – ' She stopped, aware that she was babbling.

'We're all shocked,' Miss Pink said comfortably. 'Nasty thing to happen to someone you know. There's still the original theory: that someone stole the Chevy and either Andy doesn't know yet, or he has an innocent reason for not reporting it. Comparatively innocent.'

'What are the police doing now?'

'Inquiries?' Miss Pink sighed. 'They tell you only what they want you to know.'

'What do you think? With your experience you must know the routine.'

Miss Pink looked embarrassed. 'Every case is different, but I assume here that finding Andy will be the priority – and they'll be going over the Chevrolet again. The important thing is to discover what that car was doing between when Carl passed it on Tuesday afternoon and when it was rammed in Portland on Thursday evening.'

'There was a woman driving it then.'

'Someone wearing a skirt, yes.'

'You're not suggesting it was a transvestite!'

'Just setting the record straight.'

'It was a woman.' Miriam was emphatic. 'The witnesses said so. A woman runs differently to a man. Certainly that points to the Chevy being stolen. I don't know that I particularly care if Andy's a killer, but I'm fond of Lois.'

Miss Pink asked, with seeming casualness, 'What is the situation there?'

'Between Lois and Andy?' Miriam hesitated. 'It's not easy to explain. They lead their own lives, and yet Andy keeps coming back; maybe she represents security for him, a mother-figure.' She considered that. 'Financial security,' she amended. 'Andy likes his creature comforts, but then' – her eyes widened – 'he was living dangerously: bringing that girl here. It was deliberate: he walked in as if he owned the place, with that slut trailing behind him!'

'Why do you call her that?' Miss Pink was genuinely curious.

'Why, you saw her! The awful dress, heels about four inches high, made up like she was on television— '

'What did she have to say?'

'I have no idea. I didn't talk to her. Obviously she'd never been in a nice home before, never seen caviar.' Miriam gave a snort. 'Thought the champagne was flavoured pop! Can you believe that? She was a ghetto kid. Andy probably paid her to come to the birthday party just to embarrass Lois.'

'Apparently Andy and Gayleen were living together.'

'What? So they were. So he got tired of her, shot her and cleared out.'

'He'd shoot a girl because he was tired of her?' Miss Pink was incredulous.

'Well, you know how these things happen.' The tone was light but the eyes stared fixedly at Miss Pink. 'It doesn't have to be a crime of passion,' she went on in that artificial voice, 'more like an accident, then the guy panics and has to get rid of the body. But it was an accident in the first place.'

'You want it all ways. A man hits a woman and she falls and strikes her head on something unyielding, and she has a thin skull? But Gayleen was shot.'

'Yes, well' – Miriam looked away – 'it does look rather bad for Andy, I must admit.'

Miss Pink took the mugs to the sink, poured herself a sherry and settled in a chair on her deck to commune with the view. She had rid herself of her guest by simulating exhaustion, but as the sea and the rocks and the distant cries of birds threaded the sunshine she knew that she hadn't needed to pretend fatigue. She felt inundated by the speculation that seethed in Sundown. Now she thought resentfully that it was none of her business. A girl had been murdered and a man was missing. The man was married to a woman who had a close circle of friends in a village where Miss Pink herself was a stranger. More than a stranger; with the identification of the body (and it looked as if it would be identified if it hadn't been already), with the disappearance of Lois's gun, the situation had become so delicate since this morning that she felt like an interloper. Had she not extended her tenancy for a second week she would have been due to leave tomorrow morning. As she started to ponder the question of calling Boligard Sykes to cancel the extension she felt the first twinge of a headache.

She got up and went to the kitchen. The concentration needed to follow a recipe would allow of no distractions. Drink would help, and music.

An hour later she was accompanying Schwartzkopf in an aria from *Cosi Fan Tutte* and stirring her version of a ratatouille when someone said loudly, 'I said, "It smells gorgeous." What is it?'

Lois Keller stood in the living-room smiling with appreciation: at the smell, Mozart, her neighbour's unsuspected prowess – it was immaterial; Miss Pink recovered her equilibrium and went to turn off the stereo. Lois protested and it was tuned to a whisper. She was alone and appeared to be relieved when she was asked to stay to dinner.

Miss Pink regarded her guest benignly and forbore to ask where Chester was. 'I seem to have got through the bulk of this while I was cooking,' she remarked, as she poured the sherry. She felt the other's eyes on her and guessed that Lois was reconsidering her decision to remain. And did she really want to hear Lois's speculation on the latest developments? She smiled serenely and waited for the other to take the initiative.

'Good sherry,' Lois said. 'I was wondering: do you work professionally? I mean, do people retain you to investigate – problems?'

'Not exactly.' Miss Pink recalled that a recent journey along a variant of the California Trail had been underwritten by a publisher concerned to find a missing author* but, 'I'm not a professional investigator,' she amended.

'And probably all the better for that. You see, I have a problem; more than one, but the one that bothers me is, I had a gun and it's disappeared. Do you know about Gayleen?' Her tone didn't change with the question and Miss Pink was taken by surprise.

'Er – what aspect of her?'

'I assume you know as much as we do.' There was no sarcasm implicit in the statement; Lois's presence at Quail Run demonstrated people's desire, if not their compulsion, to talk to Miss Pink. 'You know about the body being found?'

'Yes.' She was herself again. 'Has it been identified?'

* *Rage* (Macmillan 1990)

'It's Gayleen. Laddow called me. The manager of the motel identified her. She was shot. You know that? There's the snag: the gun's missing from my night table.'

'Are you saying she was shot with it?'

'I've no idea. And the police don't know yet. They recovered the bullet but that doesn't mean anything: it could have come from the same model but not from my gun. It could have been so deformed by the impact you can't tell.'

'What did you want me to do?'

Lois stared at the sea for a moment and then she laughed without amusement. 'I came rushing along here to ask you to find the gun. At least, that's what I thought I wanted you to do, but I'm moderately intelligent; what edge would you have over the police? They have all the advantages where finding things is concerned. And people.' She shivered. 'No, my subconscious reason for coming here was because you're a stranger – basically uninvolved. You might be able to throw light on the subject, see it in perspective. Everyone else has an axe to grind, but you' – she smiled, her eyes pleading – 'you're just the ship that passes in the night.'

'Why did you keep the gun in your night table?'

'Well, you never know; we've had the odd break-in on this coast, and I don't keep a dog . . . Grace was happy for me to have it, so was Chester. It didn't do any harm to keep a gun beside my bed. Of course one would use it only as a deterrent.'

'What did your husband think of your keeping a gun in your bedroom?'

'Oh, he gave it me. Because he's away so much. Said he didn't like to think of me in the house on my own.' She smiled. 'My husband is a sensible guy and he's familiar with urban areas; he's more aware of crime than most people.'

She stopped and appeared to be waiting. Miss Pink saw that, despite the avowed intention to seek some kind of revelation from herself, Lois needed prodding. 'How do you find Laddow?' she asked.

'Charming. A perfect gentleman: an English type, in fact – no, a mix of Latin and Anglo-Saxon. But Hammett makes one feel somewhat uncomfortable: watching, not saying much. Laddow's old-fashioned, even a bit redneck in his attitudes. He seems to be wondering if he's strayed on to the set of some sophisticated movie: out of *Marienbad* by *La Dolce Vita*? A wife tolerating her husband's casual affairs while she's enjoying a liaison with an elderly roué. Two old ladies united in lesbian bliss, another old lady just taken on a new gigolo having put the last one out to grass; I tell you: Laddow feels a bit bewildered.'

'Is any of that true?'

'Of course not; it's how he sees it.'

'What makes you think that?'

'Because that's how any outsider would see it.'

'I didn't.'

'You're different; you have a high IQ. But Andy sees it that way.'

'Does he? Your toleration of his affairs, the elderly roué?'

'Well, the first – but not Chester. He and I are good pals and the friendship is platonic. Andy wouldn't care anyway; now *there* is the only sliver of truth: we tolerate each other's foibles and we lead separate lives, more or less.'

'What are your foibles?'

Lois raised expressive eyebrows. 'My work. It consumes me – when I get going, that is. I can't even attend to my house guests properly.' She pondered. 'I shouldn't have them when I'm into a book.'

'You invite people to stay when you have a book on hand?' Miss Pink was astonished.

'Not at all.' Lois drank the last of her sherry, put down the glass and glanced absently at the bottle. Miss Pink refilled their glasses. 'I didn't expect Andy to bring anyone to my birthday party,' Lois went on. 'But in this case things turned out all right, although I shall always wonder whether I drove Gayleen away. I must have shown my impatience that day when she was pouring out her woes— '

Miss Pink had been momentarily puzzled but now her face cleared and she interrupted: 'You mean, the day they left, the day they were last seen' – she bit her lip – 'by Carl.' She went on more firmly, 'You said she talked about herself, had all kinds of jobs, never kept one for long.'

'I sanitised that part.'

'Sanitised? You edited it?'

'For the company. Actually what Gayleen was best at was being a stripper. She was proud of it: told me all about timing and the kind of music and how you pretend to despise the voyeurs (my word, not hers) and how they loved it: being treated with contempt. She was on crack too. Apparently Andy rescued her; he does things like that: picks people up, dusts them down, sets them on their feet.' She smiled ruefully. 'I'm not saying it's totally disinterested; the girls are always striking and my husband is no angel, I'm afraid, but do his motives matter if he gives them breathing space, long enough for them to recover some self-esteem?'

'But not a very healthy activity.'

Lois gasped. 'I don't think she was suffering from anything like that – '

'I didn't mean medically; I was thinking that if she was mixing with street people: being on crack and working as a stripper, it could be dangerous: being involved with her.'

'For Andy, you mean. That's not a pleasant thought, Melinda.'

'You asked for objectivity.' She got up and went to the kitchen. 'Shall we eat now?' she called. 'There's a bottle of rosé here in the refrigerator; if you'll open it while I dish up . . . '

'The police will have asked you this,' she said later, 'but I don't know what you told them. When Andy and Gayleen left, did they say anything that would throw light on where they intended to go?'

The ratatouille had been a success and now they were seated in the living-room, coffee and brandy at their elbows, watching the clouds turn pink as the sun set behind the fog.

Lois held her brandy as if her hands were cold. 'Gayleen did say she didn't want to go back but I related that to her enthusiasm over the house and everything. She thought the cabin was cute and the house was stunning. I rather wondered if she was angling for an invitation to stay on when Andy went back, but it didn't occur to me that she might have a reason to fear returning to Portland.'

'What did Andy say when he left?'

'Nothing. I mean, literally. I didn't see them go. Heard the car, that's all. This is how it was: they were leaving that day and he went for a quick hike because Gayleen never woke up till past noon. When she finally got up that day she came down to the house. I was trying to work out a problem with plot and I wasn't averse to listening to problems unconnected with my work. Besides, let's face it, she was splendid copy. But she got stuck into a bottle of wine and stayed on; Andy didn't come home and at some point I'd had enough so I told her she didn't have to go but I was going upstairs to work. She said that was all right with her, she'd watch television, maybe go for a drive. I considered suggesting that she wasn't in a fit state to drive but' – Lois grimaced, acknowledging she had been at fault – 'I let it go. I went to my workroom, put some music on the stereo and – quite honestly – I forgot all about her. Like I said, I can't even look after my guests.'

'When did you discover that they'd gone?'

'I don't know. Some time late. I finished work, wandered downstairs to get a bite to eat, saw she wasn't there; it didn't mean anything at the time. Why should it? We're pretty informal in Sundown. I showered and changed, came down to the Tattler – oh, I did see the Chevy was gone, so I just assumed they'd left – for good or for the evening, I didn't think. I was in such a dream at that moment I wasn't really *there*.'

'When did you find out the gun was missing?'

'Oh, my God, the traditional scene! When Laddow asked me today if I owned a firearm and could he see it, I went upstairs and it was gone! It was like being punched in the stomach. The immediate reaction was that it had been stolen, but now I'm not so sure; if I can lose myself so completely in my work, could I have forgotten putting the gun, say, in a safer place, and it will come to light eventually?'

'You'd much prefer to believe that.'

'Why, of course. Wouldn't you?'

Miss Pink didn't respond immediately and when she did it was indirectly, and as if she arrived at the answer by communing with herself. 'Guilt is like a cancer,' she said thoughtfully, 'and it spreads laterally. You admit you feel guilty about Gayleen: asking yourself if you rejected her in favour of your work. You retreated to your room. I don't expect she felt rejected, or did she? I didn't know her. Now you're asking yourself if, by leaving a firearm in your bedside table – the obvious place – you made it available to the person who – But if that gun killed Gayleen, you know, as a criminologist of sorts, that when a person intends to kill, the weapon is immaterial; if he doesn't find what he needs in one place, he'll find another elsewhere. He's an opportunist.' She thought about that. 'Is he? I was assuming premeditation . . . and it wasn't a gun that was responsible for Gayleen's death but the man who pulled the trigger. You can't be taking the blame for him?' Miss Pink turned her full attention to her guest.

Lois said coldly, 'How could I do that? We don't know who it was,' but as she spoke her eyes widened, she swallowed and looked away.

Miss Pink said sadly, 'And you came to me for comfort. I'm sorry.'

'It's been a help talking about it. Look' – suddenly she was desperate, her eyes boring into Miss Pink's – 'I know exactly what you're thinking. Isn't there a crumb of comfort?'

'For you, yes.' Miss Pink was grave. 'You're not responsible. You've forgotten free will. No one forced your husband to take up a dangerous pursuit, and since he knows street people, what they're capable of, he knows the risks better than most of us, definitely better than you do; you know crime only from theory.' She considered repeating Leo's assertion that Andy Keller was a man with a self-destruct button, and rejected it. Instead she said, 'I have the feeling that if you've told the police what you've told me, they aren't all that surprised either. I suspect you've always anticipated trouble yourself.'

'Actually, I didn't; I just drifted along: unheeding, happy – well, contented. We would have divorced in time, I guess, had one of us had enough energy to spare from our writing – remember he's a writer too – enough energy left to start proceedings is what I meant to say. Meanwhile' – she shrugged – 'everything in my garden was lovely. And actually, it could have been in his too. Careless, that's what he is. But this is utterly ridiculous! I'm being morbid. I've mislaid the gun – and Andy is in Hollywood. He left the car with Gayleen. She ran into trouble. She was expecting it. That's the most likely scenario, isn't it? All right, I see you're having difficulty answering that one. I'd better leave you and go back to my work.'

'Where's Chester?'

'He went home. He's a bit of an old curmudgeon and – er – in this particular respect we're not seeing eye to eye.'

Miss Pink didn't have to ask which respect she was referring to: she had witnessed Keller's boorishness and seen Chester's face when he looked at Lois. There was no doubt where his sympathies would lie, and there would be anger too. Chester Hoyle wouldn't have much time for his lady's feelings of guilt. These two could well have quarrelled – and Lois had come running down to Miss Pink for sympathy, and got the same dusty response. But of course, thought Miss Pink, this isn't merely a lovers' tiff: the usual eternal triangle (ridiculous dated phrases); there was a murdered stripper involved, and Lois suspected her husband.

Chapter 8

'You can't put out a description on a guy who may be innocent and who could have influence.'

'That doesn't answer my question.'

Miss Pink and Hammett, an unlikely couple, were strolling along the edge of the tide towards the cliffs of Cape Deception. Ostensibly they were discussing those features of the case that had been made public and were therefore debatable. In reality Miss Pink was hoping to discover what had taken Laddow away from Sundown again, leaving Hammett to do – what? Investigate the inhabitants by way of a show of friendliness?

He had found her on the beach taking photographs of the stacks. It was extraordinarily calm today, the fog had slipped back, the sun shone and the tide was making unobtrusively; a few miles ahead, under the point, the sea lions were singing their wild chorus.

She had exchanged a few remarks with Hammett about photography and then she had started on her morning's walk, not really surprised when he accepted an invitation to accompany her. At this stage in the proceedings it was unthinkable that a detective should be given the day off. He appeared to be idle but this meeting wasn't fortuitous, of that she was sure; he wanted something from her, but since he remained silent and appeared to be waiting, she had to start the ball rolling. In the guise of local resident, however temporary, she asked the obvious question: what was being done to find Andy Keller?

Walking along the firm sand at the edge of the water he said, with a show of reluctance, 'We're looking for him, of course. After all' – his eyes were ingenuous behind the wire-rimmed spectacles – 'he could be a victim.'

'There was always that theory: that they had picked up a

hitch-hiker who killed both of them.' Her eyes followed an oyster-catcher. 'But he couldn't get two bodies in the trunk. So that means— ' She checked, pondered, and became chatty. 'Tell me: when you went away yesterday morning, did you discover anything on the road north?'

'We came back because we learned that a girl's body had been found in Portland.'

She sighed. He was a harder nut to crack than his boss. 'I know that, but bodies are being found all the time in large cities. What made you think that this one related to the body that had been carried in the Chevrolet?'

'It was possible. A female body had been in the trunk; there was make-up: traces of lipstick, powder, hair gel, so we needed to follow up all reports on female corpses. This one was found Thursday. We did some phoning Saturday but it was the weekend; some people keep their weekends sacred in Oregon.' The tone was censorious. 'However, we did manage to find the pathologist Sunday morning. He hadn't made the connection yet but there was this suggestion it could be the same girl: the one on the lot could be the one was in the Chevy at some time. He was right: the woman at the motel identified her. She was worried; they were supposed to be back on the Monday, and she was bothered about her rent.'

'Gayleen was alive on Tuesday afternoon,' Miss Pink murmured, 'and the body was found – when on Thursday?'

'First light, near enough. Night watchman going home. It had to have been dumped in the dark because it was obvious to anyone passing in the daytime.'

'Did *rigor* set in when she was in the trunk of the car or afterwards?'

He didn't question that. Had Laddow checked up on her experience in such technical matters? It was immaterial. He said, 'The position of the body when found suggested that it was in the trunk when *rigor* set in.'

She blinked at his choice of words. 'And lividity?'

'It would appear— ' He stopped and – amazingly for him – he giggled.

She smiled. 'What were the conclusions, Mr Hammett? I don't mean the pathologist's findings; what do you think?'

He sobered but he remained circumspect. 'We figure that, from the location of lividity and *rigor*, she was put in the trunk

89

soon after she was killed and probably kept there until the body was thrown out on the vacant lot.'

'So someone was driving around for over twenty-four hours—'

'Could be as much as thirty-six hours. The place was badly lit but it wasn't remote. There would be people about in the evening. Probably dumped in the early hours of Thursday, shortly before it was found.'

'And it was driven around – Portland? – all the time. That seems amazingly reckless. Suppose he'd been involved in an accident before he could get rid of the body?'

'Criminals do stupid things, ma'am.'

'Quite. Was there any luggage in the car when it was found?'

'None. It had been stripped of everything valuable.'

They walked a little way in silence until he glanced ahead, then sideways. 'The tide's coming in,' he said uneasily. 'How far did you intend to go?'

She looked at the steep and friable slopes under Cape Deception and the strip of sand that disappeared into debris below the point. At high water the headland dropped straight into the sea. 'We'll turn back now before we're cut off,' she said.

But instead of retracing their steps she walked across the drift of tangled weed that marked high water and sat on a bleached log. He sat beside her, his profile a little owl-like, she thought, observing him benignly. Had anyone been watching them he would have been justified, observing those companionable backs, in concluding that there was a special relationship between these two.

'Before you contacted the pathologist yesterday,' Miss Pink said, 'had you made any headway in tracing the Chevrolet after it left Sundown? How about the people on the roadworks for example: did they remember the couple?'

'No. There were quite a few cars on the road, and the Highways people were packing up early because of the rain. Besides, an old brown Chevy isn't noticeable.'

'The roadmen packed up early?'

'Yes, but they had to leave people to direct traffic and drive the pilot car because the notices say the road's not closed till six, so a few stayed on.'

'Did you have time to make inquiries north of the roadworks, between there and Portland?'

'Inquiries are being made. It could be a while before anything turns up; it's over a hundred miles to Portland – the quickest way – and we don't know which way they went. We turned back at Moon Shell Beach; that's about twenty miles north of the roadworks, and we'd found no one who remembered them stopping at pumps or to get something to eat. That doesn't have to mean anything; they could have gone straight through without stopping, or picked up a passenger without anyone seeing. Or they could have been seen, even seen picking someone up, and no one's come forward because they don't know it's important.'

She considered this and her face lit up. 'So Mr Laddow is working from the other end! Of course, it's obvious. I'm getting old.' He wasn't taken in by that; he nodded acquiescence and squinted along the strand towards the village not, she noted, as if he were bored, more as if he were expecting something to happen.

'Have you traced the woman driver who ran away?' she asked politely.

'Not yet. I mean, she may have been traced but I'm in the dark at the moment.' His tone changed, became harder: 'It's more straightforward this way: something to get your teeth into. Here we were just after background, but even the background – at least, the only kind that matters, is in Portland.'

She gave no sign of her surprise at this. 'Sundown is the kind of place where nothing happens,' she said. 'That's why it's popular among older people.'

'Amazing, isn't it? An enclave of retirees – and mature careerists' – indicating that he recognised she was not retired – 'except for their younger relatives: Grace Ferguson, Jason at the bookstore, Oliver Ramet.'

'Harper. It's Oliver Harper.'

'Of course it is. He'll be a relative from her side of the family.' He was still interested in the strip of sand between them and the village, and suddenly she knew the reason. As she considered this, pretending to be absorbed in the antics of some turnstones on the rocks, he said, 'He's not running this morning.'

'No.' Useless to simulate perplexity. 'But he goes anywhere; they all do: Grace, Miriam, Lois. I've met them on the headland, in the forest— '

'Oliver Harper,' he said heavily. 'How did he get to Portland that day?'

She gaped at him. *This* she had not been expecting. 'Did he leave Sundown on the Tuesday?' she asked weakly.

'He left on Monday, according to his hostess.' No more coy assumption that Oliver was a relative; the gloves were off.

'I remember.' Her memory returned with her balance. 'Miriam said he had a telephone call. Grace Ferguson left on Monday too.' She smiled. 'One suspects he got a lift with her; she's a personable young lady, I've heard.'

'Very likely.' He went on as if it were an afterthought, 'Miriam says not, but then he wouldn't be likely to tell her, would he? I wonder what he has to say for himself. We haven't spoken to him yet, apart from that first evening when he waited on us in the restaurant. Since then he always seems to be somewhere else when we turn up.'

So why wasn't he concerned that she would go back to the village and warn Oliver that the police wanted to talk to him? Because, she thought wryly, Oliver knows that already, and the police are fully aware of it. But then, if Oliver was quietly enjoying his stay in Sundown, regardless of a police presence, he had to be as innocent as he looked, didn't he?

Lunch was a ham sandwich in the bar, sharing a table with Fleur. They were waited on by a plump girl in shorts and wearing her hair in a French braid. Miss Pink remarked that she hadn't met everyone in Sundown yet and Fleur, without self-consciousness, said she'd met everyone who mattered.

'I haven't met Grace,' Miss Pink pointed out. 'Andy and Gayleen I saw but didn't speak to.' She had given Fleur the gist of the morning's conversation with Hammett but had omitted mention of Oliver Harper until Fleur, who had listened intently, asked, 'What did he want from you?'

'Well, it's ridiculous, kind of police gossip, you know? He tried out a theory on me; that's what he was doing: pointing out that Oliver was on the road when Andy and Gayleen left.'

Fleur stared, then comprehension dawned. 'Ah, the hitchhiker. That won't do. Oliver left the day before, and probably with Grace. She would have picked him up once he was out of sight of Miriam. And Willard, of course.'

92

'Willard would tell Miriam that Oliver had left with Grace?'

'Naturally.' Fleur sipped her apple juice and looked at Miss Pink without expression. 'I'm going to have a brownie. How about you?'

'No more, thank you. I have to walk this afternoon and burn off these calories. Why don't you come with me?'

'Sorry, another time. I'm expecting delivery of Gideon's new book.'

'Yes? When is publication date?'

'As soon as the book arrives; we don't bother with dates. I have to take advantage of the few visitors left on the coast.'

'Does he do book-signings, that kind of thing?'

'Probably, locally, in LA. Not up here; he's much too rich and grand.'

'What's he like?'

'In appearance he's not particularly remarkable: middle height, clean-shaven, glasses, wears good but not striking clothes. Otherwise he's steady, kind, reliable, and not at all like his work which, you must admit, is sexy, fantastic and violent. He says that's his dark side showing.'

'Is he an engineer?'

'I – don't know. I mean, about his past life, what he studied; it could have been engineering. Why do you ask?'

'Because of the draughtsmanship.'

'Yes, of course. It's a talent, he says. Discrete, just something he can do. And the plots: well, comic strips don't need plots, only action. That's what he says.'

'Actually he sounds rather nice.'

'Why the surprise?'

Miss Pink spread her hands, searching for words, but all she could think of was 'puerile' and 'juvenile'. Desperately she said, 'Even the name, Gideon d'Eath, is designed for sensation.'

'It's a good old English – well, French name.' Fleur's cheeks were flushed. 'Didn't you ever hear it before?'

'D'aeth, I've heard of. I'm not sure where the lower case comes, but definitely with the vowels transposed. I'd make a guess that your man spells it the other way deliberately. It will sell a lot of books.'

'Which is what it's all about. Why do you write gothics?'

Miss Pink nodded soberly. 'Quite. I have my house, my cats

and a pleasant garden, all run by a housekeeper and a gardener, and costing a fortune. The gothics make the fortune. They are, of course, my Gideon d'Eath.'

That afternoon, looking for somewhere to go that she hadn't been, she climbed the trail to Cape Deception, emerging on the summit to a vista that was breathtaking, not only in its extent but by virtue of the peculiar quality of the light. The humidity could have had something to do with this, concentrating the sunshine prismatically so that the heat was intense but like a mild steam heat, not the roasting aridity of the deserts. Distances were hazy: south down the cliff-plunging coast, north across the pale dunes, west past crumbs of stacks in peacock water to where the fog bank slept on the shining sea. And yet the damp haze increased the sense of space rather than limiting it and, to the observer on Cape Deception, the world behind its drapes of gauze was infinite.

She was glad she was alone; it was restful to sit quietly, not to have to examine statements and reactions, to observe, without appearing to do so, the movements of hands and facial muscles. And why should she be doing that anyway? This was an investigation but not her investigation; she was hag-ridden by the writer's consuming curiosity that never, for one moment in company, will lie dormant. Only on Cape Deception could she relax, relieved that Fleur was miles away at this moment, unpacking books. What an odd picture she had drawn of Gideon d'Eath: unremarkable in his appearance and dress, yet perceptive and clever, and all at variance with the phrase 'rich and grand' that rolled so easily off Fleur's tongue. Otherwise she hadn't missed the fact that the shadowy figure outlined by Fleur bore a resemblance to Chester Hoyle. Miss Pink regarded the stacks without seeing them, speculation, if not curiosity, working overtime.

Laddow did not return that day but he was in contact with his partner. This was achieved neatly and without overt rudeness. People left messages at the motel but even if Hammett were in his room the result was the same: after a brief and innocuous exchange he would go down to the bar and use the call-box.

Next day Miss Pink went looking for owls over in Coon Gulch. She was unsuccessful and she had the feeling that there was not enough old-growth timber there to furnish the cover favoured by spotted owls. She returned to Sundown disgruntled and thinking that tomorrow she would strike out, not leave for good but go north past the roadworks, have a look at a new stretch of coast, perhaps find the entrancingly named Moon Shell Beach.

She let herself into her house, dropped her pack, went to open the doors on the deck – and stood motionless, her hand raised to the catch.

Someone was creeping through her fuchsia hedge: stooped and furtive, a black object held in one hand and reflecting the light. Backing carefully, Miss Pink caught sight of a second figure, but this one was upright, facing her, hands lifted, elbows pointed, the face hidden by binoculars. Sadie and Leo: stalking birds in Quail Run's garden. She exhaled with a gasp and went to the kitchen to fill the kettle.

' —were waiting for you' – Leo was saying, already talking as she led the way into the living-room – 'and we saw a black-headed grosbeak. No good you going out; it's gone now. You're making tea? Great. We just said, before we saw the grosbeak, we were dying of thirst and you'd be sure to be drinking tea at four o'clock, but you weren't here. Where were you?'

'Coon Gulch. I was looking for owls.'

'There aren't any in Coon. We could have told you that. We were there the day of the birthday party – Lois's. We're going – somewhere on Thursday though, not tomorrow because we have to go to town for groceries.'

Leo exchanged glances with Sadie who said gently, 'We may know where there's a pair of owls. We would be happy for you to join us.'

They sat down in the living-room. 'Are you sure?' Miss Pink was diffident. 'Is that what you came to see me about? I'd be delighted; not to put too fine a point on it, I feel honoured.'

Sadie dimpled. Leo said, sounding surprised, 'It wasn't that, actually. We came to tell you about the latest developments. They found the driver.'

'And the man she got the Chevy from,' Sadie said.

'And who sold it to *him*. It's all tied in with drugs and prostitution. You were right – someone was right; it was stolen. Andy doesn't come into it at all.'

'He doesn't?' came Sadie's old-lady voice.

Miss Pink said, 'Would you mind going back to the beginning and giving a little more detail? The driver: is that the woman who ran away after the accident?'

'That's it.' Leo nodded, her mouth full of shortbread.

'She left her fingerprints all over the car,' Sadie contributed. 'And like Leo said, she's a prostitute – Bobby – I forget her name.'

'Robin Neal,' Leo said. 'It's not important.'

'And she ran away because she's on probation for dealing in crack, and hadn't reported, or something.'

'After coming out of prison,' Leo put in, anxious to get the technical part correct.

'Yes.' Miss Pink was patient. 'And she ran away because she guessed, or knew she was driving a stolen car. Where did she get it?'

'It's all supposed to be aboveboard,' Sadie said, 'but no doubt if there's a nasty smell in the car someone told you to get washed, you don't wait for the police to come along, ask questions: "What's that smell in the back of your car, ma'am?" Even though it wasn't the girl's car, it belonged to her – ' Sadie looked at Leo.

'To her pimp.' Leo was angry; if nothing else she was a feminist. 'He'd told her to take it to a garage to be washed. Laddow said that would include a respray and new plates because it would be obvious to this guy that the car was stolen. He got it too cheap. Laddow found the pimp, you see, and *he* said he bought the Chevy from a guy in the street, a drug addict.'

'Mr Laddow brought a little pressure to bear,' Sadie put in sweetly. 'Would that be what they call third degree? No' – as Miss Pink shifted uneasily – 'not Mr Laddow. However, the pimp agreed that there had been an odd smell in the car and he noticed the trunk had been forced. He thought probably the previous owner had carried a dead animal in there, like a dog? Deer, maybe?'

'Have they traced the drug addict?'

'Not yet,' Sadie said. 'That will be why Mr Hammett left. He's gone to Portland to help Mr Laddow break the pimp.'

'Really, Locke, your choice of words!'

Chapter 9

'So you see,' Lois said, 'we were right all along; it *was* stolen. Probably from the airport?' This last was addressed to Chester.

After dinner people had drifted down to the Tattler for brandy and reassurance. Miss Pink arrived to find Lois and Chester, Fleur and Oliver in the bar, Lois obviously relieved that the theft of the Chevrolet seemed to remove the site of Gayleen's murder to a location well away from Sundown.

Chester said, 'We'll know more tomorrow. But maybe not; there's no reason why Laddow should keep us informed. It's a city crime.'

'It started here,' Fleur pointed out.

'I doubt that,' Oliver said, adding thoughtfully, 'I doubt it very much.'

'Yes,' agreed Lois, 'it goes back into her past. And yet to look at her you'd never have thought that she was a – involved in that kind of thing.'

'What kind of thing?' Fleur was aggressive.

'Why' – Lois looked uncomfortable – 'prostitution, crack. Are you suggesting that she wasn't, Fleur? That it was a coincidence: a mugging perhaps?' She looked at Chester. 'We didn't consider that; it would have to be a coincidence: a girl on crack is shot and then found – no, carried – in another addict's car. A car which had been driven by another addict,' she amended carefully.

'Oh no!' Chester exclaimed. 'There had to be a connection between Gayleen and the addict. That's obvious.' People nodded agreement.

'How long has Andy been miss— away now?' Oliver asked, almost casually.

'He left on Tuesday,' Lois said. 'So he's been away a week.'

'He could be out of the country,' Oliver pointed out. 'It's only

97

one stop to Mexico; maybe he went to LA: someone asked him to go down, work on a script in Acapulco, wherever. He could be gone months.'

'The police are looking for him,' Miss Pink said.

They registered varying degrees of surprise but Lois was more than surprised, she was angry. 'Why?' she asked. 'And why wasn't I told? They're *looking* for him?' She turned on Chester, mutely questioning.

'I thought you'd know.' Miss Pink was apologetic. 'Hammett told me yesterday.'

'But the car was *stolen*,' Lois said firmly as if explaining it to a child.

Miss Pink gave the ghost of a nod. Oliver said, 'Lois, dear, they're not necessarily looking for him as a killer.'

There was a charged silence. As on other and similar occasions they waited for Lois to speak; after all, he was her husband. She said weakly, 'What else did Hammett tell you?'

Miss Pink struggled with recall. 'Mostly he was telling me how they came to connect the body on the waste ground with the Chevy: it was traces of make-up . . . and then there was the fact that she'd been put in the trunk not long after she was shot, carried in it . . . The murderer was stupid— '

'Why?' Lois asked.

'Reckless, pathological. A psychopath?' Miss Pink pondered her own question. 'I don't think so; there's too much planning . . . On the other hand, if the killer was a drug addict and an opportunist, no planning need be involved, just luck; that is, assuming there is a drug addict, and Gayleen wasn't killed by her pimp. I wonder.' She was staring at Lois, who responded as if she'd been addressed rather than the company at large.

'She didn't look like a prostitute.'

'You think not?' Oliver asked.

'Not really,' Fleur put in. 'She was too healthy – despite the crack, and that could have been boasting: a need to shock the bourgeoisie. She was emotionally immature – very much so.'

Miss Pink looked at her, hesitated, and continued, 'Then Hammett said they were working backwards from Portland, trying to trace the woman who ran off after the Chevrolet was bumped.'

'And?' asked Oliver.

'And what?'

'You stopped suddenly. Go on: trying to trace the woman driver – '

'And once they found her they would hope to be able to retrace the movements of the car back to – well, ideally to when Carl and Fleur saw it leaving Sundown.'

Attention switched to Fleur, even Oliver's attention. This evening they seemed volatile as children, for which Miss Pink was thankful; she'd had an odd feeling there that Oliver knew she was holding back, and what she was withholding was information that concerned him and the fact that (if he'd spent the night somewhere en route) he could have been on the road next day, when Andy and Gayleen might have picked up a hitch-hiker.

At nine o'clock next morning the coast was blanketed in fog and Miss Pink drove with her heater on and the windows closed. About fifteen miles north of the village she came round a bend to see twin red eyes flaring in the gloom and, stopping in time, prayed that following vehicles would have heeded the warnings, 'Flagman Ahead' placed along the shoulder.

More vehicles arrived, stopped, and waited like patient animals. After a while the line edged forward and moved left as the tarmac became single-lane. Machinery loomed on the right, faintly yellow, and there were glimpses of people in fluorescent orange. The convoy crept over mud and gravel with a low vegetated bank on the left above the drop. The cars kept as far away from the abyss as possible.

At the end of the roadworks they came back to the correct side, passing the pilot car with its huge notice, 'Follow me', and the line of traffic awaiting its turn. The northbound cars picked up speed, Miss Pink wondering idly how they closed the stretch at night, and then remembering someone saying that they put earth-moving machinery – bulldozers and the like – across the single lane. There could be no way round the obstructions: the precipice was on one side, steep slopes and the landslip on the other. They closed the road at six; she must make sure she was back by then. She'd looked at her map and seen that a detour would involve roughly four sides of an irregular figure: around 180 miles of paved road, although there were forest tracks that were only a third of that distance. But what stranger would venture on sixty miles of dirt roads in the dark, roads that could have been washed away since the map was produced, had fallen out of use or were even barred by locked gates? No, she had to be back by six.

It was important to keep an eye on the time because at this moment she didn't think she would be coming back early. She wanted to stay out until the fog cleared and here it was ten o'clock and still no sign of movement in the dense cover. It was frustrating to see nothing more of the country she was driving through than the low gnarled shore pines and what looked like banks or barrows that must be tangles of vegetation.

A sudden confusion of coloured lights ahead: the familiar twin red eyes waxing bright, the exciting, disorientating effect of flashing police lights: red, white, blue. She slowed and stopped; this was not her day.

But in a way it was. Waved forward, then halted by a large Highway Patrolman, she lowered her window and heard an unexpected question, but one for which she realised she should have been prepared.

'Good morning, ma'am. Were you on this road last week: Tuesday, 22nd, in the afternoon?'

'Ah,' she said, 'Andy and Gayleen,' and was, of course, directed to pull off the road, where Laddow came to her five minutes later, unable to conceal his disappointment as he approached and saw whom they'd caught in the net. He looked chilled and hesitated for only a moment before getting into the warm car.

'What is all this about?' she asked and, anticipating a reluctance to answer, went on, 'You might as well tell me; you know it will be all over Sundown, if not the whole coast, by this evening, including television.'

'You're right.' His tone sharpened. 'You're always right.' He stared through the windscreen at the pines and the fog all in shades of grey. They were in a big lay-by among other cars, some unmarked, others police vehicles. Out on the highway the stationary cars were perceptible only by virtue of their headlights. 'We traced the Chevy back to here,' he told her: 'Moon Shell Beach.'

'This is Moon Shell Beach?' She peered as if she could pierce the fog. 'I thought you got this far when you were working north.'

He pursed his lips. 'We turned back from here because we

100

phoned from a call-box up the road; that's where we got the word about the girl's body and came back to ask for descriptions of her clothes, remember? We attached no significance to Moon Shell Beach. We didn't know it was important until now.'

'There have been more developments? The latest we heard was that there's a drug addict who is supposed to have sold the Chevrolet to a pimp.'

'He did, if you can believe them, and I think, in this case, we believe all of them because murder is involved and everyone's very much concerned not to be charged as an accessory, let alone as a principal.' He grinned like a shark, searching her face. He saw that she understood and went on, 'So I think that here we have a true story, give or take the odd omission.' He paused, apparently assembling his thoughts. 'We start from here,' he said slowly. 'The addict was on Moon Shell Beach that day – some of these beaches are *not* resorts, ma'am, not family places like Sundown; I'd steer clear of them if I was you.'

'Drugs?' She was astonished. 'On beaches?'

'Oh, yes. It started in California and, like all the wrong things: multiple murder, drugs, cults, you name it, it's spreading. Anyway, here's this guy – Kelsey's the name – came down with someone else in the other guy's car; friend disappears with a girl, leaves Kelsey without a lift back to the city. What does Kelsey do? Why, he wanders up to this Vista Point of course, looking for someone to give him a lift home, and there are several cars parked, and a guy just getting into one of them, hand on the door handle. So Kelsey shouts, comes over and asks for a lift back to Portland. Other guy takes his hand off the door, says, 'Be my guest' and walks off.'

'This is the Chevy?' Miss Pink asked. 'Empty? Abandoned?'

'Well, no one in it, no one *obvious*. So Kelsey walks round to the passenger side – he's had an invitation, hasn't he? – gets in, thinking the owner, the guy he took for the owner, will be back, he just went to the bathroom, keys are in the ignition, everything ready to go, but the guy doesn't come back. After a while Kelsey gets to thinking the guy's not going to show because he was planning to steal the car, and the real owners are down on the beach some place snorting coke and here's their car, keys in the ignition, luggage in the back, and Kelsey with scarcely a dollar to his name – and he could get five hundred for the Chevy and, who knows what's in the luggage? Cameras, maybe.'

'So he drove away.'

'He drove away to Portland and next morning he takes the Chevy to a crooked dealer he knows but *he's* not buying a car with a locked trunk – did I say there was no key to the trunk on the key ring?'

'No. And the trunk was locked at this point, here in this lay-by.' Her eyes were glazed.

'And you couldn't get at the trunk by taking out the rear seat because it was jammed, so the dealer forced it – and guess what he found.' The clown's face registered horrified amazement.

Miss Pink humoured him. 'Gayleen's body,' she said.

'Correct. And Kelsey's thrown out of the garage, out of the area, warned never to show his face again . . . We've seen the dealer: straight as a ruler so far as the world's concerned. Funny thing though' – frowning fiercely – 'he didn't report it to the police. Still, that's by the way. Now Kelsey's driving around Portland with a body in the trunk, but he's greedy, and he's not very bright. He's got a car and a Nikon to sell (he'd gone through the luggage during the night) and the only people know about the corpse are the dealer and the killer, and neither of those is going to talk about it. So he waits till after midnight when there aren't many people about and he gets rid of the body and in the morning – this is Thursday – he sells the car to a pimp, and the rest you know – except that seeing as it's hot in Portland right now, the car began to smell. But the pimp, he was greedy too, and after all he could always say he thought the previous owner's dog died and he had taken the body to the pet cemetery which is, in fact, exactly what he did say.'

The fog was lifting, the shore pines showing against blue, not grey, wet bark catching a glint of sunshine.

'So the body was in the trunk at this spot,' she said. 'The Chevy never got to an airport; it was stolen from here. Where is Andy Keller? Are you thinking in terms of his being the killer? No, you're looking for his body. That's what all this is about.' She gestured at the other vehicles.

'We're doing two things; we're trying to find someone who was passing here last Tuesday afternoon, who may have seen something— ' He checked as Hammett came quickly across the gravel. Laddow opened his door. Miss Pink opened hers, got out and stretched. Over the roof of the car she saw the excitement in Hammett's eyes. He turned his back, talking urgently. The two of them walked away and she followed. A cluster of people in plainclothes and uniforms, women among them, gathered about the detectives like acolytes and everyone crossed the road and moved along a track that was green with lank grass but marked by wheels. There was a smell so foul that it made the eyes water: not just skunk but dead skunk. There was litter and used tissues: an unpleasant place, the kind of place where unpleasant things happened. On either side was a matted mass of scrub. A densely wooded depression lay below, while chaparral climbed the slopes above to gaunt rocks on the skyline.

The track dipped and turned and after some fifty yards ended at a wall of jungle. Cars that had come this far would have to reverse; there was no room to turn.

They stopped before the end of the track. A uniformed man in his shirt sleeves was waiting there with a yellow Labrador on a leash. The crowd stood like an audience, Miss Pink peering over shoulders. Laddow and Hammett advanced to a small post like a surveyor's post which had been stuck in the ground. They squatted on their heels and Laddow parted the grass blades with the delicacy of a surgeon. After a moment they straightened and stared at the dog. Its handler was expressionless. Laddow asked a question and Hammett responded. They stepped back and everyone retreated as a man came forward and started to take photographs. They returned to the road and an orange tape was strung across the mouth of the trail.

The people around Miss Pink were talking without inhibition. Not Press, she thought; they were all from Forensics and the Medical Examiner's office: detectives waiting their turn to gather evidence from what to all appearances was the scene of a crime. She listened to the talk.

' . . . no doubt,' a voice was saying. 'You didn't see him: he was digging in that grass like he'd buried an old bone there.'

'He's that good? It was supposed to be a downpour that night.'

'All I know is what I saw. That dog says there's blood, maybe it washed off the grass but it's still in the dirt underneath. It'll show in the samples.'

A third man approached and said feelingly, 'We've got to search *that*?'

Everyone looked at the fecund jungle on the inland side of the highway.

'No way,' someone said. 'It was only a week ago: drag a body in there, the track's got to show. Look at it, man; that stuff hasn't been disturbed this season.'

'We'll search. Wanna bet?'

The dog was sent in although it was obvious that no body could have been deposited in this place, not without leaving a trace. Miss Pink watched and waited, anticipating the moment when Laddow would have her continued presence brought to his attention and he would be forced to ask her to leave. Forced, because it would mean he'd have to speak to her again, but after a while she realised that there was nothing, or nothing fresh he could say. She guessed that, until the laboratories had analysed the samples, the foetid trail could tell them nothing more.

She guessed correctly. When Laddow came back to the lay-by and saw her standing by her car he blinked in surprise. He had forgotten her, moreover it appeared that he hadn't seen her among the horde of technicians.

'I'm sorry,' he said, 'I was called away. I'm leaving now. Did you want to see me about something?' People were getting into their cars, starting up, pulling out on to the road.

'Was the girl killed over there?' She indicated the mouth of the track.

'You've been talking to someone.'

'Listening. I'm not deaf, Mr Laddow.'

'Yes, well' – he was grudging – 'the dog is interested in the place. We've taken samples; it could turn out to be where he killed her, yes.'

'He? You mean – ' She let it hang.

'There's no other body here. He put her in the trunk, reversed the car to this spot and walked away, leaving the keys in the ignition.'

'Then he would have to hitch a lift northwards, or south.'

'Or east: another few miles and the road crosses the coast range to Portland, and to the interstate.' He stifled a sigh. 'He's got eight days' start on us.'

'You're pretty certain now?'

He looked at her. 'He left Sundown with the girl. She was

dead at this point, and she was almost certainly killed here; even if rain washed away the blood the dog was on to something. But there's no second body. I never did believe in a hitch-hiker; that was his wife: wishful thinking. Who wants to believe her husband's a murderer?'

Chapter 10

'How was she shot?'

'I didn't ask.'

'Why not?'

Miss Pink regarded Leo Brant in surprise, not at the other's belligerence, which was her natural manner, but at her own omission. In imagination she recalled that meeting with Laddow yesterday at the Vista Point above Moon Shell Beach.

Sadie said, 'I'm amazed he gave you any information at all, but then you invite confidence.'

'Quiet!' Leo ordered. 'There he is.'

The others looked where she was looking and saw the pileated woodpecker lurching up a snag, its crest flaming in the sunshine. They held their breath but it was no good; three people and three rucksacks were alien objects in the bird's territory. A plastic bag flapped, the woodpecker gave a shriek of alarm and dived for the timber.

'Time he got used to us,' Leo grumbled. 'He sees us often enough.'

'He's always spooky,' Sadie pointed out. 'She's much more amenable.'

'How do you tell them apart?' Miss Pink asked.

'She doesn't have the red whisker,' Leo said. 'But it's easiest to distinguish them by behaviour. You can't always see the whisker against the light – or its absence.'

'Are you a superlative birder or do you just have eyes like a vulture?'

Leo looked at her friend. 'Which is it, Locke?'

'Something of both,' Sadie said, then, gently probing: 'So we still don't know what calibre gun was used on Gayleen.'

Miss Pink wrenched her attention back to the question of firearms. 'Not yet. And who's going to ask?'

'No one now. Poor Lois.' A pause. 'And poor Andy,' she added. 'It had to be a crime of passion.'

'What the hell difference does that make?' Leo glared. Miss Pink stared at the canopy where the woodpecker had disappeared. The words hung between them.

They had climbed out of the timbered basin by way of Porcupine Gulch to lunch on Pandora Ridge. There were places here on the crest that were clear of trees and they had stopped on a rock platform from which there was an extensive view. This was mostly forest, although there was the sea to the west and Cape Deception north of the cove, but all the land was covered by trees except for a ribbon of cliffs under the cape. There was a certain variation in texture because creeks and canyons had their counterparts in spurs and the timber traced such irregularities meticulously; the far side of the basin was a design of shaded folds, soft as green velvet.

'He didn't tell you much,' Sadie remarked after a time. 'He merely confirmed what we were all afraid of.'

Leo turned slowly. 'Since when were you bothered Andy Keller would turn out to be a murderer? What about "Spotted Owls Roasted"?'

'Don't, Leo.'

'He deserves all he got.' She checked in astonishment. 'What am I saying? He's the one that got away, except he hasn't; Laddow traced him pretty quickly to Moon Shell. Andy had to hitch from there; once it goes out on television, whoever gave him a lift will come forward within minutes.'

'He's had over a week to get lost,' Sadie said.

'Now where would he go?' Leo looked at Miss Pink. 'Stay out in the boondocks, he's noticeable. He'll hole up in a city, don't you think? San Francisco or LA?'

'He needn't be noticeable in a wilderness area,' Miss Pink pointed out. 'A certain type of criminal could do it; it's been done often enough. And there are all the marijuana growers in the coastal ranges; he could well find sanctuary with them.'

'Well, there's one thing' – Leo started to pack her rucksack – 'he's got to stay hidden, so he can't come back here. We've seen the last of him, thank God. Why are you looking at me like that, Locke? What did I say, apart from the obvious?'

'Only that it's a good thing there wasn't a second body.'

'Don't be ridiculous. Everyone hated that man. He was mean.'

'Don't talk about him in the past tense; it's borrowing trouble.'

When everything came to be known about this day, Miss Pink was to wonder why they had talked in this way, but at the time she paid it no more attention than she did any of the speculation rife in Sundown, and an hour or so later she forgot it completely, at least for a while.

Their business here was the spotted owl and below them now, on the northern slope of Pandora Ridge, dropping towards Bobcat Creek and Porcupine, was the old-growth forest of hemlock and spruce and red cedar. The party, with Leo leading, descended Pandora to the point where the subsidiary spur broke right, pointing towards the village. They were back in the trees and shortly they came to the signpost that pointed in two directions to Sundown. Here, instead of continuing to follow the spur as Miss Pink had done shortly after her arrival, Leo dropped steeply down the trail that would take them through the old-growth. Within half a mile they came to the lip of the big landslide.

Miss Pink looked up. 'The higher trail can't be far above,' she said. 'I remember looking down the gash but I couldn't see this path. It must have been hidden by that crag.'

In the middle of the slide was the cause of the trouble: a trickle of water (which would be a torrent in rain) that drained past a ragged outcrop with angular chunks poised on either side. A few more inches of soil would wash away in the next storm and more rock tumble into Porcupine Gulch. From raw indentations in the slope it was obvious the whole mess was extremely unstable.

'There was a fall here quite recently,' Leo said. 'We tried to dig the path out again.'

'Not to say "dig",' Sadie protested. 'We didn't have shovels. We cleared the trail with our hands.'

The landslide was about sixty feet wide and the trail started as a thin line marked by deer. The women walked along this without a pause but treading carefully; it was a long way down to the bottom of the slide and the angle was not consistent. There were more outcrops below, and drops.

'I'll stop in the stream,' Leo warned – and not superfluously. To tread on the heels of the person ahead in this place could be sufficient to upset delicate balance. At least one of them might fall.

They edged round the foot of the outcrop and stopped in

108

wet rubble and water. Miss Pink glanced up at the poised blocks and swallowed. Rocks shifted under her feet. Leo intercepted the glance. 'We pushed down the worst rocks,' she said cheerfully. 'Those we left are wedged; you gotta believe it. No way would we have been digging out a path right under them otherwise.'

'It was the first thing we did,' Sadie assured her. 'Knocked off all the loose boulders, and then we dug out the trail.'

Miss Pink yawned with tension and looked at what they called a trail. Sadie watched her anxiously. 'You should have seen it before we dug it out again,' she said. 'The last rockfall must have happened in the storm we had – remember: last week, soon after you came?'

'I was here,' Miss Pink said absently, watching Leo who was staring down the line of the slide. 'I got caught in the rain.'

'Good job you weren't here when the rock fell,' Sadie said.

Miss Pink frowned. Leo said, 'It's only ravens. Let's move; my boots are leaking.'

They continued to the sweet haven of the trees and a good earth trail, but instead of walking on, Miss Pink paused and looked back.

'I heard that rockfall,' she said. 'I must have been coming down the spur. There was a tree dropped earlier in the day, and then there was the woodpecker, and a red-tail. Curious' – she stepped back to the very edge of the slide and looked down – 'the red-tail was around here. And now,' she mused, 'there are ravens.'

'I said so.' Leo was impatient. 'Come on; it's owls we're looking for.'

Miss Pink was focusing her binoculars. Sadie and Leo exchanged glances and then, resigned, making the best of it, they concentrated on what might be in the canopy.

'Those ravens are feeding,' Miss Pink observed.

Leo blinked. Sadie said, 'There'll be rodents and things got caught in the landslide.'

'The rockfall,' Miss Pink corrected. 'The landslide was years ago. But anything caught in the rockfall would still be fresh.' She stepped back. 'You look,' she told Leo.

The other squinted down the slide. 'Yeah, they're pecking.' She focused her binoculars and was still for quite a while. She lowered them. 'They got something big. Like a deer's leg.'

'No deer ever got caught in a rockfall,' Sadie said.

'Well, cow then.'

There was no response; they all knew that there were no cows in this forest. The other two looked at Miss Pink, who said, 'We don't all have to go. You look for the owls; I'll go down the side, through the trees.'

'You can't,' Leo said. 'It's a jungle: all down-timber and enormous logs. You'd never get through. It has to be some old carcass.'

'I'll go down to Porcupine then, turn up the trail and cross the creek. The landslide must go almost to the water, so it can't be a quarter of a mile from the trail.'

'Quarter of a mile – in this!' Leo gestured at the timber, meaning the under-storey rather than the trees.

But Miss Pink was adamant and, out of courtesy as much as common sense, they wouldn't let her go alone. In fact, she wasn't sorry to have company. It was quiet and dim under the great trees: the fronds of the sword ferns were motionless, the hanging lichen unstirred by any breeze. There was no movement, no sound of bird or squirrel, only the thud of their boots in the dust, the creak of a rucksack strap, the whisper of denim against a twig. This was an alien place and Miss Pink found herself thinking of Gideon d'Eath and the mythology that he had stolen from the old world, when all the time a native magic lurked here in the primeval forest that fronted on the Pacific.

They came to the creek, crossed it by a log bridge and climbed the far bank to turn up Porcupine Gulch. They agreed to go for about three-quarters of a mile and then to start looking.

In the event the landslide wasn't all that difficult to locate when three people were searching for it although, predictably, it was the far-sighted Leo who caught the glimpse of pale stone high under the spur a mile away.

'You don't want to come, Locke,' she said firmly, 'not with your knees.' And Sadie sat down to wait while the other two started to work their way to the creek.

The terrain was appalling: they could scarcely take one step without being forced to climb a log or boulder, which might not be anything on the uphill side, but below, the drop was sometimes impossible and they'd be forced to retreat. And always, under the obstruction, there was the danger that something, disturbed by their progress, would shift and roll, trapping a limb. In the end they took the easiest line, regardless of the fact that they might come out a long way from the foot of the landslide.

They slid into the bed of the creek and clawed their way out on the other side. They paused for breath, streaming sweat, and Leo turned to Miss Pink: 'I had an awful thought. If there is – anything – then we killed it, rolling down rocks when we dug out the trail.'

'I doubt it.' Miss Pink tried to sound equable but she was panting heavily. 'Were there ravens that day?'

'I didn't notice. Who bothers with ravens?'

But it was the birds that brought them to the landslide. As they blundered through the undergrowth above the creek they were unable to see their goal but they could hear the ravens croaking. Rock appeared through the tree trunks and the ferns: raw, angular, sunlit. The birds flapped away and the women came out on a titanic rubbish dump: rocks, splintered branches, uprooted bushes and, at the lowest extremity, trees leaning drunkenly into the forest.

They clambered over the debris to the centre, the fall-line. Sticking out of a mass of gravel was a leg.

'A leg,' Laddow said coldly. She had finally reached him on the telephone that evening. He was in Portland. 'An animal's leg?' he asked, sounding as if he would like it to be that but knowing it was hopeless: a ridiculous question. She hadn't run him to earth in order to tell him she'd found a dead deer.

'Not with a Hi-Tec boot beside it,' she said.

'Oh, so it could be – The boot need have nothing to do with— '

'There was a foot inside it, sort of.'

'*Sort* of? What d'you mean: "sort of"?'

'The ravens. They're scavengers – but they couldn't get at the rest of the body.'

'And you didn't?'

'It's more or less cemented in by the gravel. We thought we should leave it anyway.'

'A Hi-Tec boot,' he repeated thoughtfully. 'Can we get a car in there? A helicopter?'

'I'm afraid you'll have to walk.'

'Why did you call me?' He was suddenly wary.

'The police had to be told, and we know you, and then you were engaged in Sundown.'

'Are you keeping something back – like this discovery points to someone we know?'

'Andy Keller's missing.'

'I see. You think he came back.' She said nothing. 'We'll be down tomorrow,' he said.

'I forgot to ask— ' She stopped. He'd rung off.

She asked the question next morning as the detectives, exhausted, splashed water on their faces and drank from Porcupine Creek regardless of bacteria.

'What kind of gun was used to shoot Gayleen?'

Laddow was too worn down to orientate himself. Hammett who, being lean, was suffering less, said, 'A .22. Why?'

'Was Mrs Keller's revolver a .22?'

'It was.' Laddow glared. 'It doesn't mean she was shot with that revolver, but she could have been. You know' – a thought had struck him – 'I don't want this body to be Andy Keller.'

'No,' she said, 'I can see that.'

They turned to the bank, the men going straight up to an eroded overhang, Miss Pink working diagonally out of the creek. Unable to cope with the overhang the others slid back to the water and followed her.

The ravens were there again, showing them the way to the landslide, taking off in alarm at the noise of their approach, perching high to watch and wait.

'Oh, yes,' Laddow breathed, looking at the leg which was no more than splintered ends of bone. 'Where's the boot?'

'Here.' She indicated a small stone structure like a dolmen. Carefully Hammett removed the capstone to expose the boot: grey and white, grubby, the laces still in their eyelets but not tied, the thing smelling foul.

Hammett was carrying a small pack. He produced a pair of gloves and, picking up the boot, peered inside. He grimaced and replaced it in its nest of stones.

Laddow said, 'Take some pictures and then we'll move these rocks.'

They stood aside while Hammett busied himself with a Nikon.

'Do you understand this?' Laddow asked. 'You're the hiker.

See anything like it before? You have to *think*.' as Miss Pink hesitated.

She responded calmly. 'I've seen a lot of bodies in mountains and so on, the result of falls . . . But the nearest I've come to anything like this was in avalanche debris. It looks similar, except that this is gravel and rock rather than snow.'

'You figure it's natural – no foul play?'

'My dear man!' She was shocked.

'Look' – he was testy – 'I'm not the expert here, not at least until we uncover him – or her – although that's a big boot, a man's, wouldn't you say? I'll be more at home' – he grinned like a bear – 'when we've got him out, but right now, ma'am, I need to know about avalanches. Do you follow me?'

'Yes. So far as I can see, everything looks natural. He could have fallen by – accident . . . ' She trailed off.

'You thought of something?'

'Only that there's so much rock on top of him, but then that happens too: a boulder comes down after the victim's fallen and brings a lot of subsidiary stuff with it.' She had remembered Sadie and Leo clearing the trail above, but she would let them tell it, not her.

'Right,' Hammett said with relief, 'I'm finished.'

'We haven't started yet,' Laddow said, and Miss Pink withdrew to sit on a rock and watch them work.

They hadn't brought a shovel and they wouldn't have used one anyway; they cleared the ground like nurserymen gently exposing the roots of a cherished plant that must be removed without a scratch – or without further injury; scratches bore no relation to what had happened here. The body was so battered and crushed that not only was it unidentifiable, its sex was in doubt until they could work it out to their satisfaction. It had been a man.

They retreated to join Miss Pink, bringing with them the stench of putrefaction, or rather, intensifying it, for with the disinterment the whole place stank.

'No way,' said Laddow morosely, 'no way can anyone identify that. Levis and a T-shirt: nothing distinctive.'

'Clean up the jaw and see if it can be wired together,' Hammett suggested. 'Try it out on his dentist.'

'You have the boot,' Miss Pink said. 'It's odd that there's no pack and nothing in the pockets.'

'Pack?'

'Rucksack. You went through all the pockets?'

Hammett said, 'He's face upwards, we haven't moved him yet. What about the hip pockets?'

Laddow sighed and stood up. She watched them walk slowly back to the body. The ravens were watching too and she shivered in the sunshine.

Hammett eased the body off the rocks, trying to be gentle, but he had an extremely difficult task before Laddow could work his hand underneath. To Miss Pink, observing their movements with her senses dulled, time had stopped and there was just space and silence, the sun shining on the stones, black shadows in the forest, and two men trying to find something that would tell them about the third.

Hammett was lowering the body, Laddow was getting to his feet holding a small object in gloved fingers. They came back and he showed it to her: a key on a ring with a dark wedge of plastic on which was printed in neat white letters: Fountain motel. Portland, Oregon, and a telephone number.

Chapter 11

'He came back.'

'When?'

'The same night. He walked back – through the forest?' Laddow looked at Miss Pink. 'Is that possible? How far is it?'

She considered the question. They were sitting beside Bobcat Creek, drying their hands after washing themselves for the second time. Washing skin made little difference; the smell clung to their clothes.

'I didn't bring the map,' she said, 'but I would guess that if he'd taken to the forest trails he'd have to cover at least fifty, sixty miles to get back to here. He couldn't do it in less than two days on foot.'

'He could have got a lift,' Hammett said.

'Not that night,' Laddow put in. 'The road would be closed at six.' He pondered. 'He had to call somewhere before he reached this point – ' he gestured upstream. 'Where's his parka and haversack, where's his billfold?'

'It wasn't in the car of course.' They stared at her. 'In the Chevrolet,' she elaborated, 'stolen from Moon Shell Beach.'

Now they looked at each other. 'Like I said,' Laddow repeated, 'he stopped off somewhere.'

'And his hat,' mused Miss Pink. 'But he'd never wear that when he was hiking.' There was silence from the listeners. 'What happened to the Stetson?' she asked brightly. 'Did the drug addict find it in the car and sell it? That hat cost money.'

'It's a detail,' Laddow said, not answering the question. 'Why is it important?'

'Because he was wearing it when he left Sundown.'

'He was,' Hammett said, and looked meaningly at Laddow.

Miss Pink, poking at dry gravel beside a log, said, 'I don't

115

see how he could have covered the ground, even hitching back to Sundown, because the rain stopped overnight.' They turned to her like hound dogs. 'The storm,' she explained. 'It started to rain on the Tuesday afternoon but it stopped some time during the night. There's been no rain since. Surely the gravel round the body washed down after he fell.'

'It could have been brought down by the stream,' Hammett pointed out.

Now she felt compelled to tell them that Sadie and Leo had been trundling boulders down the slope in an effort to make the trail safe.

'Why didn't you mention this before?' Laddow asked grimly.

'I didn't relate it to the body. Would the rocks fall that far?'

'That's it!' Hammett exclaimed. 'He fell from a trail. How far above is it?'

Relieved not to have to speculate on the actions of Sadie and Leo, she concentrated on distances, but Laddow was off on another tack. 'When were they up there?' he asked.

'I didn't ask. I had the impression— '

There was a scream from the far side of Bobcat. Hammett gasped, Laddow gaped at Miss Pink. 'Red-tailed hawk,' she murmured. 'It's always around – ' She frowned, remembering. 'There was a tree came down that day around lunchtime and afterwards the red-tail kept calling, and then there was a rockfall.'

'Where? When?' Laddow was excited.

'I was above . . . way up near the top of Pandora Ridge. The rock fell away from below me; it could have been in the old landslide. The time? I don't know; I didn't look at my watch.'

'Try to remember,' Laddow urged. Hammett looked puzzled.

'It was after lunch and before the rain started.' She shook her head. 'Early afternoon, two, two thirty, at a wild guess; I can't do better than that.'

Hammett had waited impatiently for her to finish. 'But Keller was seen much later,' he reminded Laddow. 'Four, around there; he was travelling fast to catch the roadworks, remember? That's what Linquist and Fleur Sanborn figured. If she heard a rock come down, couldn't be anything to do with Keller. He was alive long afterwards.'

'Just coincidence,' she murmured. 'It was an odd day all round.'

'How: odd?' Laddow asked.

116

'Well,' she gestured vaguely, 'the atmosphere; it's intimidating when you're alone. And then: a big tree falling without human agency, the hawk screaming, the rockfall.' The voices, she might have added, but didn't, self-conscious about her age, anticipating the way they would look at each other, or try not to; old ladies hearing things: trees, rocks, voices.

'You can't get away from it,' Laddow said, watching her. 'If that was Keller in the Chevy around four, he wasn't killed when you heard a rock fall around two or two thirty, was he?'

'Why is it important when he died? Is there some suggestion that it wasn't an accident?'

'When there's a long fall involved there's always the question of whether the victim was pushed.'

Fleur stared at Miss Pink in consternation, then tossed back the rest of her whisky. They were in her sitting-room behind the gallery where the west wall – mostly glass – fronted on the ocean but neither of them was interested in the view. Miss Pink had been telling her about the discovery at the foot of the landslide. It was only now, after a long shower and a lazy bath, at a distance from the events of the day and summarising them, that questions surfaced which had not been apparent at the time.

'What I really came to ask you,' she said, 'was how did they appear when you saw them in the Chevrolet leaving Sundown?'

'You mean, if he killed her only a few miles north of here, something should have been apparent when I saw them?'

'Well, *could* have been apparent. Quarrelling perhaps? Was – did he appear to be angry? You said he was driving too fast. You're an expert observer; can't you recall the scene? You'd been painting on Cape Deception. Presumably the rain drove you home.'

'Not really; the light changed. It was bright early on: a luminescence behind the fog, but that faded so I packed up, came down slowly, reached the road, or rather, their road-end, around four, I seem to remember. They came out of the loop road just as I reached the junction. Andy didn't stop – the idiot – didn't even slow for the Stop sign, just pulled out on the highway, burning rubber, and was away. Angry? Could be: driving like that. If anything had been coming he could have killed them both.' She clapped her hand over her mouth and stared, wide-eyed, at Miss

117

Pink. She lowered her hand. 'And yet,' she said, 'they died quite differently.'

'Wait a minute. You saw them at Lois's road-end: the northern junction.'

'Of course. He wouldn't come out the south end of the loop if he was going north, would he? Oh, I see: you're wondering what I was doing up there instead of coming straight home to the village. I went to look at a pool in the forest: Salamander Tarn. There's a gorgeous maple on the bank and I needed to work out the best time to paint it. That's why I was at that end of the village – outside it actually.'

'You were walking along the left side of the road?'

'Naturally. Why?'

'So Gayleen was the passenger, and she was on your side, and Andy, who was driving, was on the far side?'

'What *is* this? Oh, I get it: you're trying to make me visualise it as it happened, how they looked, were they quarrelling.' She thought about it. 'You can't see much behind those tinted windows; I think they're stupid, lethal, they ought to be illegal, specially windshields.'

'You're certain Andy was driving, not the other way about?'

'Oh yes, outlines, you know. You couldn't mistake her hair and his Stetson – and shades! Shades *and* tinted glass, can you believe that?' She considered her own question, then said slowly, 'You're not interested in their behaviour, but in their appearance. Why's that?'

Miss Pink didn't answer but asked another question: 'That Tuesday evening, when you came along to the Tattler and Miriam told us Oliver had gone to Portland, you asked if he left with Gayleen and Andy.'

'Did I? But Oliver left the day before – '

'Did you ask that because you thought someone was in the back of the Chevy?'

'I can't remember that far back! And why, for heaven's sakes?'

'I don't know.' And Miss Pink did look bewildered. 'It's an extra vehicle we need, not an extra person.' She caught Fleur's eye. 'You didn't see the body,' she went on in a more practical tone. 'Water had been the agent . . . I thought he couldn't have fallen after the storm but Hammett pointed out that the stream could have brought down gravel. Can I use your phone?'

'Sure. Providing you explain what you just said.'

'Let me get one thing straight first.' The telephone was beside her on an end-table. She dialled a number. 'Sadie – Melinda here . . . Yes, and it appears to be Andy . . . A key, a room key to the motel in Portland where they were staying . . . They're bringing it down this evening, I understand . . . Oh, no; a long fall like that: he'd be killed instantaneously – tell me, when were you there: rebuilding the trail? . . . What time did you start work? I see.' She stared absently at the stacks beyond the windows. 'I don't think so; they'll go to Lois first . . . Why? Because he was her husband!'

'What was that about them rebuilding a trail?' Fleur asked as she replaced the receiver.

Miss Pink told her. 'They went up the following day, Wednesday, and they got down to work around midday. Andy's body had to be there already, at the bottom of the slide.'

'I don't see— '

'Because the body was under all the debris. Whether the water that bound the gravel and stuff together came from rain or from the stream is immaterial; he was under rocks as well. If he'd fallen after Sadie and Leo knocked off the loose blocks, he'd be on top of them.'

'Meaning he fell before they got up there, before noon on Wednesday – but he had to be at Moon Shell around five the previous day. How did he get back?'

'That's what I meant when I said we needed an extra vehicle.'

'"Not an extra person"; you said that too. But you do need another person for your theory because someone has to drive the other car – ' Fleur stiffened and held her breath. Miss Pink waited. After a while the younger woman tried to speak, croaked and coughed. 'Excuse me. May I offer you another drink?' The tone was artificial.

They sat and looked at the view, Miss Pink sipping, Fleur drinking whisky as if it were lemonade until she said, 'Well, she's done nothing seriously wrong, has she? OK, so he called her and she drove up there in her Jeep and fetched him back to Sundown. He could have told her they'd quarrelled and Gayleen drove off in the Chevy. It's as simple as that. She didn't have to know he'd killed Gayleen. You can't be an accessory if you don't *know*, can you?'

'I wouldn't think so.'

'Did you say the police are with Lois now? Let's call Chester.'

'No.' Miss Pink was sharp. She went on more gently, 'Let's wait a while, allow things to sort themselves out somewhat. You see, your theory of collusion, even innocent collusion, won't wash. By the time Lois got there the road would be closed, and Andy would have to walk from Moon Shell to meet her. *He* could walk through the roadworks of course, but she couldn't drive past them. Suppose he did walk: he couldn't have left Moon Shell much before five and he had some twenty miles to cover to the roadworks. But Lois came down to the Tattler around – what? Ten o'clock?'

'If he'd run that twenty miles from Moon Shell . . . Or even got a lift from a tourist who didn't know the road closes at six, hadn't seen the notice . . . '

'There are lots of notices – and would he risk running along the road and have a local see him?'

'A local could have given him a lift.'

'If so, he'll come forward. There's something else you forgot. Would Lois believe a story that he allowed Gayleen to drive off with all his luggage in the car?'

'He could have told Lois he stopped at Moon Shell to use the bathroom and Gayleen drove off: they'd quarrelled and she acted impulsively. Look at her; you'd say that was in character.'

'Your theory depends on too many strokes of luck, or coincidences, or both.'

'So what's the police theory – or is that a silly question?'

'Not at all, I would think everyone's asking it. I think they'll be reserving judgment until after the autopsy.'

Fleur gave a sick grin. 'From what you told me that's going to be a bummer. How could they tell – anything?'

'Only if they found, say, a bullet in the skull.'

'Like a .22? You think he committed suicide?'

Miss Pink shrugged. She hadn't meant that but it was another possibility. Fleur elaborated: 'He was a guy would do anything for attention, like a naughty kid; you know: even opprobrium is better than no attention at all – and Andy enjoyed being offensive.' Miss Pink said nothing. 'There's the gun,' Fleur continued thoughtfully. 'If it was suicide, the gun would have to be nearby, wouldn't it? Except Sadie and Leo rolled rocks down. You'd almost think— '

'Yes.'

120

'No!' Fleur shook her head vehemently. 'That's ridiculous! So what if they covered up evidence – it was just a coincidence that they happened to be there the day after he died.'

Miss Pink thought that Fleur might be literally correct, but was it coincidence that Leo and Sadie had covered up evidence?

'Did you get the impression that the trail had been washed away or – ' She ground to a halt and regarded her listeners expectantly.

'No,' Leo said. 'There was a kinda gouge right there where the trail should be.'

'Enormous,' Sadie said, 'like a boulder weighing a ton – more, a few tons – had sort of cartwheeled. Didn't we say there'd been a rockfall? Are you thinking what I'm thinking: that Andy started it, climbing maybe?'

Miss Pink had gone straight from the gallery to Sand Dollar. Sadie and Leo had heard nothing, could discover nothing, and had been avid to learn the result of Miss Pink's second visit to the bottom of the landslide. Lois, they told her, wasn't answering the phone. They had been appalled at the news that the body was that of Andy Keller, but they weren't bothered by the mystery of how he'd covered the ground so quickly from Moon Shell Beach. What did bother them was still the matter of their having trundled boulders down on the body, but Miss Pink was postulating that the earlier rockfall was the one associated with his death; the action of clearing the trail had resulted merely in a kind of interment, no harm done.

'Except we may have buried the gun,' Sadie pointed out.

'So what?' Leo grunted. 'Accident or suicide, what's the odds? My God, am I glad they can't get a chopper back in there! And people aren't going to hang around a place a body's been for ten days, end of August. The owls shouldn't be disturbed too much, always assuming there are owls in that old-growth. The ones we went up to find yesterday,' she added meaningly.

Sadie said, 'Don't let Mr Laddow hear you talking like that. He may hold the view people are more important than owls.'

'I'll argue that with him any time, but there can't be any argument a pair of owls is more important than Andy Keller's corpse.'

The telephone rang. It was Chester Hoyle, and he wanted to speak to Miss Pink.

'I've been trying everywhere to find you,' came his voice. 'Can you come up here: to Lois's place? Laddow just left and she needs to talk to you badly.' His voice dropped. 'She's bothered, Melinda, apart from the shock of it all. Laddow's acting weird. He seems to be implying that she's involved in what happened – you know: collusion?'

It wasn't until she was walking along the road to the Keller place that Miss Pink reminded herself that she was about to call on a widow who had only this evening learned that her husband had died a violent death. She was devoutly grateful that Chester would be there but she was also curious to see how Lois, sophisticated, honest, respectable, was responding to the shock. And, belatedly, she wondered where Laddow and Hammett were.

Chester opened the door to her. At the other end of the house, Lois was doing something in the kitchen: 'Making sandwiches,' Chester explained on a false note. 'She won't relax.'

Miss Pink crossed the parquet firmly but with a certain wariness.

'Hello, Melinda.' Lois raised her eyes. 'Good of you to come. Sit down. Have a drink.'

Miss Pink stood her ground and offered her condolences. Lois, pale and drawn, her eyes huge, thanked her, swallowed and turned to the stove, her spine as stiff as a plank. Miss Pink sat down and accepted a drink from Chester.

'We're drinking too much,' he said on that same false note, with a meaning glance at Lois's back.

'Small wonder,' Miss Pink murmured, and waited to see how the conversation would go, which subjects might be acceptable, but Chester only repeated that he had been trying to find her all over the village.

'I was with Fleur,' she explained and, with a glance at the deck where the glass doors were open on the afterglow, added inanely, 'You all have such magnificent views.'

'The houses are built that way. The original owners came here for the ocean.'

Lois approached with a tray and he relaxed a little too obviously. 'We haven't eaten since lunchtime,' he said.

'Laddow,' said Lois, 'smelled. Oh, my God!' She pushed the tray at a coffee table and rushed upstairs.

Chester sighed heavily while Miss Pink sorted out the plates

and napkins and poured coffee. 'How did she take it?' she whispered.

'She wouldn't believe it at first even when they told her they'd
found the motel key on the body. But then there were the
boots . . . She believes it now. So you see the – accusation –
no, the suggestion from Laddow that she *harboured* Andy, a
killer, doesn't really bother her. It's me who's bothered.'

'They can't charge her with being an accessory if she didn't— '

Lois returned, her face stiff, bearing herself with the kind
of defiance worn by the bereaved who are defying themselves
to break down rather than the company to pity them.

'It doesn't matter, Chester,' she said. 'A good lawyer would
make mincemeat of it.' She sat down, looked to see that her
guests had helped themselves, took a sandwich and addressed
Miss Pink. 'I haven't bothered to call my attorney. Any charge
would be ridiculous. What do you think?'

'There's the question of how he managed to get back here
so quickly from Moon Shell Beach.' Miss Pink spoke carefully,
wondering how far she could go in any discussion of the dead
man's movements, leaving it to Lois.

'They'll have to look elsewhere then, because I certainly didn't
bring him here. I didn't see him again after breakfast that day
when he said he was going for a hike because Gayleen was still in
bed. By the time he came home I was working, so he left without
even saying goodbye.' She clenched her jaw and looked away.

'Laddow is sceptical,' Chester said and then, in a rush: 'The
man's out of his depth; he's a *police*man; a woman like Lois is
a closed book to him – her domestic arrangements too.' He was
embarrassed.

'Euphemisms, Chester.' Lois turned to Miss Pink. 'He means
my relationship with – Andy.' She didn't like saying the name.
'What Chester is trying to say is that Laddow can't understand
how people like us can have what he thinks of as permissive
attitudes. And it *was* unusual,' she added with warmth, 'and
I do feel guilty; it was a form of selfishness. I couldn't be
bothered with— Now, wait a minute' – she was chiding herself –
'look who's going in for euphemisms! Let's put it this way:
my work is the most important aspect of my life – oh, there's
Grace too. Andy came a poor third after work and Grace, so he
had to make his own life and I didn't pay him all that much

123

attention. Now I feel so guilty, and Laddow can't understand any of it.'

Miss Pink had followed this carefully. 'How does his incomprehension relate to the – investigation?'

'Gayleen? He put forward a theory that she was blackmailing Andy – who killed her in a fit of rage, and then he brought me in to clear up the mess, which makes me an accessory. Who cares? About the accessory bit, I mean.'

Chester shook his head. 'I can't see her blackmailing him.'

Lois said absently, 'She was simple, but someone else could have been manipulating her. Laddow has a point there.'

'Like someone who guessed Lois was rich,' Chester explained to Miss Pink. 'And then, if Gayleen could manipulate Andy, he could get money out of his wife, d'you see?'

Miss Pink said, 'That seems an unusually devious form of blackmail.'

'Laddow was trying to find an explanation for Andy bringing Gayleen here,' Lois said. 'They've talked to people, those two; they've listened to everyone, and they've formed an exalted view of us, all of us: like we're old money – old for Oregon, cultured, mannered. On the other hand there's Gayleen: a stripper, uses crack, needs money – apparently was a prostitute. The police can think of no other reason Andy could have brought her to my party except he was blackmailed into it.'

'It makes sense,' Chester said.

'Did he try to blackmail you?' Miss Pink asked.

'No – no, not *blackmail*. He asked me for money; he always does – did, but he didn't threaten me, offer any kind of ultimatum. I didn't get the impression that he was forced to bring Gayleen here – and when she talked to me, she had to be a marvellous actress to pull the wool over my eyes although— ' She stopped.

'Yes,' Chester said. 'She never stopped enthusing over the – opulence in which she figured you live.'

'She was awed, poor child. Silly child. Although since one doesn't know how she died, that could be unfair.' She was still protecting Andy.

'That's another thing,' Chester said. 'It was the same calibre gun shot Gayleen as is missing from Lois's bedroom, and the inference is that Andy stole it or— '

'Or I gave it to him,' Lois said.

'Laddow extended the blackmail theory,' Chester continued, 'to include Lois directly. Gayleen had something on them both, he suggested, or Lois involved herself because her husband was being blackmailed, and they plotted to dispose of Gayleen. And that would make her more than just an unwitting accessory.'

Lois smiled coldly. 'It would make me a conspirator to murder.'

'It had to be blackmail.' Miss Pink was cheerful. 'There can be no motive for your needing to kill Gayleen. You have the ideal life. But then what could she blackmail Andy with?'

Lois shrugged. 'Laddow was on a fishing expedition. That's what I've been trying to explain to Chester. Like I keep saying: it isn't worth calling an attorney.'

Suddenly it seemed that the subject died. They had finished eating (Lois had scarcely touched her sandwich); Chester had filled their glasses, they were silent until Miss Pink said, 'I don't think you need me; you seem to have coped with Laddow's vague threats very well on your own.'

Chester's jaw dropped but he didn't speak. Lois said, 'He had another theory but that was so way out it was fantasy. Wasn't it, Chester?'

'Yes, but nasty. Fantasy, of course, like you say.'

Miss Pink sipped her wine. 'You tell her, Chester,' Lois urged. 'I didn't take it in properly. I was tired and still in shock, I guess.'

'It was ridiculous,' he protested. 'Laddow was saying it was possible Andy never left.'

Miss Pink, who had not forgotten the first stonefall, the one after the tree fell last Tuesday, before the rain started, looked politely interested, and then saw that Chester was mutely begging for this theory to be refuted. She obliged. 'If Andy never left, who was driving the Chevy?'

'That's the point!' he cried. 'But suppose it was true: that someone else was driving when Carl and Fleur thought they saw Andy, what's more natural than that it was someone Gayleen knew, came to pick her up, take her back to Portland: some hippie type from Moon Shell Beach, hitched to Sundown because Gayleen told him she'd be here? Could be her boyfriend, even her pimp.'

'Could be,' Miss Pink agreed. 'What makes that so fantastic?'

Lois grinned. 'That's Chester's theory,' she pointed out. 'Laddow figures the driver could have come from here.'

'From right here!' Chester said heatedly. 'And he was looking at Lois when he said it. Which is why we need you.' He regarded Lois fiercely. 'She won't have it; she doesn't care. I can't persuade her to get legal advice but I did convince her to bring you in. She needs protection.'

Lois ignored him. Miss Pink objected. 'What we all need right now,' she said, 'is a good night's sleep.' She stood up and, taken by surprise, the others followed suit.

Lois said politely, 'Thank you very much for coming. We'll see you tomorrow.' She made to turn away, remembered her manners and accompanied her guest to the door.

'I'll walk you home,' Chester said, and turning to Lois, 'I'll not be more than half an hour.'

'Go home, Chester; I'm going to bed.'

'Leave the door open. I'll sleep in Grace's room.'

'Dear man.' She touched his arm before starting up the stairs.

As the door closed behind them Miss Pink asked, 'Does she have sleeping pills?'

'Lois! Never took one in her life. Won't have even an aspirin in the house. You don't have to bother about her taking a pill on top of alcohol. She'll be all right once she gets over the shock, and I'll be there tonight if she needs to talk. It's this guilt business is the problem, you see that. Neglected her husband in favour of her work, blaming herself because he got involved with unsavoury characters. Believe me, Melinda, that guy was rotten from the start: married her to get himself an easy living, and never gave up his bad old habits.'

'Are you telling me he was a criminal?'

'No, he was a parasite.'

They were walking along the road, avoiding the potholes by the light of his torch. Miss Pink asked curiously, 'What do you think happened?'

He was quiet for a moment. 'It *is* difficult,' he confessed. 'Either he did come back – Andy, I mean; he killed Gayleen, got back somehow, and maybe spent the night in the cabin without Lois knowing, then went hiking next day and fell – or he didn't leave at all, and it was someone else drove Gayleen away. And shot her, of course, because the person who was driving the

Chevy had to be the murderer. Didn't he?' His tone had grown increasingly diffident and now he stopped walking and faced her in the starlight. 'What do *you* think?'

'I'm not going to be like Laddow and put forward a host of theories. We all need sleep. Truthfully, Chester, I don't want to consider it at this moment.'

'Will you tomorrow?'

'What?'

'Consider it, and help Lois.'

'You think she needs help?'

'She's in a spot. She's too close. If Andy killed Gayleen and came back it's almost certain he touched base, as it were; spent the night in the cabin. Perhaps' – his voice faded as he turned and looked out to sea – 'perhaps he did come to her and she's concealing it. And then again, if he had the accident on the Tuesday, then the guy who drove Gayleen away had to come to the house to pick up the Chevy. No way can Laddow see a guy doing that without Lois knowing. He has no concept of how an author works: retreating into another world.'

'And the stereo going, which would mask the sound of an engine.'

'Exactly. Please help, Melinda. She's a rich woman, she can pay – but of course she'll say she doesn't need you, technically speaking; I'm sure she was very grateful for your company tonight. However, I'm not poor; suppose I – er – engage your services?'

She smiled in the darkness. 'Let's sleep on it. I assure you: I'll put my oar in if necessary. I'm all for justice.' Her tone was deliberately light.

Chapter 12

Miss Pink rose early and sat on her balcony drinking French Roast and wondering how the police would react to her becoming involved in their investigation. When Leo telephoned, asking if she would join them for another owl-hunt, she had difficulty orientating herself. 'No,' she said. 'I'm not going back there.'

'Not *there*!' Leo protested. 'We don't have to go near the landslide – well, not the bottom of it.'

'Another time – '

'What happened? What did Lois want?'

Miss Pink hesitated. This was bad manners even for the outspoken Leo. 'I think,' she said carefully, 'we need to talk. What time will you be home from your hike?'

'If it's that important we won't go.'

'I have things to do. Can I call you this evening?'

There was an empty silence: Leo had put her hand over the mouthpiece. Suddenly she was back, with a change of tone. 'This evening will be fine; we'll be home.'

Sadie, thought Miss Pink, was a restraining influence.

As she put the telephone down someone knocked at the door. She opened it to Laddow who greeted her as effusively as if she were his favourite aunt. He accepted her offer of coffee and a seat on the deck but although it was early and he looked fresh (she wondered how much sleep he'd had) he sat down with a sigh and regarded the dazzling stacks as if they were a reward for some arduous task just completed.

'I'll never forget this place,' he pronounced, shaking his head in wonder. 'I could spend the rest of my life here.'

'I don't think Mr Hammet is so appreciative.'

'Oh, Hammett. He's away to Portland.' It was tossed off carelessly but he was waiting for her reaction.

'He's gone back – to work from the other end?'

'The other end? No, no; just to be present at the autopsy: chain of evidence, you know. He supervised the removal of the body so he has to accompany it to the morgue.'

'I'm sorry for him. And for the pathologist.'

'What? Oh, yes. Terrible, wasn't it? I can do without aged cadavers. In such an environment too!'

They were silent, sipping their coffee, waiting each other out until she wearied of the game. 'So, after a night's sleep, which theory do you favour, Mr Laddow?'

Expressions flitted across the mobile features: surprise, amusement, respect. 'Mrs Keller summoned you after I left?'

'Not to say "summoned".'

'No, that was impertinent. Which theory do you favour?'

She studied his face which now appeared totally ingenuous. 'I wouldn't like to form an opinion from the facts as they stand,' she said. 'And who's to say they are facts? Where is the gun and Andy Keller's Stetson?'

A change of expression was, by now, predictable, but before his brows rose and his eyes widened, she had seen a spark of genuine surprise and knew that, behind the mask of astonishment, he was watching her carefully and, no doubt, catching every nuance in her voice.

'We haven't found them yet. Why do you attach importance to the hat?'

'Because it hasn't been found? I'm not sure. Did the drug addict mention it?'

'This came up before. No, ma'am; we went back to him. He swears there was no Stetson in the car. Why should he lie? You're thinking someone else wore it, maybe?'

'You suggested it.' She was equable. 'Don't you have a theory that Keller never left Sundown and someone else drove the Chevy away?'

'I think you arrived at that theory independently. Who was driving?'

She blinked at him, her lips parted.

'Who was driving the Chevy?' he elaborated.

'The murderer, presumably.'

He smiled. 'You could be a lot of assistance to me.' The tone was silky. He was, of course, employing a double bluff, but behind it she scented a triple stage, and two could play that game.

'These people are my friends,' she said stiffly.

'Even if one is a murderer?'

'Why couldn't it have been Andy Keller?'

'Several reasons.' He was serious. 'One: he couldn't have covered the distance from Moon Shell Beach to the landslide in the time. Remember, he had to – fall, before the rain stopped. Two: that type don't commit suicide. Anyways, there was no weapon near the body— '

'That could be there: under the rocks.'

His eyes sharpened. 'We're looking for it. Three: the man was fit, strong, a hiker. Do hikers fall off trails? I don't know; that's your department.'

'It happens all the time. It's not fitness or experience that count but lack of concentration. Anyone could fall off that trail.'

'OK. Now suppose he did come back: where's his billfold and his Stetson? No, ma'am; Keller never left Sundown. Someone else was driving that Chevy: wearing his hat and shades – someone Gayleen knew. That person could say: "There's Fleur; wave to her. There's Carl from the Tattler; give him a wave." It was someone she trusted, someone she'd obey automatically, like her boyfriend's wife.'

'Oh, come on!' Shocked, she lapsed into the American idiom. 'Gayleen trusted her boyfriend's *wife*? You're not listening to what you're saying.'

'But they were on excellent terms! Everyone knows that.'

'So why kill her?'

'Yes. Why kill her?' The silence lengthened. 'Why?' he repeated. 'Who wanted Gayleen dead?' He looked at her without expression. 'You got to have a very strong motive to kill someone.'

She moved impatiently, wanting to deny it, refusing to do so, knowing that she could well implicate someone she didn't want implicated. She didn't like the significance of that. She said, 'This hypothetical driver: did he leave fingerprints? Silly question. I mean, are there fingerprints on the car that shouldn't be there?'

He grinned. It was still a silly question. Nevertheless he responded seriously. 'The only prints were those of the girl who was driving in Portland, the prostitute, and those of her pimp, the drug addict who stole it originally and the crooked dealer.'

'No others *at all*?'

'No others on the steering wheel and none elsewhere although you'd expect Andy's and Gayleen's. No, before the addict stole that car, it had been wiped clean: doors and trunk, everything, but there were smudges too, like someone wore gloves. In August?' She absorbed this, staring at the cove without seeing it. 'You could help us,' he repeated quietly. 'You know them; like you said: they're your friends. Don't you want to clear them of suspicion?' The tone indicated that she could accept it as a joke – a sick joke in the circumstances – but there was the tacit acceptance that, should she take him seriously, there were no witnesses to the conversation. Laddow, as Lois pointed out, was a fisherman.

'A glorious day,' Eve Linquist agreed, lowering herself to a chair in the window of the Tattler's sun-room. 'All right for some,' she added serenely, nodding towards Fin Whale Head.

'What's he after?' Miss Pink asked.

'Snapper. He'll bake it for dinner if he catches one. Can we tempt you?'

'I'd be delighted.' She thought quickly. 'Maybe Sadie and Leo will come.'

'Why not? They'll be birding, nice day like this, no fog. Sadie will be glad of someone else to cook dinner for her. I should go for a walk myself, get some exercise. That'll be the day. And there's that other guy: diving into his little shed again, working on his masterpiece. Lot of exercise he gets.'

Miss Pink was just in time to catch sight of Boligard Sykes disappearing into his cabin.

'Clever guy,' Eve said. 'Driven.'

Miss Pink regarded the round innocent face, the braided hair, the pale eyes that met her own. 'Driven?'

'"Driven by demons": his own expression.'

'I see. What is he working on now?'

'I don't know. An ocean epic, no doubt; like some old guy fishing below Fin Whale Head and hooking a great white shark. No, that's been done; a wolf-eel then.' She smiled placidly.

'You don't think he has talent?'

'Oh, he'll have talent. Is that sufficient? He has enormous application – concentration for all I know; look at him now: he'll be in that shed till dark, except for lunch – Mabel insists he go home for lunch – but where's the end-product?' She didn't sound interested. 'Who cares?' she added. 'It gets him out from under Mabel's feet.'

'Well-trained,' murmured Miss Pink.

'If you're going to live with them you gotta make sure they're occupied. You're not married so you never had the problem, but everyone here 'cept Sadie and Leo – and they don't count – they've had to work something out.'

'So your husband cooks and fishes,' Miss Pink mused. 'Boligard pens epics, Jason has his bookstore. Miriam, being a widow, doesn't have the problem. Lois?'

'Miriam would have the problem eventually except that Oliver will go before he's thrown out. Lois was kinda similar. Andy left. You say they're doing the autopsy this morning. When will they know the result?'

'That depends on the damage. It will be interesting to see if he was shot with the same calibre weapon as the one used on Gayleen.'

'Which was the same as the one Lois – *what*!' Eve gasped. 'Andy was shot?'

'Didn't you realise?' Miss Pink was all innocence. 'That he comm— he could have committed suicide?'

Eve looked away, biting her lip. 'I see,' she said softly, her eyes straying to the headland. 'He killed Gayleen and then himself. With a .22, you said: a revolver.'

'They recovered the bullet that killed Gayleen. They will say only that it's a .22. But it wasn't a rifle.'

'Oh, no, not a rifle.' Now they both stared at the rocks below Fin Whale Head.

'Who else owns a firearm?' Miss Pink asked.

'I don't know who has a .22. Leo Brant has a .45, Boligard's got a shotgun, my old man has a deer rifle; Miriam – I don't know anything about Miriam's firearms, if she has any. Are the police asking everyone if they have a gun?'

'They won't trouble. If someone said Carl owns a rifle, they wouldn't come to you.'

'You mean they question people about their neighbours?'

'Naturally, that's how they get a lot of information.'

'But that's monstrous! They *believe* what people say? Suppose there's someone has it in for you, for his neighbour: tells lies, vindictive folk, like that?'

'You mean, someone might say you had a .22 revolver, or owned one at some time, or that Carl was seen with Gayleen one evening?'

'That's gross. Someone said that?'

'Just a scenario demonstrating spite. That was what you meant, surely?'

Eve turned troubled eyes on Miss Pink. 'I did mean that kind of thing but I hadn't followed through. Does this have anything to do with Carl being the last person to see them?'

'Andy and Gayleen?'

'Of course. It wasn't as if he saw them here; it was on the road, for heaven's sake! The Highways people at the roadworks must have seen them after Carl did – and then Andy had to come back here because that's his body in the landslip.'

'Yes, that's his body – evidently; there's the key of the motel – '

Eve's lip curled. 'Isn't that just like the guy: shacking up with a prostitute.' She stiffened. 'I hadn't thought of that: he'd be living on her earnings. Disgusting. You know what he was before he married Lois? He came from some scrappy old ranch over in the east: Wallowa, Stinking Water, wherever: the boondocks.'

'How did they meet?'

'At some writing seminar Lois was helping out with at Eugene. Andy had worked his way through school – he had all his wits about him, you know; he wasn't dumb. He called himself a screen-writer but he never sold anything till he married Lois. It was her had the contacts; she had the money and the nice home too. You know something: when Andy first come here, he was like Gayleen at that party, didn't know ought from somp'n – as they say. Kept his hat on indoors – like he did the other day, remember? Lois broke him off of that but he reverts when he wants to annoy, like ordering beer with his dinner, and that day: keeping his hat on to shock, so's that whore would see him as the local playboy.'

She stopped speaking and Miss Pink stared blandly at the ocean, wondering how her companion would recover poise unbalanced by rage and sloppy grammar.

'He was a farm boy,' Eve said heavily. 'And Lois is a pushover where a handsome face is concerned.'

Carl came plodding along the sand in his waders, carrying two large fish.

'Snapper?' Miss Pink asked eagerly. 'Eve told me to come down to dinner. Aren't they magnificent?'

'Pretty good,' said Carl, preening. 'Any news?'

'Not yet. I assume we'll be told the results of the autopsy. Laddow doesn't seem to be trying to conceal anything from us.'

'What do they think happened?'

'He used the same gun as the one that killed Gayleen.'

'I don't get you.'

Small wonder; she had been deliberately ambiguous. She blinked at him.

'You mean the same guy shot them both?' he asked, puzzled. 'Or – what do you mean?'

She looked unhappy. 'The theory – one theory is that he shot Gayleen and turned the gun on himself.'

'No.' He shifted the fish to his other hand, thinking, looking towards the village. 'No, that guy never killed himself. Not out of remorse he didn't.' He shook his head. 'Never. Andy Keller was a guy was torturing little animals soon's he could run fast enough to catch 'em. He loved hurting people, thrived on it. Kill himself? Not him. I'll tell you what though: someone coulda known he killed Gayleen and so they finished him off, stop him doing any more harm: like shooting a rabid dog.'

'You mean someone with a rifle followed him into the forest and shot him as he was crossing the landslide?'

'Why not? Shot with a rifle? You didn't say that before.'

'It's a possibility.' They started to move towards the village. 'Mrs Linquist says he came from a ranch in the east,' she said chattily. 'He did well for himself.'

Carl stopped. 'You think so?' The tone was sour. 'Maybe. It didn't rub off then. Got himself a rich lady and a beautiful home and all them Hollywood glamour jobs mixing with movie stars and like that but he was still poor white trash. Always was, always would be.'

'You sound like a Southerner.'

'Maybe so, but they got some good labels for folks down there, and I tell you another thing, ma'am' – he was fierce, glaring at her – 'they got *class* in the South, and trash knows their place. Don't get me wrong; I'm not referring to the coloured people, but the poor whites. That's all that boy was, and this village is well rid of him and his ways. Tell you another thing: ain't no one gonna help the police find out the guy who shot him.'

Miss Pink said in surprise, 'I believe the police are assuming it was an accident; he could have slipped off the trail when it turned slick in the rain.'

'Oh, so the rifle were your idea. That's all right then.' They resumed walking. 'And no one's got nothing to worry about.'

Miss Pink, on her way to the Surfbird motel, thought she would avoid Fleur by creeping round the back of her cabin. Few people in Sundown fenced their properties and there were little paths everywhere. Unfortunately there was also a great deal of undergrowth and, seeking to keep a discreet distance from the house, she found herself confronted by a riot of brambles and poison oak. Forced to retreat and take a paved path under the cabin walls she came to an open window and saw movement inside. Opening her mouth to call a greeting and apologise she saw that the room – a bright bedroom in white and pastel shades – was unoccupied and on the bed under the window sheets of paper were lifting in the draught, anchored by a book. She glimpsed print on the loose sheets and black and white drawings. On the book jacket there was a drawing and the large capitals of title and author. The format was familiar and unmistakable.

She went back to the beach, came to the access path and took the conventional way to the village. Passing the bookstore she saw that Jason had customers. A few yards further, Fleur was talking to some people in a Mercedes. As Miss Pink approached they drove away.

'Hi!' called Fleur. 'Been hiking?'

'Just along the shore.' She glanced casually at the gallery. 'Busy morning?'

'It isn't actually; things are winding down now, end of the season. How about you? I heard you were up at Lois's last night.'

'You did? Who told you?'

'Sadie, of course. We're all bursting to know what happened. Does one ask?' Fleur studied her face. 'Perhaps not.'

'Why not? I hesitated because Chester and Lois recounted several of Laddow's theories and he had to have been fishing, or perhaps talking just to get them talking.'

'But – hell! When Lois heard only yesterday that Andy was dead! Why, Laddow probably brought her the news. Come inside' – as Miss Pink glanced round – 'we can't talk here.' Cars were parked between the highway and the gallery and people were moving about them.

As they stepped into the big room with its scintillating colour, Miss Pink asked, with a wary look at the doorway leading to the back quarters, 'You're alone?'

'Of course.' Fleur was puzzled. 'I live alone, Melinda.'

'I know you do. Just wanted to make sure; not at all nice: one or two things he hinted at – Laddow.' Fleur was staring at her, but Miss Pink was accustomed to disguising pertinent questions with a mist of gabble. 'Laddow is insinuating Lois is involved in Andy's death,' she said.

Fleur showed no surprise. 'That's what *I* said: she was an innocent accessory.'

'Yes, innocent. So you reckon Andy wouldn't tell her he had killed Gayleen, just pretend they'd quarrelled, in which case why would he allow the girl to drive away in his wife's car?'

'I said, she drove off while he was – otherwise engaged.'

'And you're sticking to that.'

'I have to. There can't be any other explan— ' She trailed off. 'You said the police had several theories. There are other explanations? Do I want to hear this?'

'There was a theory about blackmail: Gayleen having something on Andy and forcing him to try to get money out of Lois – '

'That's possible. Andy was greedy as the devil, but for my money anyone trying to blackmail Andy is asking for trouble . . . I see, you're saying he killed Gayleen because she was blackmailing him.'

'It's an idea.'

'So Laddow thinks Lois is protecting Andy – that's back to square one, except he says she's involved. OK, so she's involved, but innocently.'

'I said "involved in Andy's death".'

'What?'

'Laddow is talking about Andy, not Gayleen's murder.'

136

'Jesus Christ! You're telling me Andy was murdered too? No, last night we agreed on suicide.' They hadn't, but Miss Pink didn't interrupt. 'When did the result of the autopsy come through?'

'It hasn't so far – '

Fleur wasn't listening. 'But Andy was dead before – the rain – stopped.'

'The suggestion is that he was dead before it started.'

There was a long silence. Fleur broke it. 'So that was why you wanted to know – not what Andy looked like, but what the driver of the Chevy looked like.'

'Could it have been someone else?'

'Now you've got me confused. For God's sake, who? I only saw shades and a Stetson. Could have been anyone.'

Through the windows they saw people approaching the gallery. 'Saturday afternoon,' Miss Pink murmured. 'I'll leave you to it. How are the sales of the new book going?'

'Fine.' Fleur spoke absently. 'I sold eight already.'

'Good. When's the next one due?'

'How did you – who – ' Her eyes were jittery. 'I don't work – I don't know; we only just got this one from the distributors. For God's sake, I'm only the agent here – nothing else.' She was angry now and there was fear behind the anger.

Miss Pink moved towards the door. 'Boligard's beavering away at his,' she said casually, standing aside for the customers, smiling at everyone as she stepped out into the sunshine. So what was the book on Fleur's bed, and the proof-sheets fluttering in the draught? Did she proof-read d'Eath's books? If so, why get so angry about it?

There were no police cars on the Surfbird's court; in fact there were no cars at all and the only signs of life were an open door and the strains of Sinatra belting out his old black magic.

'Hi, stranger,' shouted Mabel Sykes as a shadow fell across the floor. She straightened a bed corner and switched off the radio. 'What can we do for you? You've never come for a room!'

'Not far out,' Miss Pink said. 'I want to extend my contract for another week.'

'Why, of course; it's lovely having you here. Boligard's down in his den but I'll tell him.'

'Nice-size room.' Miss Pink nodded her approval, glancing about her, allowing an inquisitive gleam to show.

'This one's the boss's,' Mabel said possessively, and they looked around with the conspiratorial air of women surveying a man's quarters.

Nothing is so impersonal as a motel room yet some people, and Miss Pink was one of them, can make a home out of one of these boxes within a few minutes of taking possession. Not Laddow. This space, like its tenant, was bland, the only personal objects being a pair of twill trousers in the alcove that served as a wardrobe, moccasins on the floor, a toothbrush and paste beside the wash-basin. Mabel had removed used tablets of soap and put new towels in the rack, emphasising the neutrality of the place.

'Not even a hair brush,' observed Miss Pink.

'He keeps that in a drawer. But no pyjamas.' Mabel grinned, her eyes dancing. 'Isn't that exciting: at his age, sleeps in the raw?'

'He's not that old . . . but this man is secretive.' Miss Pink seemed to be talking to herself. 'Perhaps in the circumstances he has to be. He's a policeman. And he doesn't trust a soul.'

Mabel's grin had faded but as Miss Pink stopped speaking and eyed her with what might be taken for polite inquiry, an invitation to confirm or deny Laddow's lack of trust, she smiled broadly. 'Well, he certainly don't trust me,' she agreed in her fruity voice, brimming with confidence. 'And nor does that Hammett. I gotta clear up after him every day like I was his mother: clothes dropped all over, towel in the tub, wringing wet, everything filthy, but not one personal thing around, if you take my meaning, nothing to show what kind of guy he is at bottom, except untidy – and gets himself into some very dirty places.'

'He couldn't help that; it's hot weather – when it's not foggy.'

'Yeah. Can you smell it in here?' Mabel was concerned. 'I got all the windows open for a through draught and I'll leave them that way.'

'Perhaps I'm imagining an odour. It could be me. Although Lois said Laddow smelled but she didn't tell me I did.'

'Poor Lois.' Mabel picked up her vacuum cleaner and moved towards the door, shaking her head. 'It's a terrible thing to happen in Sundown. I knew that girl was trouble soon as I set eyes on her; you shoulda seen that dress, it ended here' – she indicated her crotch – 'lovely legs though, if I say it myself; it's all they want, isn't it: men? That Andy Keller: it was obvious all along he'd come to a bad end.'

'Oh?' Miss Pink stood in the doorway looking very English and a bit silly. 'What was obvious?'

Mabel decided it was time someone broadened this old lady's perspective. 'That guy,' she said seriously, 'should never have gotten married; he was after all the young girls – and this place, in the height of summer, is like a honey pot and him the bee. Walking around with no clothes on, or almost: the poor guy was looking every which way. Is there a word for a man who's a nymphomaniac?'

'But he was married.'

'You think that stops 'em? You think married men don't play around? Not my old man,' she added quickly. 'Not that Boligard's without those kinda feelings but with an author it all goes into the books, like that guy d'Eath: Jason says as d'Eath is probably as laid back as Chester Hoyle on the surface, then he has to put all the sex into his books, like sub – sub-something.'

'Sublimation?'

'Yeah, how d'you know?'

'I know the theoretical side, the labels. I've been to lectures.'

'You have? So what would you say was the intellectual label for Andy Keller: a guy looks at every female like a bull at a heifer? You're not going to believe this' – as Miss Pink hesitated – 'he'd try it on me, and I'm no spring chicken, although, like he said: large ladies are comfortable, and comforting.' Her smile was smug and reminiscent as she pulled her lacy jumper over her plumpness. 'What would you call a man like that?'

Miss Pink shrugged. 'The Greeks had a word for it – '

'What? Oh, I see: a joke.' Mabel's smile was uncertain. She changed course. 'So, they figure it was an accident,' she observed carelessly and then, with a sly grin, 'They don't make their private calls from here.'

'Accident is possible: falling off the trail when it turned slick.'

'I heard suicide was one idea. He killed Gayleen and then himself. They often do.'

'They?'

'Murderers. I mean, a guy like Andy Keller: he's not going to spend the rest of his life in a cage, is he? No women.'

'There's a lot of homosexuality in prison.'

'Tcha!' It was like a reaction to a blow in the solar plexus.

'It could be suicide,' Miss Pink admitted. 'They're looking for the weapon in the landslide.'

'Good.' Mabel seemed to think that more was demanded of her. 'All that kind of information goes over the public phone,' she emphasised. 'The one outside the bar.'

'Yes, Jason mentioned it.'

Something flickered in Mabel's eyes. 'You reminded me.' Flustered, she stooped again to her vacuum. 'I gotta get the dinner on. We're having a beef borsch tonight. Will you join us?'

Miss Pink declined, saying she was entertaining Sadie and Leo, and took her leave, reflecting that early afternoon was an odd time to be starting preparations for dinner, thinking that, once you started to probe in this village, to penetrate behind the façade, you realised that the friendliness and the good humour were just that: a façade. The villagers were like Laddow and Hammett whose mobile features and steel-rimmed spectacles masked observation platforms and intricate thinking machines, impersonal as a motel room. But there was a basic difference: the police were without emotion; the residents of Sundown were all emotion.

Chapter 13

It was a beautiful afternoon: warm and bright, the air smelling of salt and pine resin. Miss Pink, dawdling along the loop road, entering Miriam's drive, binoculars round her neck, thought, like Laddow, that the place had magic even outside the forest: a different kind of magic.

Miriam's front door was closed and there was no response to her knock. She followed an old brick path round the side of the house and as she edged past the ferny pool (no naked cement for Miriam) the schnauzer rushed yapping round a corner.

'Down, Oscar!' The terrier stopped and glared. Willard Smith stood up from among the ferns and touched his faded ball cap politely.

'Good afternoon.' She was affable. 'Is Mrs Ramet at home?'

'They went to Salmon. They'll be back this evening.'

'I'll call her.' About to turn away, she checked. 'What fine blooms! *Agopanthus*, surely?'

'That's right, ma'am. They does well here. There's one there though, in back, is looking sick. I'll have him out come fall.'

'It's not noticeable among all the others. These petunias make a good show. How do you do it?'

'I feeds 'em well. 'Course, this is the best part of the garden: round the pool and along the front of the house. I tries to keep it looking nice.'

'It does you credit. A garden this size is a full-time occupation.'

'You gotta garden? Where?'

'In England: damp, a short growing season but warm: warm for England, that is. The soil's very acid. Azaleas mostly; we're proud of our azaleas.'

'Come and see ours.'

She followed him eagerly. A person shown azaleas in September

141

is accepted as a kindred spirit. Who but a gardener appreciates plants when their flowering time is over?

As Willard Smith showed her round Miriam's property which, like all good gardeners, he considered his own because he had the cherishing of it, she was not hearing the words but observing the man. His looks were not all that remarkable of themselves: regular features, a smooth tanned face, blue eyes, white hair; the remarkable thing was that it was a boy's face: that of a fourteen-year-old lad. Yet the hair, the slight stoop to the shoulders, and something indefinable: deference, good manners, the affinity with plants, all these indicated age. She thought he wouldn't see sixty again.

Where gardens were concerned he was as knowledgeable as herself although their experience was different, living on different oceans, at different latitudes. They found this diversity absorbing and half an hour passed before they reached a small cabin masked by rhododendrons behind the house. He asked shyly if he could offer her a beer: a mark of respect; had he considered her a lady he wouldn't have offered anything, but she was a gardener and sexless so he offered beer.

They sat on rockers on his tiny deck and studied a hedge of pyracantha. 'That'll be full of waxwings shortly,' he told her. 'Soon's the berries is ripe.'

'We grow stuff specially too. The finches love giant hogweed: greenfinches, goldfinches and such.'

'What's hogweed?'

She told him and went on to tell him about greenfinches, and how European goldfinches differed from the American species, to confide how she gloried in the variety of the West, in its extremes: the great horned owl larger than an osprey, elf owls like sparrows, a pileated woodpecker the size of a crow.

'Where d'you see him?' Willard cut in.

'Above the landslide in Porcupine Gulch.'

'When were you up there?'

'The day after I arrived. A tree came down at the same time. Does that happen often: a tree fall on its own?'

'It happens. You see all those old logs everywhere; no one dropped 'em, been there hundreds of years some of 'em; it can take five hundred years to rot one of the big ones, you know that?'

142

'I didn't. Fascinating.' She stretched her legs and sighed bliss-fully. 'You have the perfect environment here: temperature, humidity' – she smiled – 'even from the human point of view: a small village, friendly people.'

'You're seeing it from the outside. We got our problems. This old house now: looks nice, don't it, but them planks'd be falling apart if I didn't treat 'em every two years. And motor cars! You gotta hose down a car every day or it'll rust. It's the salt. I tell her: she's gotta get a man to do the painting and the washing off; I got my work cut out with the garden.'

'Yes, I see the snags. And labour must be at a premium on the coast. There's too much on this property for one man to attend to.'

'Otherwise,' he said, 'I found my niche.' He sipped his beer and rocked gently. 'I got everything a man could possibly want: a little house and a big garden. What else is there?'

'Companionship?' she ventured.

'I got the garden!'

No two ways about it, Willard was simple. Delightful, but how could he be persuaded to gossip about people when the only relationships he recognised were those with plants? And Miriam and Oliver might be home at any time. 'How much say do you allow Miriam?' she asked bluntly. 'In my garden we discuss every move.'

He gave it serious thought. 'Not much,' he admitted. 'Colours, maybe; yes, colours. She'll say she wants something bright round the pool, show up against the ferns; like skyrocket – the pool area being all wild – and I says no, too damp for skyrocket there; we'll try some cardinal flowers.'

'Who wins?'

'Why, me of course. She wants skyrocket, she gotta have it on a dry bank, like up the back: have as much as she likes there, 'cept I can't have it interfering with the fritillaries. You should be here in spring: see them scarlet fritillaries. I stole 'em; stole 'em and saved 'em. Know what I did? I gotta friend down in California. He told me about this land scheduled for sub-development and there was scarlet fritillaries on it. I had her drive me down there and me and this guy, we goes into that place even before they puts the survey posts in and we digs up every plant we can find, then we divides 'em equally, him and me. How d'you like that?'

143

'Clever. Very clever.' It could have been the first time she'd heard of a practice that she'd followed all her life: saving plants from the bulldozers. There was a pause, and then she asked him if he grew fruit and vegetables.

'No, just what you see. I couldn't manage with vegetables as well as everything else.'

'Why don't the others give you a hand? Oliver could do the simpler jobs, the unskilled labour.'

'*Oliver*? I'd never have him in my garden!' He was amazed. 'He don't know a fritillary from a nettle.'

'He could paint the house, wash the car.'

He shook his head, astonished at her lack of perception. 'You can't have talked to him, ma'am. That Oliver, he's like all kids his age: no time for work about the house; he got time only for sports and like, being company.'

'Yes, he's good company; a well-mannered boy. He has respect for age; I like that.'

'So does she. He waits on her hand and foot; now that's something I never did. But she's a helpless little thing and she misses having someone look after her, know what I mean? She's not a woman can live alone, always has to have someone in the house.'

'No one should live alone. I don't.'

He eyed her for a moment. 'You're different. Men can protect a woman, see? That's why I'm here. I wouldn't live in the big house, did for a while but when it came time for me to move on, she built this little place for me, so I agreed to stay because I didn't want to leave the garden. It's like family, isn't it: a garden? And now the only way I'll leave is when they carries me out. I stay; the others, they just pass through, like migrating birds; they come down to feed a whiles and take off again. He'll go shortly.' He nodded towards the big house.

'Then what?'

'Someone else'll come by. Meanwhile I'm here.'

'You know something, Mr Smith? You're a happy man.'

'Oh, sure.' But he was startled. 'Aren't you? If you're not, change your circumstances, ma'am; you can always do that.'

She beamed at him. 'I don't need to. Like you, I can't think of anything else I want.' But, looking towards the sea beyond the rhododendrons, her eyes clouded. 'I've made friends here,' she said. 'I would like to see this nasty business cleared up for their sakes. Your garden is peaceful; it drove all thoughts of Andy Keller and that poor girl out of my mind.'

'You got no call to concern yourself.' He was phlegmatic. 'It's nothing to do with any of us; not even with Miz Keller, nor Grace. If he shoots a girl and then himself or falls off the trail, 'tisn't Miz Keller's problem − 'cept the shock of it, like losing a dog or a cat. She's got her friends around.'

'How do you think Andy died?'

'I don't think about it. I got no call to. He were found dead at the bottom of the slide and we're well rid of him. Mean piece of work, that Keller. It's all one to me whether he put the bullet in his own skull or someone else did; he's dead and that's all as matters.'

She was sitting on her deck drinking tea when she heard the sound of feet padding up her front steps and smiled. She had expected one of them but hadn't been sure which would appear first.

'Anyone home?'

'I'm on the deck, Oliver.'

He came round the outside of the cottage bearing a package. 'The mistress's compliments, ma'am, and will you dine with us?'

'How naughty you are.' She loosened the wrappings to reveal a bottle of Tio Pepe. 'And how kind Miriam is. Sit down. Do you drink China tea?'

He was dressed for running and his brown legs were beautiful below the skimpy shorts. 'You will eat with us?' he asked anxiously.

'I'm sorry. I'm dining with Sadie and Leo.'

His face fell. 'We've been looking forward to it, discussing the courses all the way back from Salmon. Stupid of us: as if you'd be free at such short notice. May I use your phone before Miriam gets into high gear?'

He went indoors and she followed to fetch some glasses.

'She's devastated,' he announced when he came back. 'Oh, you've opened the sherry. I'm supposed to be running and I adore Tio Pepe.'

'You'll run like a deer.'

145

'To Circe and all tempters.' He raised his glass. 'You've conquered Willard's old heart.'

'He won mine.' She was unruffled. 'I had an enchanting hour in his – your garden.'

'He's a character. His flowers are his children.'

'So I gathered. He attributed gender to a lily.'

'I'm sorry we missed you. Miriam would have liked to show you around. Were you waiting long?'

'But I had a delightful time with Willard! He could talk till the cows come home.'

'He's usually so taciturn; he doesn't have much time for people – '

'He was extremely amiable – '

'For me, I mean.'

'Are you sure? I got the impression you were – that you were considered as one of the flowers; you know: a bit exotic, needs training, should do well in the right soil?'

'Really? How sweet. He said that?'

'Just my impression.'

'I'm amazed. I thought he resented me.'

'Why should he?'

'You know these old retainers: they get a bit possessive over their employers, think of themselves as one of the family, jealous of house guests, that kind of thing?'

'He said nothing disparaging about anyone except – ah!'

'What?' The ingenuous mask slipped momentarily, the chiselled lips thinned.

'Except for Andy Keller, but then no one has a good word to say for him. Did the man have no redeeming qualities at all?'

He was thoughtful, relieved at the change of subject. 'Miriam says he could be charming when he tried – but she's susceptible – and he could lay flattery on with a trowel.' He snorted in derision. 'He'd never have got to you though; I saw you watching him: in the Tattler that lunchtime. You got his measure.'

'He was a bully.'

'You can say that again – and he was clever with it; he'd back people up against a wall – psychologically speaking – and just as they were about to lash out at him, he'd fade away. I'm mixing the verbal with the physical here but you know what I'm driving

146

at. He was a coward, he always avoided the physical side.' He grinned. 'You saw his nose?'

'I saw it had been broken.'

'He tangled with the wrong guy. He was at a party in Portland, at Grace's home, probably gatecrashed it; she wouldn't have invited him. He musta thought the guy she was talking to looked ineffectual: small, with eye glasses. Andy said something to Grace and this guy drops him: smash, right on the nose.'

'Wait a minute. You mean, he said something – rude? But he was her step-father!'

'You didn't know Andy.' He was expressionless.

'Do you have Grace's address?'

'No need. She's coming home this weekend. You want her to confirm what I told you. Now, why is that?'

She filled his glass and he made no comment; he was more interested in the conversation than in running. 'The police are trying to involve Lois in Andy's death,' she said. 'Even, by implication, in Gayleen's. Chester is being protective and asked me to try to find out what happened to her gun.'

'Oh yes, she lost her revolver. Kept it in her night table.'

'Everyone knows everything in Sundown,' she murmured, sipping her sherry.

'Just about. We know all each others' secrets, yes, but we don't talk about them.' Was this a warning?

'So Hammett said. Have the police got to you yet?'

He smiled slyly as if he'd taken her point. 'I was grilled by Laddow. It appears that my going to Portland the day before Gayleen was shot is suspicious. They don't have much to go on, and I'm not a respectable person. They need a scapegoat.'

'But you didn't leave the same day as Gayleen did.'

He opened his mouth and closed it again. He drained his sherry. 'It's rather awkward,' he muttered, boyishly embarrassed.

'You went with Grace?'

'Now what makes you think that?'

'Because you and she are the only unattached young people in your circle here . . . There's talk. And you don't have a car but Grace has, and you left around the same time.'

'And Willard's been talking.' She didn't contradict him. He sighed and settled back in his chair. 'Miriam's very good to me; she never had any children and I kinda take the place of a son.

147

But she's just a little possessive . . . Some mothers are like that; mine was, oh wow, was my mother jealous! Nothing to it,' he went on airily, 'to the Portland trip; I needed to get away for a while, mix with my own age-group, so – yes – I went to Portland with Grace. There, is that a sin?'

'Of course not. That's fine.' She beamed at him. 'So you have an alibi.'

'For what?'

'Didn't you realise why Laddow needed to question you? He's investigating murder, my dear. Someone shot Gayleen, and with a .22, and Lois's .22 is missing so everyone in Sundown is a suspect in Laddow's eyes. When did you come back?'

'There's no way I can be tied to it. I came back next day – no, the Wednesday. You remember: I met you on the beach. I hitched partway home on the Tuesday afternoon and then came on early the next morning when they opened the road.'

'Tuesday you were in Portland?'

He smiled knowingly, nodding at her. 'The day they both died I was in Portland. All day. Laddow has the times. And Grace is my alibi. Miriam doesn't know yet,' he added grimly, 'and there'll be all hell to pay when she finds out. However, they say it rains all the time in Oregon in the winter. Guess I'll be moving on in the fall.'

'Arizona is a good place.'

He brightened. 'Yeah, Tucson. No ocean though.'

'LA? Malibu?'

'I'm not cut out to be a California beach boy; too much competition.'

'The Virgin Islands.'

'Now you're talking! The Caribbean.' He grinned happily at her. 'I'll think about that.'

'I heard you write screenplays.'

'I'll write anything. I'll do anything.' He was very chipper now, probably visualising lonely widows in the Virgin Islands. 'I'm versatile. But I have to have a background and on the coast it's screenplays.'

She was reminded of Gayleen telling Lois how a stripper exploits voyeurs. Aloud she said, 'So ostensibly you had something in common with Andy Keller.'

'Ostensibly.' His eyes narrowed and for a moment she saw,

or sensed, below the gaiety and the gloss of charm, below the ability – and the willingness – to amuse, something dark and careful. 'Andy and I didn't discuss our common interests,' he told her. 'We preferred to avoid each other.'

'No mistake about it,' Leo said firmly. 'The hoots rise in pitch – ' she turned from the Tattler's bar and, throwing her voice, imitated an owl's call to perfection, or so it seemed to Miss Pink.

'Just as we'd decided to call it a day,' Sadie put in. 'She'd kept saying she'd heard it; I hadn't, but then my hearing isn't all that good – '

'Your hearing's perfect; you were talking to yourself when it called in the morning, that's why you missed it. I heard it well enough.'

'But you weren't sure. So she insisted we stay up there, just under the crest of Pandora, between the north-west spur and that deep depression that's absolutely choked with old-growth.'

'They'll nest in there,' Leo told them.

'Difficult to find an old nest in the fall,' Boligard said.

Leo turned on him. 'We wouldn't look for a spotted owl's nest at any time! Hell, we're bothered about going to look for the *birds*. 'Fact, we have to consider how often anyone's going to use that trail in the future.' She glared at them, challenging them to assert their right to use the trail. 'There's been enough disturbance as it is; that depression's within a mile of the slide and they were all over it today looking for that damn gun.'

'It is a nuisance.' Sadie shook her head.

'Nuisance? It's sacrilege!' Leo was beside herself. 'Made me wish for an earthquake, have the whole mountain come down, sweep 'em all off, leave the owls in peace.'

Leo and Sadie, summoned by a note in their door, responding by phone when they returned excitedly from the successful search (except that they hadn't actually seen the spotted owl) were drinking cocktails with Miss Pink. Eve was serving them, Boligard had stopped by on his way home, Carl was putting the finishing touches to the snapper in the kitchen.

'They're in to dinner,' Eve said.

'What!' Leo cried. 'Not the guys who were searching the slide?'

'Hammett and Laddow.'

149

'Hammett's back?' Miss Pink exclaimed. 'Did they tell you the result of the autopsy?'

'Laddow just called to say they'd both be down to eat this evening; he said nothing about the autopsy.'

They exchanged glances, a ripple of unease running round the circle. Leo voiced the feeling: 'I didn't expect this; I was looking forward to a gourmet meal and now it looks like we're not going to be allowed to concentrate on it.'

'You don't have to ask them,' Boligard pointed out.

'Oh, come on!' Leo was derisive. 'And sit there wondering what the answer is all through dinner, with the two guys who know only a few feet away?'

But they could and did concentrate on their dinner. When the detectives appeared – in time to have a drink before they went in the dining-room – Laddow told them that the autopsy had produced no revelations. Too much damage had been sustained in the fall, he said, and a lot more in the succeeding rockfalls – he didn't look at Sadie and Leo – and if Andy Keller had been shot, there was no sign of it, and no bullet in the body.

Chapter 14

The party broke up early. The snapper was a success but as always when the police were present, there was a constraint on conversation. They could talk about wildlife and the coast, they could not gossip; above all they couldn't discuss the case.

After dinner, taking their coffee in the bar, Hammett asked permission to join them, which seemed odd until they realised that Laddow was not going to follow. Laddow had disappeared and it was obvious that Hammett had been directed to stay and listen. He could have heard nothing useful. Leo showed signs of belligerence over the disturbance to the owls but he was so bewildered ('It's a very *big* forest, ma'am; surely there's lots of room . . . ') that she thawed a little as she lectured him on habitat and behaviour, and that led to ecology and the question of diversity. Miss Pink, who had had a hard day herself, noticed that Sadie was nodding blissfully in her chair, and by nine o'clock the party broke up. Leo drove everyone home, the police car having disappeared from the front of the Tattler and Miss Pink not fancying her steep little footpath in the dark.

She entered her cottage, switched on the lights and went to draw the curtains. As she did so the telephone started to ring.

It was Miriam. 'Ah, at last! Are you alone? I'm on my way down: I have to talk to you.'

She was at Quail Run a few minutes later, arriving at the door in pink sweats and slightly out of breath. She declined brandy, said she would like a cup of herb tea but settled for Lapsang Souchong. In the kitchen she asked casually about the evening at the Tattler and Miss Pink said it had been dull owing to the presence of the police. Had Miriam heard about the autopsy? The results were inconclusive.

151

'So they still don't know whether he shot himself or fell off the trail?' Miriam said.

'I don't know if they ever will.' Miss Pink responded absently, slicing a lemon.

'It's obvious: he shot Gayleen, came back here and shot himself. And I know why he did that,' she added darkly. 'He told Lois and she finally threw him out. She wouldn't tell the police, but she wouldn't have him back neither.'

Miss Pink made the tea and carried the tray into the sitting-room. They sat down, she filled a mug, passed the lemon to Miriam: all this in silence, a charged silence. At length she said, 'That behaviour is in character, would you say?'

'Definitely. I'd do the same thing myself.'

Miss Pink suppressed a smile but Miriam was sharp. 'Wouldn't you?'

'In her shoes probably I would.'

'It's the most likely explanation, isn't it? It fits the facts.'

'The facts.' Miss Pink considered them, aware that she was being closely watched. 'Actually,' she said in some surprise, 'it does. You're assuming that Andy phoned Lois from Moon Shell Beach and she drove north to meet him – but how did he get to the roadworks? She could take a car only as far as the south side of them; he had to travel twenty miles.'

'Either he got a lift with a local resident going as far as the north side of the works, or at least a good part of the distance, and he ran the rest of the way, or he got through before the road was closed. Or even' – her eyes glazed – 'Lois went round the back way over the forest trails.'

'It's a matter of timing. Laddow will have gone into all that. You know that Lois says she didn't see him after they left. She didn't see him then; she was working.'

'But she would say that, wouldn't she? No way is she going to admit that he confessed to her, so she's going to maintain she isn't involved in any way.'

'To avoid being charged as an accessory? I wonder.' Miss Pink was silent, following a train of thought. She nodded to herself. 'It would be much better for everyone concerned if Andy was the one who killed Gayleen.'

'Why d'you say that?'

'It lets everyone else off the hook. If it wasn't Andy, who

152

could it have been? Who didn't have an alibi for that Tuesday afternoon?'

Miriam gave a gay little laugh. 'Well, I know someone who's in the clear, and that's Oliver. He was eighty miles from Moon Shell Beach.'

'That's not an alibi.'

'What! Why not?'

'An alibi is someone who – or something that proves you were not at the scene of the crime when it was committed.'

Miriam was very still, then she said coldly, 'As it happens, he was with Grace Ferguson. He's rather taken with her; I don't think anything will come of it' – again that tinkling laugh – 'Oliver hasn't a cent to his name, and Grace does very well out of her boutique, not to speak of her "expectations", as they used to say, from her mother. However, with the profit there is in the rag trade, I'd be surprised if Grace doesn't end up richer than Lois. But as for that day in Portland, Oliver was with Grace.' It came out hard and defiant.

'Did he tell Laddow that?'

'Of course.'

'Then he has nothing to worry about. I told him that.'

Miriam eyed her. 'So he confessed all to you, did he?'

'I can't think why you're so worried.'

'Worried! Me! What gives you that idea?'

'What brought you down here tonight?'

'You sound positively hostile, Melinda. It's you been questioning my household behind my back, getting Oliver drunk so he tells you what he told the police, God knows what else besides; waiting till I've gone to town to sneak up and interrogate Willard about my household, soon's my back's turned— '

'You're repeating yourself.'

'Shit! What are you doing here? You working for Laddow?'

'For Chester.'

'*What!*'

'I'm trying to find out who took the gun from Lois's night table.'

'Why?' The knee-jerk response indicated that she no longer considered the significance even of that question.

'One would think it probable' – deliberately pedantic – 'that the person who stole the gun killed Gayleen.'

The careful tone seemed to calm Miriam. She had listened,

had got the meaning, and now she asked, 'So why wasn't it Andy?'

'A number of circumstances.' Suddenly Miss Pink looked very tired. 'And your hostility exhausts me. Why are you so bothered that Willard and Oliver should have talked to me? *You* have an alibi; it was your party at the Tattler that Tuesday evening. How could you have been at Moon Shell Beach shooting Gayleen?'

Miriam's hands flew to her mouth and she stared, currant-eyed and vulnerable. '*Me*?' she gasped. 'They think I killed her? Why on earth?'

'Someone did.' Miss Pink was quite composed. 'Someone had a motive. Who wanted Gayleen dead, and why?'

'But why should I— '

'Why should Oliver?'

'He had nothing to do with it. He was with Grace! All the time: day *and* night!' She was strident.

'He wasn't,' Miss Pink said.

Miriam collapsed like a rag doll. She said nothing, fingering her lips. Miss Pink got up and fetched brandy and glasses. She poured a generous measure and pushed it across the coffee table. 'He must have some kind of alibi,' she said.

Miriam drank some brandy. As it took effect, her mouth tightened and her eyes started to snap again. She said firmly, 'Oliver had nothing to do with the death of that girl.' She regarded Miss Pink intently. 'I'll never make you believe it, will I? But it's true' – she looked away – 'Grace will bear him out – of course she will: he was with her! I'm sorry for what I said about you coming up to the house; I've – we've all been under considerable stress; I mean: murder in our midst, concerning one of our closest friends. You have to forgive me, I was overwrought, but I do assure you, Oliver is – had nothing to do with any of this' – the little laugh again – 'after all, what motive could he possibly have?'

'Who needs a motive?' Laddow asked. 'The courts don't, but we do need evidence. That boy's lying. He's clever and plausible, and slippery as an eel, but then you'd expect that, seeing as he's a con-man, and rich widows are notoriously paranoid about indigent young men. They gotta be clever to get past the guard of old ladies like Mrs Ramet. I might break the girl though. She arrived last night.'

154

'Grace is here?' Miss Pink was interested. 'I've been looking forward to meeting her.'

'Lovely girl,' Laddow mused. 'Her and Oliver; two of a kind on the surface: the beautiful people.' A tiger swallowtail sailed past the balcony: lemon and black and misty blue. 'They fit this place,' he added, his eyes following the butterfly.

'You've interviewed her?'

'I met her last night. Had coffee at the Keller place: reported to Mrs Keller how things were going.' His face was bland. 'Grace is very laid back; maintains young Oliver left Sundown with her on Monday, stayed until around four on Tuesday afternoon.'

'She didn't work at the boutique on Tuesday?'

He smiled, appreciating her perception. 'She did. She says she called him at her apartment to arrange dinner, what she should bring home, but he said he was leaving shortly. It was then just four o'clock. Her mother didn't seem surprised that her daughter should be on intimate terms with Oliver Harper.'

'Well, in these days . . .'

'What I meant was, no one ever hinted at a relationship there.'

'Naturally. Oliver is afraid of Miriam. He'd need to be discreet.'

'Quite. He's lying to lead her astray, not us. For instance, where did he spend Tuesday night? He says he hitched back to the roadworks, found an empty shack used for when it rains and slept on a bench till six when he couldn't stand the cold any longer and started walking. He got a lift soon after eight. I don't believe a word of it; that guy was up to some mischief in Portland—'

'He told you where he really was—'

'No, but I'll find out. Not that it matters; young Oliver didn't kill Gayleen – I don't think – he's too shallow, got too big an eye for the main chance. This was a crime of passion.'

'There's also the question of timing –' She thought about that. 'More important: Andy's death wouldn't fit at all if it was Oliver who killed Gayleen. You've not mentioned the .22; I take it you found nothing at the landslide.'

'Nothing at all – nothing.' Obviously it was a sore point. 'Why would a guy be up there in the rain – cold rain on the Oregon coast – in a T-shirt and Levis just? Where's his parka? Like I said, he never left. He was there before the rain started—'

'Not necessarily. Did you never consider that he might have gone up there deliberately in order to kill himself?' She expounded on Miriam's theory. 'A potential suicide might walk out into the storm without a parka,' she pointed out.

He was thoughtful. 'It fits. But then Lois is lying. I guess she would at that – or would she? There are no children to protect, like not wanting 'em to know their dad's a murderer. Would she be bothered about public opinion?'

'I don't know. To be the widow of a man who killed a prostitute . . . perhaps he was living on her earnings – and Lois is something of the *grande dame* in Sundown . . . ' She frowned, ignoring him, recalling her own experience of village life in Wales and England, trying to relate it to Oregon. 'Privacy,' she said suddenly, 'that's why she would lie: treating the police as intruders. This is her business, family business, and nothing to do with you.' She turned to him, sincere and questioning.

He nodded. 'You could be right at that, ma'am.'

'Incidentally did you ever work out how Andy might have reached the roadworks from Moon Shell Beach?'

'You mean, if he *did* leave Sundown. He woulda had to get a lift. It's possible that in the rain and bad visibility some tourist would miss the notices saying the road closed at six, so there could be some traffic, and he thumbed a lift. He would have phoned his wife from the call-box up the road from Moon Shell, the one we used when we were making preliminary inquiries.'

'So what do you do now? Assume Andy killed Gayleen and committed suicide?'

There was a furtive light in his eye and he looked away quickly. 'It's Sunday.' He was expansive. 'Lovely day for the beach.' He met her gaze and blinked. 'A few loose ends to tie up,' he muttered and then, with an artificial smile: 'I'll see you around, ma'am.'

He took his leave with no word of where he was going and no mention of what Hammett was up to on this beautiful morning. She had the feeling that the net was tightening on this section of the village: on the loop road where there were five households, six if you counted the Surfbird motel, but that they were not greatly interested in all six. Obviously Laddow had visited her so soon after breakfast, not to impart information but to obtain it. Someone had told him that she had talked to Miriam and her menfolk yesterday, and he was interested in Oliver, surely not in Willard. She considered this last and dismissed it; he might be but

156

she wasn't concerned. Willard was one man who would never be guilty of a crime of passion except, perhaps, if someone uprooted his fritillaries or tramped his *agopanthus*.

It would seem that the investigation was tapering off to an anti-climax, but was that the impression Laddow was trying to create? Murder and suicide: was it possible?

'Suicide?' Jason repeated, and laughed unpleasantly, then he flushed and turned his back on Miss Pink, flicking at the book-shelves with a feather duster. 'Could be.' His voice was muffled. 'He was a bully, and bullies are cowards. He'd be afraid of prison; afraid of other prisoners, is more like it.'

'I never met him.' She was leafing through a dictionary. 'A bully at his age?'

'Any age. That guy was obscene, accusing – making allegations . . . He had a filthy mind, and so what, even if what he said was true, it's not a crime – but it wasn't true. He made things up.'

'He accused everyone of something; he'd see a wisp of vapour and make a conflagration out of it.'

'Smoke and fire, you mean: where there's smoke . . . You know' – Jason stepped towards her, dropping his voice, glancing outside – 'I figure that fella had something on everyone here: invented, I mean; he'd kinda probe a weakness like a dentist probing a tooth and if that person, his victim, winced, he'd twist until he drove folks crazy. Like my dad: he was always on at him about Hemingway, because Dad's *like* Hemingway, see? And could he turn the screw! Sounds trivial, don't it, but it wasn't to Dad. He's an artist, an author; it's his whole life, and here's this son of a bitch not just laughing at my dad, but sneering at Hemingway!'

'I see. And he would have jeered at Oliver for – what? Suggesting he was being kept?'

'Gigolo is the word. *He* used it.' Jason's eyes were flashing.

'And Sadie and Leo – '

'You guessed it, and they're old pussy cats, those two; I love 'em. Leo nearly floored him one time. He used to ask her how the wife was.'

'Very nasty. He wouldn't have spared you either.'

He said nothing but his expression was eloquent as he struggled

157

to find a response that would convey his feelings without shocking his listener. Finally he said, 'I heard as how you were looking for the one who stole Lois's gun. I tell you this, ma'am: if it happened he didn't kill himself and someone else finished him off, there's no way I'd help you find out even if I could.' He smiled. 'But I don't know nothing' – acting the country bumpkin – 'only we lost a torturer in this village. Some loss.'

'The same response as Willard,' she murmured.

'Oh, you talked to Willard. Now there's a fine guy. I'm very fond of Willard. There – I can say it now. Coupla weeks ago I wouldn't have dared. He's dead now and can't do no more harm. I hope he roasts in hell for his sins.'

'He feels things deeply,' Boligard explained. 'He takes after me that way rather than his mother. Mabel's an extrovert.'

Sunlight poured through the doorway of his shack and dust motes danced in the beams. Miss Pink sat on a worn sofa under the window and contemplated her host affably. She had, she told him, been a little shocked by Jason's vehemence regarding Andy Keller.

'The trouble with that guy,' Boligard went on, 'was he was frightened of involvement.'

'With women?'

'No – well, probably' – he was dismissive – 'I meant life. Andy Keller was shallow; he skimmed the surface of life like a water bug.' He made a movement to turn to his desk, probably to make a note, but thought better of it.

'A most evocative expression,' Miss Pink said. 'And appropriate from what I've heard. I didn't know him, of course.'

'You can take it from me, ma'am: Andy Keller was afraid of life, of people – and now you come to raise the subject: of women too. He was a man used money and people as a shield. Why d'you think he kept coming back? Well, of course, you wouldn't know, and they' – a nod towards the village – 'they wouldn't have gossiped to you, at least where that kinda thing is concerned. But that guy always had itchy feet, and he'd go away for weeks at a time, ostensibly to Hollywood – maybe for all we know he did go to LA but he certainly wasn't working on screenplays because he never had a dollar in his pocket. He had, but he didn't earn it. And now we know how he came by that money, don't we?'

'So why kill the goose that lays the golden eggs?'

'Kill Lois? No, you mean Gayleen, although when you come to think of it, Lois surely gave him more money than he ever could collect from that poor slut. That's what I mean by using people: he never earned an honest dollar in his life. He was a parasite: living on women.'

'I see that, so if Gayleen was a source of income, why did he kill her?'

'Pimps are notoriously violent.'

'I agree, but their violence is seldom fatal; that's the last thing they want. Even those men who beat up their girls try not to mark their faces.'

'That's very nasty.' He shook his head in disapproval. 'How do you know about such things?'

'It's common sense.'

'Oh yes? I'm not much of a person for the sordid side of relationships.' He smiled wryly. 'I leave the mean streets to Lois.' His eyes were wistful as he intoned, '"Down these mean streets a man must go . . . " It's good, but it has none of the power of the Master.' His gaze dwelt on a section of his shelves where the Hemingways were at eye-level. 'There was a man,' he said quietly, 'a man who worshipped nature in all her aspects, and the elements: mountains, deserts, the ocean. Nothing will ever be written to surpass *The Old Man and the Sea*: a peasant alone with the ocean and the monster of the deep.'

'Rather like *Moby Dick*.'

'No, ma'am. Melville was writing about evil and Moby Dick was the devil. Hemingway celebrates life and death; look at *Death in the Afternoon*! He was a man who took what life had to offer with both hands, who exposed himself to everything: the good and the bad, the beauty and the dangers – what a guy! The guy who said that when you'd taken everything life had to throw at you – he was talking about grief, and problems and failure – when you're beaten to your knees and you can't go no further, you stand up and you come out fighting, throwing it back, and when you got nothing left you throw yourself.'

Miss Pink nodded acceptance of the sentiment rather than the interpretation but Boligard wasn't finished. 'Beside him,' he went on, 'we're all second-rate people.'

'Really?'

'Yes!' He'd caught the scepticism. 'You, me, Fleur, Lois. I don't care what you say: he was a *writer*. We pen our mediocre works in his shadow. I mean, mediocre in comparison, of course. Do you class yourself with Ernest Hemingway, ma'am?'

'No.' She was firm.

'We can't all be geniuses.' He stood as she got up from the sofa. He smiled at her. 'Each one of us has his niche; we have to fill it as best we can.' He was totally sincere; Boligard had loyalty, no matter what it was directed towards. He was a man of dignity but in one sense and as far as his neighbours were concerned, not a man of discretion.

Fleur was alone in the gallery. 'Lunchtime,' she explained. 'Once people have eaten I'll have customers again till around four o'clock. What are you doing?'

'Tying up loose ends,' Miss Pink murmured. 'Trailing along behind Laddow, who appears to be concentrating on the people who live on the loop road. That gets him off your back.'

'He was never on it. Come inside and have some coffee.'

They went into the brilliant sitting-room. Fleur closed a door in passing but not before Miss Pink had caught a glimpse of an unmade bed.

They sat side by side and observed the ocean as they talked. This position, not facing each other, gave to their conversation a dreamlike quality, assisted by the fact that Fleur seemed to attribute to her guest powers – or at the least, information – which she didn't possess, only a hint dropped by Boligard.

'You're tired,' Miss Pink said. 'You should go out.' Looking towards Cape Deception.

'Not this afternoon. Sunday's always busy but particularly now: the last days of summer.'

'Did you finish the proofs?'

'Yes, they were— ' She stopped, and there was no sound except the calls of gulls which seemed to come from a distance, drowned in a flood of sunshine. She continued quietly, 'What is this: "proofs"?'

'How did I know about Gideon d'Eath? People talk.'

'Someone's been imagining things.' Miss Pink made no answer to that. After a while Fleur asked, 'What are you going to do about it?'

'Nothing. It's not my business. Unless it's tied in with Andy's death – or Gayleen's.'

Fleur turned and stared at her. 'How could it be?'

Miss Pink returned the stare. 'Blackmail?'

Fleur looked back at the stacks: rock towers in molten light, their shadows black on the quiet water. When she spoke her tone was empty, drained of emotion. 'No, he hadn't asked me for money. That would have come, of course: demands. He lived like that. But for the moment he was enjoying his power: flicking at me with a knife, as it were, whenever I came within his orbit. "Death from a thousand cuts." Who said that?'

'Would your sales have suffered had the truth become public knowledge?'

'I'd reached the stage of asking myself that but I was so orientated to the legend of this nice steady – father figure? – man beavering away in California – and then there was the dichotomy: *that* I needed to hang on to: the divorce of the subjects. My paintings are my life; they're *me* – my love, if you like; but those silly fantasies I do with another part of my mind. And you've never been poor, Melinda; I can tell that by your confidence. Gideon d'Eath isn't just a matter of being able to shop at Nordstrom and Neiman Marcus; it's this.' She gestured at her well-appointed room. 'I was raised in a ghetto. My father drank himself to death and my mother was left with a family of four young girls. We were so poor we lived in a shack among Mexican wetbacks outside of San Diego. Nothing wrong with Mexicans, or wetbacks either, just their poverty. Two of my sisters died of tuberculosis and my mom of hard work. My last sister took to drugs and regularly goes to a detox centre. I can spare a bit of money there. I'm the one who got away. So I'm rather obsessed with this compulsion never to go back. Maybe no one would be bothered about a middle-aged spinster turning out to be Gideon d'Eath but I wasn't taking any risks. However, I didn't kill Andy. I thought about it . . . ' She smiled. 'When part of your mind is preoccupied with thoughts of violence and death, even in fantasy, if you're being tormented in reality, you're liable to get mixed up. I admit I visualised Andy Keller being decapitated by someone like my Gideon d'Eath wielding a great sword, or a nice furry monster tossing him over Fin Whale Head . . . ' She turned back to Miss Pink. 'Are you suggesting

161

Gayleen was killed because of her association with Andy? That he told her what he knew about some – or one of us, so the person who killed the blackmailer had to kill her as well because she was an accomplice, or at least a confidant? Why are you staring at me, Melinda? What did I say? You suspect me.' She shrugged. 'I'm not bothered; I didn't do it.'

'I know you didn't.'

'So? Where are you going?'

'For a walk.'

But as she left the gallery a car pulled in from the highway and stopped beside her. Leo was behind the wheel. She spoke urgently: 'Miriam wants you to go up to her place. They're after Oliver.'

'Oliver? Why?'

'Or Miriam, or both of them. Collusion? How the hell would I know? Get in. She seems to think you can help.'

Leo dropped her at the house and drove away. Willard Smith was dead-heading roses beside the open French windows of the sitting-room. He nodded in a perfunctory manner and she guessed he had stationed himself there deliberately; in a garden as well tended as this there would be few dead-heads. As she walked along the brick path Miriam emerged from the sitting-room. She was a bad colour under her tan. At her elbow Oliver smiled uncertainly. He was wearing a blue work shirt with the sleeves rolled up to reveal a Gucci watch in steel and gold.

Miriam said, without preamble, 'We have a problem with the police. They're pushing Oliver; despite everything they seem to think he's involved with Gayleen's death.'

'Do sit down, Melinda,' Oliver said. 'Can I get you a drink? Coffee?'

Miriam glanced at him distractedly. Miss Pink declined refreshment and they all sat down. Beyond the windows Willard stooped and straightened, the snip of his secateurs loud on the soft air.

'How do they go about involving you?' Miss Pink asked.

'Just the timing.' Oliver swallowed. 'I wasn't around when Gayleen was shot.'

'What he means,' Miriam rushed in, 'was he wasn't here. He was in Portland. But Laddow says he was at Moon Shell Beach.'

162

'He doesn't *say* that.' Oliver was gentle. 'He implies it.'

'That's the same thing.' Miriam turned on Miss Pink. 'What can we do? At what point do we pick up the phone and call a lawyer – or does that suggest Oliver has a reason to need one?'

The young man looked uncomfortable and Miss Pink tried not to stare at his expensive new watch which, she thought, could have left little change out of five hundred dollars. She guessed that Miriam did not as yet know where he had spent Tuesday night (when he claimed to have slept in the roadmen's shack) so she concentrated on the more important issue as she saw it. 'What's your alibi for the time of Gayleen's death?' she asked. 'Presumably that's between four on the Tuesday afternoon and the time the car was stolen. When would that be?'

'Laddow wants to know where he was between four and six,' Miriam put in, glancing at Oliver like an anxious mother offering her son a cue.

'I was making my way out of Portland,' he said. 'I was in Grace's apartment just before four because she called me around that time.'

'So the first thing Laddow did was to ask her to confirm that.' It wasn't a question but Miss Pink waited for a response.

'Of course she confirms it,' Miriam said shortly.

'Then what's the problem?' Miss Pink looked confused.

'The same as everyone else's,' Miriam said angrily. 'Alibis! Everyone can confirm what everyone else says. Look at us: all living with others; Carl and Eve, Boligard and Mabel, Willard and me – and Grace and Oliver were together. So we're all suspect because no one believes what a person's partner says. Relatives and such' – she glanced at the window – 'will always confirm each other's movements. That's the theory; the police trust no one.'

Miss Pink was interested. 'Did Laddow mention those other people: Sadie and Leo, the Linquists, Sykeses and so on?'

'He did, didn't he?' Miriam appealed to Oliver.

'He did say that partners alibi each other.'

'He was getting at Oliver, needling him,' Miriam explained.

'Hi, Grace!' came Willard's shout. Their heads snapped round and in the silence that followed they sat like alert cats. There was a crunch of light tyres on gravel and a girl's voice: 'Hi, Willard; how're you doing?'

'I'm fine – ' He moved past the window and out of sight. Oliver stood up.

'Wait!' hissed Miriam, and glanced at Miss Pink. 'They're old friends,' she said wildly, 'Grace and Willard. He'll be filling her in.'

'*What*!' Oliver giggled inanely, but he stayed where he was, watching the window.

'Do sit down, sweetie.' Miriam grasped his wrist. 'Or get the drinks. Do *something*.' She got up herself, recollected her manners, said, 'Excuse me, something to eat,' and blundered out of the room.

'Oh, God!' Oliver whispered, and looked helplessly at Miss Pink who fluttered her hands in a vague gesture; she was merely an observer. His eyes brightened as a girl appeared at the window, a girl with red hair and green eyes, wearing little white shorts and a halter top. He introduced her with some warmth. Grace Ferguson gave all her attention to Miss Pink. Apart from the fact that he spoke, Oliver could have been a cat.

Miriam came back with plates of crackers. 'Hi, Grace,' she said. 'Oliver, get the sherry.' Her attitude towards the girl was diffident but her body was tense as a spring. She put a plate down so forcefully that crackers spilled on the table. Grace scooped up a handful and nibbled absently.

'Mom says can she have your recipe for croissants?' she asked. She turned to Miss Pink. 'I bring croissants from Portland but that's not good enough for my mother; she has to make them herself so's we can eat them hot from the oven.'

'There's nothing worse than a cold croissant,' Miss Pink agreed, aware of the other two, and perhaps Willard, hanging on her words. 'Was Laddow here this morning?' she asked, and saw a kind of relief in Miriam's face.

'He was here a short time,' she said, and the tension came back as her eyes went to Grace.

'Laddow here?' the girl repeated, and grinned. 'He's still after you then?' she asked of Oliver.

They were surprised but, where he was also amused, Miriam took offence. 'You ask that?' she cried.

'Sorry.' Grace looked neither contrite nor particularly interested. Oliver was watching her but he said nothing.

Miriam said furiously, making a demand of it, 'He was with

you; you told Laddow' – she turned on Oliver and shook his arm – 'Laddow said she confirmed it. He believes her! He was with you, Grace, wasn't he – all the time?'

'Oh, sure.' Grace shrugged. 'Don't get upset, Miriam; I'm not going to say any different.' She raised her eyebrows at Miss Pink as if to say, 'Don't take any notice; they're just kids.'

Miss Pink stood up; she could do no good here. Miriam was panicking but they must work out this problem themselves. She walked to the window. Willard was on the drive below the front steps, out of earshot. He wasn't dead-heading either; the secateurs were in his hand but he was standing stiffly, looking at a bicycle on its stand by the steps. BMX, thought Miss Pink, observing the high handlebars and small wheels. As if aware of her gaze he turned and met her eyes. He wiped a hand over his face and walked quickly round a corner of the house. She thought that in that momentary but silent exchange and before he raised his hand that his cheeks had reddened.

Grace said from the window, 'It's a lovely day. Are you hiking?'

Involuntarily Miss Pink glanced inland. 'Yes,' she exclaimed, the thought having just occurred to her, 'I shall go and look for the spotted owl.'

'Mom told me; it's great, them being in our neck of the woods.'

'Perhaps you would like to come with me.'

'I'm sorry; I have things to do.' They exchanged bright smiles, and Miss Pink looked at the cycle. 'A BMX?' she asked.

Grace blinked. 'I didn't get that.'

'I don't know what it means either, but they're great favourites with small English boys.'

'Is that so? How odd. They're used by city commuters here.'

Miss Pink was amazed. 'Why is that?'

'It's a folding bike. Didn't you know? It collapses and goes in the trunk of a car, or on the train.'

'In the – boot?'

'Sorry?'

'We call the trunk the boot.'

'You're kidding.'

'No, I'm quite serious.'

Chapter 15

The fog came back: high at first, drifting across the sun. She would have seen it coming had she been at Quail Run, would have made small preparations against its arrival: brought the cushions in from the deck, closed the windows, looked to see if there were logs for the evening fire. But she wasn't at home; she was following the trail above Bobcat Creek when the light on the forest floor dimmed suddenly and the silence assumed a different quality. In this place there was bright silence, and there was a dim, soft quietude which was more than an absence of sound, it was as if something came in with the fog. I'll never get used to it, she thought, and quickened her pace as the fading light reminded her of nightfall. And then she admonished herself; she had plenty of time, the loop trail up Porcupine and down the north-west spur of Pandora couldn't be ten miles, and she was a good walker – when everything went according to plan.

A mile above the Keller cabin she heard the water in the creek. Now came the hard part because for the life of her she couldn't remember where she had been when she heard the voices. Certainly that was twelve days ago but she had the impression that she hadn't noticed the voices at the time, that she had recalled them later in the day. And although she associated them with a creek – because one was always hearing voices in water – it seemed that the moment of recollection related to something other than water.

She sighed and shook her head and concentrated on negotiating the boulders in the bed of the creek. If she sprained an ankle here no one would know where she was. The Keller cabin had been closed when she passed; she had told Grace she was going to look for the owls but would Grace know if she didn't return?

She climbed the far bank and shortly she came on the notice

166

for Pandora Ridge, the one she had missed on her first walk in the forest. No wonder she had missed it: the sign was of weathered wood, the legend incised but almost indecipherable. When she stood back the post was all but obscured by a tangle of squaw bush and huckleberries, while the start of the steep trail to the spur wasn't visible at all.

She continued up Porcupine Gulch to the zigzags and started to climb, treading so quietly that she could hear every tiny waterfall below. The ground was very steep: cows could never keep on their feet . . . she wouldn't be happy on a horse here . . . no one knew where she was . . . no sound but the water – repetition! Her pace slackened; this was a repeat of twelve days ago, except for the voices. There were no voices. Not quite holding her breath, she kept moving, her body just ticking over, the raptor-brain watching for the rodent-memory to emerge from its hole.

Another part of the brain was crowding her: come on, come on, what was it, *where* was it? The effort needed to suppress this and remain perceptive had the effect of making her tense. Self-conscious and disgruntled, she glared at the fog and trudged on. Now the tree trunks were insubstantial, receding into grey space; the lichen hung motionless, the sound of water faded.

The trail bore right, round the headwall, and she came to the signpost where the left fork went over Pandora's crest to Coon Gulch. It was here that she had seen the pileated woodpecker – and the bird had been startled by the falling tree. She found it amazing that possibly no one, least of all herself, would ever see that fallen tree. Amazing that such an enormous object, hundreds of feet long, should lie there unknown; no one had even heard it fall except herself . . . Wrong, *they* had heard it. And then she knew where she had heard the voices.

After the tree fell she had been puzzled because there had been no whine of a chainsaw, no thock of axe on wood, no voices. But the voices she had heard had come through the sound of water, and the last water had been in Porcupine Gulch. Across from the landslide.

She continued, deep in thought, contouring on the narrow path that came to a corner which she knew was a corner only by the angle. The fog was dense now and the afternoon had grown dark. She looked at her watch. It was only four o'clock; the absence of light was due to the trees, she had reached the old-growth timber. And then she heard it: one note that seemed to go on for ever as she anticipated the next, and another, and then a chain of clear sharp calls rising in pitch. Immobile except for her eyes she searched for an oval form on a branch but knew it was hopeless: she was a birdwatcher in a fog.

After a while she moved, very carefully, because she was not watching the path, not really watching anything, but feeling, and she sensed an increased alertness, a tensing of muscles, a focusing of round dark eyes. She felt the lift of feathers, the talons unhook, releasing rough bark; broad wings were spread and the light soft body dropped and drifted silently past this figure on the trail: floating down the gap between the tree trunks to tip and slant sideways and fade from sight.

Her gaze came back slowly from the depths where the spotted owl had gone to the cause of its sharp change of direction. Totally bemused, she found that she was staring at Chester Hoyle. He approached, his face full of wonder.

'It was!' he called. 'It was, wasn't it? I heard it before I saw it; did you hear it?'

They went down together, talking like people released from vows of silence. 'Leo and Sadie will *kill* us,' he chortled, and they giggled.

'We can't come back,' she said. 'We can't risk it.'

They were sobering up. 'They can't stand the disturbance,' he agreed. 'Perhaps we should keep quiet about it.'

They came to the spur and then the start of the steep path that would end at Porcupine Creek: the lower trail that crossed the landslide. They stopped. All their elation had gone.

'I'm going down to Porcupine,' she said.

'I'll go with you.' He gestured for her to precede him.

'No.' She was smiling but firm. 'I never go first; it makes me self-conscious. I'm no guide.'

It was too silly to argue about and he took the lead. When they came to the landslide they listened but there was no sound from below. There appeared to be no one in the gully.

'Do you think they've given up searching for the gun?' she asked. 'Or could it be that it's Sunday?'

'Laddow didn't say, but then – would he? I'm sure we don't know half of what's going on. What do you think?'

'In my experience the police never, or very seldom, work

168

with a civilian. They may appear to do so, they may even ask for help, but their motives are suspect.'

'Did you get any nearer finding out who took that revolver?'

'Let's cross, shall we? We'll stop on the other side; this place makes me nervous.'

They crossed the slide, Chester still in the lead. She observed his progress while keeping an eye on her own footing. She saw that he was careful but balanced, confident but not reckless, and yet she knew that one wrong step, one push on her part, and he would commence that terrible bouncing fall into the gulch. He stopped under the outcrop and turned. A few paces from him she stopped too and they looked down, each with one hand on the rock.

'Where do you think it happened?' he asked.

'Possibly the exposed section we've just come along. Here it's comparatively safe – if he had a hold on the rock, and it's stony. I never feel so safe on steep earth as on steep scree. What do you think?'

He turned and looked along the traverse. When he remained silent she went on, 'The steep earth, I reckon. He could have been running and might have thought impetus would carry him across but the rain had made it slick.'

He nodded. 'That'll be how it happened. I wonder if Laddow thought of it that way.'

'Do go on, Chester. The forest looks so inviting from this point.'

'Oh, quite; I'm so sorry.'

'Watch it!' – as a stone spurted from his heel and clattered down the slope – 'I didn't mean to rush you.'

They proceeded, treading carefully under the poised blocks, into the trickle of water and out again. On the far side they halted and sat on the bank beside the trail, their faces damp with sweat. The red-tailed hawk called through the fog, prodding Miss Pink into speech. 'You do realise the significance of the gun?' she asked quietly.

He wasn't surprised at the question; he too could have been wondering why the searchers had left the slide. He said, 'Whoever took it doesn't have to be the one who shot Gayleen. It could have been stolen again – but Laddow doesn't think so.'

'When you postulate two thieves: one stealing from the other, are you suggesting both are in your own circle, that they are local people?'

He was quiet for so long that she thought he wasn't going to answer but then he shook his head. 'You make people think, or rather: make them realise how little they do think. That question forces one to consider motives: who took the revolver in the first place, and why was it stolen from him – or given by him to someone else, perhaps as protection but if so, protection against whom? The permutations are infinite.'

'Laddow wouldn't even start to consider them.'

'What?'

'Permutations. His theories are simplistic. He considers collusion however; Laddow likes collusion, particularly between sexual partners.'

'You're not thinking of the ridiculous theory of Andy and Lois having killed Gayleen?'

'Or of one being an accessory. No, I was thinking of Grace and Oliver.'

'We-ll – they're not sexual partners, of course, and Grace is very much of her generation. She considers the police a lesser form of life, and she might go out on a limb for Oliver not because there's anything between those two but just because he needs help, and for her that help costs nothing. The girl is totally amoral.'

'To the extent of protecting a murderer?'

He thought about it. 'That would depend on the circumstances: on the identity of the victim as well as the killer.'

'And when Gayleen is the victim?'

'Then it would depend who killed her.'

'Oliver?'

'Possibly.' It was as if they'd reached a point they had been travelling towards. 'There's no motivation,' he said, 'but Laddow would say it was blackmail.'

'He killed Gayleen because she was blackmailing him?'

'Laddow's theory, yes.'

'You mean Gayleen – and by association, Andy – were threatening to tell Miriam that Oliver is a con-man? That won't do at all; any old lady of even moderate intelligence knows – but she blocks out the knowledge – that she's buying a young man's attentions. Laddow will have to do better than that.'

170

'You got the wrong idea. It was rather more unpleasant, even dangerous from Miriam's point of view. Oliver's secret isn't a matter of sponging off rich widows but the sort of company he prefers otherwise.'

'His own age-group? Grace?'

'The opposite. He shares an apartment with a guy in Portland.'

She frowned. Someone else had implied something similar.

'He's gay,' Chester elaborated, thinking she hadn't understood. 'You see the implications: Miriam wouldn't have had him in her house the moment she found out.'

'So why hadn't Andy blackmailed him already?'

'Because Oliver has no money.'

'He has some very nice possessions. He has a Gucci watch.'

'He hadn't then. If he has now Miriam is desperate to keep him. There are a lot of younger women around who are rich and lonely and she can't compete with that. Moreover she's not a generous person in the normal way. The Gucci watch will have cost Oliver.'

'But if he was with his friend during the critical period when Gayleen was killed, Laddow has to find out – surely?'

'Laddow has to prove Oliver wasn't with Grace. He can't if she sticks to her story.'

'But so many people know he wasn't with her. Surely Lois does, and me. You don't seem to care.'

'Why should I? I'm a selfish man. My friends are in the clear.'

'I see.' And she did. Chester had trusted her with someone else's secret in order to protect his lady's daughter. 'But,' she insisted, 'what you've told me exposes Oliver. He has no alibi – at least, Grace isn't his alibi. Is the implication then that his lover can alibi him?'

'I hadn't thought about it. You may be sure Laddow has. Perhaps his lover doesn't want his name brought into it.'

'I think Oliver is going to break down and tell the police the truth rather than face a charge of murder.'

'Probably.' He stood up. 'We'd better be getting down. Seven, Lois said.'

'For what?'

'There! And I was sent to ask you. You're invited to dine with us. I forgot in all the excitement.'

'Who sent you?'

171

'Why, Lois, of course. Grace told us you were up here.'

'How did you know where to meet me?'

'Grace said you'd gone after the owls and Lois said you'd be up in the old-growth under Pandora so I followed your tracks from her cabin and where you went up Porcupine, I cut up this slope to meet you. I don't want to hurry you but seven is when we eat . . . '

'This place is a madhouse,' Lois said as Miss Pink stepped in from the deck. 'Would you believe it, those two have disappeared. There's Grace gone down to the bar for a bottle of tequila, Chester went after her and now they're both missing. You stay here; I'm not letting you out of my sight. We're having lamb cassoulet. We have another half hour to go before we eat. Come and have a sherry.'

Miss Pink sat on a sofa beside Lovejoy, the cat, thinking what a cosy domestic scene they made.

'So you saw an owl,' Lois said, handing her a glass of Tio Pepe. 'Weren't you thrilled?'

'Delighted, and so was Chester. I feel it's a privilege to be on the Oregon coast and see a spotted owl.'

'It is a privilege. I have to go up there before Leo puts an embargo on further visiting.' Her eyes sparkled. 'And she hasn't even seen the bird. It's difficult though: this problem of disturbance; there's so little habitat left. How extensive would you say that old-growth is?'

'Two thousand acres perhaps. It's not all in one stand. You'll know the extent better than I.'

'It's a while since I was there – other than the day we did Pandora from Fin Whale Head with you – but thinking of how it looks from Cape Deception, I'd say that there's adequate space for one pair of owls. The old-growth extends over Pandora and down into Coon Gulch.'

'When were you last in there?'

Lois sipped her sherry. 'I can't remember. Probably when I was looking for phantom orchids, around July some time. I wonder where those owls came from. I didn't hear them that day.'

'You weren't up there the day Andy died?'

'My God!' Lois stared at her. 'You do throw things at a

person. You're serious too. You have to have a reason. No' – she was suddenly cool – 'I worked that day.'

'I thought I heard your voice.'

'Oh yes?'

'Of course I was mistaken. In the distance a light voice can sound like any woman. Covering almost the same route today, it all came back: a tree falling, people talking, a rockfall. No doubt everyone is a little on edge. And the owl: a strange day indeed; don't you feel there's a peculiar quality of magic in these forests when the fog comes in . . . ' She prattled on until there was a step on the deck and Chester appeared, carrying a bottle.

'Grace is coming along the road,' he told them. 'I came up the trail.'

'Why didn't— ' Lois stopped.

'She took the bike.' For a moment their eyes locked, then he went to the sideboard with the bottle. 'Fog's thick,' he said and, as if on cue, the fog horn boomed.

Lois rose and slid the glass panel shut. The cat stirred, re-arranged himself and went back to sleep. She sat down again and rubbed his head. She looked at Chester who had seated himself beside her with a glass of whisky. 'Grace is a long time,' she said.

'She could have stopped. Laddow and Hammett are wandering around, on foot.'

'So?'

'Laddow— ' he began, and checked. He looked across the table at Miss Pink. Lois was looking at her too.

'Laddow will be interested in the bike,' Miss Pink said.

In the silence that followed they heard, not one step, but a trampling along the deck, and Grace was there, with people behind her. She slid the glass aside and stepped into the room followed by Laddow and Hammett. Lois stood up: the gracious hostess. They accepted her invitation to sit down but they declined drinks.

'You own a folding bicycle, ma'am?' Laddow asked.

Grace had not sat down but stood, leaning against the sideboard, regarding him with faint contempt.

Lois said, 'My husband did. I mean, there is a bike, yes. He used it.'

'So it was a premeditated crime,' Hammett said, and Miss Pink winced as the horn moaned in the fog. 'He put the bike in the trunk of the Chevy,' he went on, 'and after he killed Gayleen he cycled back to the roadworks – and through them. He could go through them on a bike. How long did it take him to ride home?'

No one spoke. Chester stared at his knees, Grace looked at her mother as if she were on the verge of tears. 'Mom?' she whispered.

Lois said, 'He called me from Moon Shell. I took the Jeep and met him at the roadworks. I brought him home.'

'And then what happened?' probed Laddow. 'After he met you?'

'On the way back he told me he'd killed Gayleen.' Her shoulders slumped; she looked very tired. 'You can guess the rest.'

'You don't have to ask her any more questions,' Grace said savagely. 'Hell, she loved the guy but no way would she take him back after that! It was bad enough— '

'I suppose they have to hear it from me,' Lois interrupted gently. 'I told him he'd got to go. He asked where. What could I say?'

'You might have suggested that he give himself up to the police,' Laddow pointed out, and they looked at him in surprise. Miss Pink thought that such a course wouldn't have occurred to any of them.

'I didn't,' Lois said. 'I told him to take the Jeep and go. We argued – well, he argued, pleaded, but at last he did go: he walked out the front door and I didn't see him again.'

'He took the revolver?'

'I have no idea. I didn't ask him where it was, what he'd done with it; whether he had it with him or left it in the Chevy or had thrown it away. That was important – beside what he told me?' Her voice rose.

'What's all this got to do with Oliver?' Grace asked in a blatant attempt to change the subject, hysteria threading her words.

'Nothing, sweetie, Oliver's done nothing criminal.' Lois glanced at Miss Pink. 'Oregon is a liberal state.'

Laddow coughed, claiming her attention. 'Did your husband give you a reason for killing the girl?' he asked.

Lois answered at a tangent: 'I don't think that it was premeditated. I assumed that he needed the bike in town: to save gas and

174

so on, easier to park it than the Chevy. But they quarrelled; they were always quarrelling, he said; I mean, that weekend. Gayleen had got the wrong idea about me: she thought I was an alcoholic, with loose morals.' Chester moved restlessly and glanced at Grace. Lois was saying, 'He told her we were divorcing but when she got here she saw that none of it was true; she also realised that no way would Andy give up all this to marry her, which was what he'd promised. So she nagged him and Andy doesn't like being nagged. They were fighting all the way north until he pulled off the road and told her to start walking. It was pouring with rain by that time and she refused, so he got out to pull her case out of the trunk and she followed, shouting at him. The suitcase came open and he went back to the front of the car, took the revolver from the glove compartment, and shot her as she was stuffing her clothes back in the case. He said he went crazy.'

'When did he call you?'

'Presumably after he'd taken the bike out and put the body in the trunk.'

Hammett cleared his throat. 'When you met him at the road-works, ma'am, how was he dressed.'

'How was he *dressed*?' He didn't help her. She frowned and said slowly, 'Why, in the red helmet and rain gear— ' She stopped, bit her lip, then said quickly: 'But that doesn't mean it was premeditated. The bike was no good to him without the helmet and the other gear.'

'What time did he leave here?' Laddow asked.

'Late, we talked a long time – hours, it seemed.' Her eyes misted as she tried to remember, then life came back and she focused on the table. 'Perhaps people would like a little brandy, Grace.' It was transparent: it was she who needed a stimulant.

Chester leapt up, caught Grace's wrist forcing her to sit down, and himself went to the drinks on the sideboard.

'Would you turn the oven off, please?' Lois asked him. 'I'm sorry about this,' she said to Miss Pink.

Laddow waited until she had sipped some brandy and then he said, 'What do you think happened?'

'I don't know.'

Hammett said, 'It would have been very dark up there, a wet night in the forest.'

'Yes, it would.'

175

'Did he take a flashlight?'

'Oh, really!' Chester exclaimed, and Grace swore.

'I expect so.' Lois was listless. 'It'll be there on the landslide somewhere.'

'With the gun,' Laddow said. It wasn't a question. He glanced at Hammett. 'We'll need a statement, ma'am.'

Grace said angrily, 'Before she gives you a statement she'll speak to her attorney. Isn't that right, Mom?' Lois blinked at the girl who went on, regarding her intently, 'Andy was family, he was my step-father. There may be aspects of this – like insurance – that you have to be careful what you say. Take advice first.'

'I think she may be right.' Lois turned to Laddow. 'I'll be available tomorrow but you do see I have to speak to my attorney first. You do understand?'

'Yes, ma'am.' Laddow looked from her to her daughter. 'We understand.'

The police left but Lois insisted on Miss Pink's staying: 'I feel as if an enormous weight's been lifted off my shoulders,' she said. 'Such relief! Now it's all out in the open and we can have our friends around us and say what we like instead of always being on our guard.'

'Speak for yourself!' Grace was furious. 'Mom, you were crazy: covering up for a dead man, for God's sake!'

'That'll do, Grace,' Chester said firmly. 'Your mother needs some peace. Besides, you did your own bit of covering up.'

'That was different. Like Mom said: Oliver was doing nothing wrong.'

'Miriam wouldn't say that.'

Lois said. 'Darlings, if you'd dish up I want a word with Melinda.' She turned to Miss Pink. 'Why were the police interested in Miriam and Oliver?'

'Laddow was thinking in terms of collusion. And he was right: you could be termed an accessory – but a good lawyer should be able to cope with that. Since you haven't made a statement yet you'll probably be advised to say that at some point during that evening you did tell Andy to give himself up to the police.'

'That's right,' Grace called from the kitchen, 'you did; you just forgot to say.'

Chester was silent. Miss Pink went on, 'And it's a well-known ploy of the police to appear to concentrate on an innocent person

176

or persons in order to lull the guilty party – in your case, one with guilty knowledge – into a false sense of security.'

'I never had any security,' Lois said. 'Of course I was going to have to tell them because of Oliver. No way could we have had him suspected of murder.'

'And there was Miriam,' Grace called. 'She was hysterical today; even made me wonder if she would claim to have killed Gayleen herself to try to lure the police away from Oliver: more like zapping them over the head with a blunt instrument, I'd say. So it was all a trick on Laddow's part: make Mom own up because she knew who the murderer was. Cunning bastards!'

'What wine are you having, Lois?' Chester asked, standing at the open refrigerator.

'Look,' Lois said wildly, 'I changed my mind. Let's hold the meal back a bit longer, right? Go down to the Tattler, both of you, *please*. I have to sort something out.' Her voice was reedy, dangerous.

Grace came out of the kitchen protesting loudly but Chester, after one look at Lois, took the girl's arm and, with surprising strength, urged her through the room and out of the door, murmuring to her as they went.

'My God!' Lois leaned back on the sofa. 'I'm not trying to get rid of them but they're too susceptible for this.'

'For what?'

'It's – squalid. He was her step-father, like she said.'

'Which could make it worse.'

'The situation could be worse?'

'Grace could be more disturbed because he was family. If she felt contempt for Andy's sexual overtures the feeling could well be exacerbated by shock, even guilt, when he was killed.'

Lois stroked her forehead with fingers that were not quite steady. 'No one should have talked to you about our family business,' she said.

'I thought that was why you sent them down to the Tattler: you needed to speak about something that would embarrass them.'

'It would hardly embarrass Chester since he told you in the first place.'

Miss Pink turned amazed eyes on her. 'Chester would die sooner than betray your confidence – or Grace's. No; Andy's – pursuit – of Grace is known to your friends.'

'That's impossible. I only told Chester.'

'Andy talked.'

Lois sat with her hands pressed against her mouth, her eyes like flint. Suddenly they softened and she lowered her hands. 'The poor stupid guy,' she said. 'He had to boast even about trying to seduce his step-daughter!'

'Not altogether stable?' suggested Miss Pink. 'Insecure, obviously.'

'He was getting worse.' Lois was letting down her defences. 'He was like a little kid; he'd do anything to get attention, anything. You saw him in the Tattler; why, everything he did was designed to shock: his behaviour, what he said, his manners – or lack of them. There was a kind of – hectic desperation about him that last weekend: an impression that he was very close to the edge. I even . . . ' She trailed off.

'Yes?'

Lois was muttering, not looking at her. 'I *didn't* tell him to give himself up – not to the police. I did try to make him go to a psychiatrist. I had the feeling that it would sort of demonstrate that he was crazy, not only when he shot her, but afterwards. What I'm trying to say is, he was on the verge of a breakdown and that weekend, perhaps quarrelling with her as they drove north, his mind collapsed. A crazy man wouldn't give himself up to the police but he might be persuaded to unburden himself, unload everything in the lap of a psychiatrist like, in another age, a murderer would go to a priest. Am I talking sense?'

'Oh yes. What did he say to that?'

'There's no straight answer. We talked for hours that night. I was terribly shocked, of course, and I could see only that he had to have help but that I wasn't the one could give it. He wanted me, like a child needs its mother, but honestly, Melinda, I didn't reject him for negative reasons – God knows, I wanted to help – but because I'd just make it worse: his dependency. He was a little boy, he reverted to childhood: weeping, on his knees, imploring' – she covered her face with her hands – 'and then he would turn on me and say I had no feelings. I rejected him, if you can call it that, because what he needed was professional trained help. Drugs perhaps: tranquillisers to calm him down. What did he say? One moment he'd be sneering at me, saying I was the one needed a psychiatrist. A little later he was begging me to take him to Portland; he'd see someone next day.'

'Did he mention suicide?'

Lois thought about it. 'Not as such. He said there was nothing left for him if I turned him away, that he couldn't have a satisfactory relationship with anyone, his work was just a contrived goal . . . No, he didn't say he would shoot himself. He had before.'

'He had?'

'Yes, there was one time when we'd had a spat about something, probably when he made up the story about Grace trying to seduce him – that was to cover his own advances, of course – and I'd sent him packing, told him not to come back. He came back, and he had another story. This time it was that a child had gone missing from a campground on the coast – which was true – but that he was responsible. I said he'd do anything, say anything to attract attention. I told him I'd had enough of his morbid fantasies – he should put them in his screenplays. That was when he broke down, said they were all a joke, that he would kill himself if I threw him out. I thought he meant it, he was certainly very sick: making up these tales. So I allowed him to stay.'

Lois looked at Miss Pink, her face drained of expression, her eyes empty. 'I loved him,' she said. She scratched the back of Lovejoy's skull and went on without a change of tone: 'When this old cat came to me, he was a stray, probably thrown out of a car by a passer-by. He'd been trying to live in the forest but he'd had a fight with a racoon or something and he had a nasty abscess on his face so he'd got pretty tacky and mean. I took him in and cleaned him up and he got well again – and I'm responsible for him for the rest of my life. Do you understand?'

'I think I do,' Miss Pink said.

Chapter 16

At eleven o'clock the night was so black that only by the wheezing of the horn could one tell that the coast was blanketed by fog. That, and the fact that no light was visible from Quail Run. Miss Pink had drawn her curtains and was sitting by the stove, not reading despite the book on the arm of her chair. When the knock came at her window she was moving to rise before the caller spoke.

'Don't be alarmed; it's me, Chester.'

He stepped into the room. There was a tray with drinks and clean glasses on a coffee table. They sat down and she poured Scotch for him.

'Were you expecting me,' he asked drily, 'or the police?'

'You; possibly Grace.'

'She won't come. She's fighting hard to keep it in the family.'

'Does she condemn Lois?'

'Never; she's her mother.'

'And you?'

He had sounded frank; now a shutter came down over his eyes. 'What course could she take except to send him away? She'd never hand him over to the police.'

She said nothing and he stared at her, then turned his head as if his thoughts could be read in his eyes. 'What did she tell you?' he asked, unable to couch it less bluntly.

She sighed. 'She sent you and Grace to the Tattler.' It was a reproof.

His eyes narrowed. It was obvious the situation was alien to this courteous elderly fellow but he soldiered on gallantly. 'She'd tell you what she wouldn't tell her own family?'

'Because you *are* family.' She noted his insistence on the relationship. 'I'm impersonal, objective. More objective,' she corrected.

'If she told you, then she has to tell the police.'

'I think the police suspect. There's that long gap between her bringing him back to the house from the roadworks and her appearance at the Tattler; it must have been around three hours. She says they were talking all that time. I suppose it's feasible.'

'It's considerably more likely that they were talking than that they went together into the forest on a wet night – ' He watched her carefully, daring her to complete the sentence.

'Oh yes, much more likely that he went up there alone. That's what her lawyer will argue, of course. How could she persuade him to go with her, or he persuade her to go with him? Maybe,' she added thoughtfully, 'there are factors we don't know about.'

'You're saying she's keeping something back?'

'From what she did tell me, I'd say she's keeping a lot back.'

'Like what?'

'Andy's behaviour, his attempts to seduce Grace— '

He made a gesture of impatience. 'Load of rubbish. Grace says he never did, never could; he was scared stiff of her. She figures he was impotent – her words.'

'It's in character. Then there was the story about abducting the child from the campground – '

'What that woman's had to put up with! It's monstrous. Go on.'

'He'd threatened suicide before.'

'He would. Emotional blackmail.'

'You must have felt like getting rid of him yourself.'

'There were times I dreamed of it – seriously. And in my waking moments I considered how it might be worked, without being caught myself.'

She said nothing. Alerted by her lack of response, her stillness, he studied her and saw that she was waiting. His eyes brightened with a thought before he voiced it, carefully.

'The important thing,' he said, 'was not to get caught.'

'He's confessed,' Laddow said next morning. 'Now he'll bolt.'

'I doubt that.' Miss Pink filled his coffee cup. 'There's no point in confessing unless he's going to stay to take the rap.'

'Ha! So you got it.'

'His so-called confession proves it.' She sketched a smile. 'It's called chivalry. Chester is a gentleman.'

'And she's no lady. But she is, isn't she? She just couldn't take that son-of-a – excuse me, ma'am – '

'Rogue,' she supplied. 'But he was much more than that: he was mentally disturbed.'

'Tell me about it.'

The police had gone early to the Keller place, only to find that Lois was awaiting the arrival of her attorney from Portland and meanwhile would say nothing. Laddow, leaving Hammett with her, had walked along the lane to Quail Run, to be accosted en route by Chester who confessed to Andy's murder. Laddow had gone along with that and, to Chester's chagrin, sent him home with the assurance that he would follow shortly to take a statement. Laddow continued to Quail Run where Miss Pink received this latest news without surprise.

'She'll get off,' he said when he had heard the gist of the conversation after he left the Keller place last night, and had read between the lines. 'In fact, how can we prove it wasn't an accident? Violent deaths in backcountry areas are hell for investigators. It may have been an accident for all we'll ever know. What are you thinking? Ah, she's told Hoyle what really happened; must have done, otherwise why should he confess?'

'He could be panicking on her behalf, thinking that somewhere there is proof – or at least an indication – that Andy was pushed rather than he fell. Something she overlooked – or maybe she was seen.'

'On a stormy night? Who goes into the forest in the dark? No, her story will be that he announced his intention of killing himself and she followed, even went with him, trying to talk him out of it. You don't agree.'

'Oh yes, that's what her story will be, or something similar.'

The telephone rang. It was Hammett. She handed the receiver to Laddow and walked to the window. The fog shrouded everything and even her fuchsias were without colour. The fog horn sounded mournfully, reminding her that she had become so accustomed to it through the previous evening and the night that most of the time she no longer noticed it.

Behind her Laddow put down the telephone and said, 'The attorney hasn't arrived yet. Grace seems to have walked out.'

'And Lois?'

'She's there, or Hammett would have said.'

182

'What are you going to do?'

'There's nothing I can do. Just wait. She won't talk until the attorney arrives, if then.' She avoided his eyes and moved to the bookshelves. He frowned and asked suddenly, 'Who is her attorney?'

'I have no idea.'

He turned to the telephone and dialled a number. Hammett must have answered. 'Get the name and number of her attorney,' Laddow grated and, when Hammett came on the line again, scribbled on a pad. He cleared the line, dialled, waited, and grimaced. He turned to Miss Pink. There was no need to comment; the line was engaged. When he did get through, the people at the law office said that Mrs Keller hadn't been in contact with them. There was no attorney on his way to Sundown.

'Now why should she do that?' Laddow asked, but the question was rhetorical; he was already on his way to the door.

Leo and Sadie arrived, breathless, interrupting each other.

'What the hell's going on?' Leo demanded. 'She knows we can't stand the animal— '

'Which is why she said take it to Fleur— '

'Locke! We still had to take the thing in the car! And that fellow Hammett: why's he answering the phone? Why won't he put her on?'

'Who brought the cat?' Miss Pink asked.

'Why, Lois of course. The note said so: "Please take Lovejoy to Fleur. Thanks. Lois," is what it said— '

' —and there it was: screaming its ugly head off; that's how we knew it was there: at our gate, in a basket thing, and tearing it to bits. We thought it had to go to the veterinarian in Salmon, guessed it could be for an operation – terminal injection, if I had my way. So we took it down to Fleur like the note said, and she knew nothing about it! She put the thing in a shed and then we tried to reach Lois. Hammett answered and told us Lois said not to come up. What's going on?'

She told them about Chester's 'confession' and how that pointed the finger at Lois. They were flabbergasted. 'I suspect,' she said, 'that the cat was dropped off because Lois is anticipating being taken to Portland— '

'Arrested?' Leo growled. 'But she'll be allowed bail!'

'They can't hold her,' Sadie protested. 'She has to get an attorney. Why doesn't she?'

'How did she get the cat to your place?' Miss Pink asked, and they stared at her, bewildered. 'Hammett wouldn't let her out of his sight,' she explained. 'I suppose that's where Grace went: to deliver Lovejoy to you.'

'That's not important,' Sadie said. 'I think we should go visit Chester. If he's all on his own up there, stewing over Lois, he needs company, poor man.'

'Particularly when he's made such a noble gesture,' Leo said drily. 'That was a stupid move if ever there was one.'

'I don't think it's of much consequence,' Miss Pink said. 'All it means is that Grace and Chester came back from the Tattler last night and Lois told them the truth – or rather, she told them the same story that her attorney will use in her defence.'

'What's the difference?' demanded Leo. 'Oh, I see: you mean the did-he-fall-or-was-he-pushed question? No sweat. He fell. We all know that.' She glared from Sadie to Miss Pink.

'Of course, dear,' Sadie said quickly.

Chester was not at his house and the place appeared to be abandoned, which was curious, because Laddow had sent him home less than an hour ago. But all the windows were closed and the doors locked, including that of the garage. Leo peered through a window and said that his car had gone.

They were worried. Leo drove them back to Quail Run and Miss Pink went to the telephone. When Hammett came on the line she told him that Chester had locked his house and left. He asked her to hold the line, and Laddow came on. She repeated the information. He said – and not, she thought, spontaneously, 'Yes, Miss Ferguson has also gone. No doubt they went together.'

After a moment she said weakly, 'I thought you ought to know.'

'I'll tell her,' he said. 'We were working on collusion all along,' and put down the receiver.

'What did he say?' Sadie urged, seeing her surprise.

'He had to be speaking for Lois's benefit,' she said slowly. 'But he must read her her rights . . . I see, a ploy to make her confess? Can he do that?'

'What ploy?' Leo asked.

'He's suggesting that Grace and Chester are in collusion. Apparently they left together.'

'Someone is acting in collusion,' Sadie said. 'Else how did that cat come to be dumped at our gate? Lois couldn't have done it because you say Hammett wouldn't let her out of his sight, so it had to be Grace. They must have communicated under Hammett's nose, probably passing notes in the kitchen.'

'Or they discussed contingency plans last night,' Miss Pink said.

'You're making them sound like criminals!' Leo stamped across to the window and glared at the fog. 'I tell you: Andy Keller *fell* down the slide.'

'I don't think anyone can prove otherwise,' Sadie murmured, and Miss Pink suggested coffee before Leo could retaliate.

There was nothing they could do. It was obvious that Sadie and Leo didn't want to leave Miss Pink, and there was no question of going for a walk when one of their circle was in danger of arrest – because whatever Leo maintained, they knew that the police were deeply suspicious, the more so because Lois had lied about her attorney – and then there was Chester's blunder.

'I wonder how he said he did it,' Leo mused, pacing the room, a mug of coffee in one hand.

'Laddow didn't say,' responded Miss Pink. 'I had the impression that the only interest Chester's confession held for the police was merely the fact of it, not the details, if there were any.'

'But,' Sadie said, 'if there were details, you'd expect them to be correct, only Chester had put himself in Lois's place.'

Leo stopped pacing and turned, her coffee slopping. 'What details?'

At the same time Miss Pink was saying, 'It could be that Laddow was more concerned to get to me and discover what we'd talked about last evening after the police left.'

'This isn't getting us' – Leo began angrily, but the telephone was ringing – 'anywhere.' She ended on a subdued note. They all stared at the telephone.

Miss Pink lifted the receiver and listened. The others heard a barked question. 'No,' she said, turning as if she could see through the front door, glancing at the fog beyond the deck. 'No, we haven't seen her . . . yes, I'll call you; where will you— ' She replaced the receiver. 'Cut me off,' she said wryly. 'Now Lois has disappeared.'

After a moment Leo asked, 'How? If the police were there?'

'Why?' Sadie asked.

'He didn't say. The bathroom window probably. It's traditional, isn't it?' Miss Pink sounded listless.

'She'll need a car to get away,' Sadie said. 'Maybe she took the Jeep.'

'There's Grace's car too.' Leo looked at Miss Pink. 'Or did Grace and Chester take both cars? We don't know much, do we?'

That situation didn't last. In a few moments Hammett was there, glancing round sharply as he was admitted. Miss Pink's surmise had been correct: Lois had left by way of a bathroom window, which had not been screened. He saw their expressions and his lips thinned.

'The screen was leaning against the wall on the outside of the house,' he told them.

'You can't remove screens from the inside,' Leo said.

'It was done before we got there this morning.'

'Are you trying to tell us she knew in advance that she— '

'Shut up, Brant!' It was quick, hard and so out of character that Leo stared at Sadie in amazement.

'Did she take a car?' Miss Pink asked.

'No, ma'am, nor did the girl; the only car missing is Chester Hoyle's.'

'So they've all gone together,' Sadie said when Hammett had left. 'And he just called in to make sure Lois wasn't here with us. Fat chance. They picked her up somewhere outside the village.' She glanced at the window. 'The fog's on their side.'

Miss Pink said nothing. They looked at her, at each other, and then they poured themselves more coffee.

In the afternoon the fog cleared and some tourists walking to Fin Whale Head found an expensive parka and a pair of safari boots on the wet sand. Under the boots was a sealed envelope with an inscription asking the finder to contact the police. Laddow found Miss Pink in her garden and showed her the note that had been in the envelope. Signed by Lois it said nothing more than that her Will was with the law firm that she had failed to contact that morning. It was a simple Will, Laddow said: she had left everything, including her house, to Grace.

He was confused and angry. 'Why?' he exclaimed. 'Why did she have to do it? We have no proof, and the guy was a psychopath anyway. She'd have got off.'

'You were keeping a pretty close watch on her.'

'We had to have a statement, that's all. I couldn't close the case on Gayleen without her evidence. Andy had confessed to her and I needed that in writing. Now she goes and drowns herself – and I thought she was an intelligent woman! It's going to break her daughter – unless – '

But Miss Pink was leading the way to her deck which was steaming in the sunshine. She brought cushions from the living-room, glasses and a pitcher of lemonade. 'Unless what?' she asked as she sat down.

He eyed her steadily. 'We wondered: did Chester get cold feet – like she had pushed one partner over the edge, did he think murder was an occupational hazard of being married to Lois?'

'And Grace?'

'Maybe she didn't like the idea of hanging around her mom neither. Maybe there was something between those two: Grace and Chester.' He saw her scepticism and went on, 'They drove off and left Lois facing a murder charge . . . ' He ignored her raised eyebrows, 'She has to have told them the truth, else why did Chester claim he did it? There wasn't any *need* unless he knew it was murder.'

Someone was mounting the front steps. Hammett came round the corner of the house and placed a key on the table. Laddow didn't touch it. Miss Pink asked Hammett to sit down and she brought another glass.

'There may be something in the house could tell us more,' Laddow said, eyeing the key. 'Hammett's closed up the place and we can't do anything until Grace comes back, if she comes back. This is a very unsatisfactory business all round. Here we got three deaths and not one statement: Gayleen's killed by Andy: Lois kills him, then herself. Case closed.'

Hammett nodded glumly. Miss Pink stared at the dancing water. Laddow's face was a mask of bewilderment. 'There was no proof,' he repeated and then, becoming aware of her silence, he turned on Miss Pink. 'Was there?' he asked, and Hammett stared.

'The proof is there in her – suicide,' she said and, seeing their confusion deepen, she went on, 'You put the cart before the horse: theories first and then working out how the actions fit although' – as Laddow stirred impatiently – 'I had the advantage of you. I heard Andy fall.'

'Oh, come on,' he began, 'you were –' He glanced at Hammett.

'You were in the Tattler,' Hammett said. 'All evening, unless you're suggesting you could have heard a rock fall as you were going home. Is that it?'

'He fell just after lunch that day.'

'Yes, of course.' Laddow was deflated. 'You were up there. Did you see him fall?' he asked without interest.

'No. I heard the rocks go down. Before that I heard voices.'

They said nothing. Their expressions were resigned, under-standing; the whole thing was an anti-climax. She saw that but she continued, 'Then Lois ran down to her house, picked up Gayleen, drove to Moon Shell Beach, shot the girl and cycled back.' Laddow and Hammett exchanged looks. 'If she drowned herself,' she went on, 'it was because of Gayleen, not Andy. She'd find good reason for killing him, but Gayleen was a different matter.'

'It was indeed.' Laddow was silky. 'So why did she have to kill Gayleen at all?'

'Because Gayleen knew she had been in the forest; she could have been looking for her hostess and discovered that Andy was missing as well. When Lois did return, with some story about Andy having been called away that morning but that she, Lois, had to go to Portland and would give Gayleen a lift, the girl would go along with that. Lois is probably telling the truth when she says Gayleen was in awe not only of her but the whole situation. However, if Andy's body were discovered – and there didn't have to be a bullet in the skull – even Gayleen's simple mind would connect where it was found with Lois coming down out of the forest and, of course, the lies Lois had to tell in order to get Gayleen to leave. Andy hadn't been called away: he was dead all the time. The girl had to be killed to silence her.'

'You *are* ingenious,' Laddow said admiringly. 'You should be writing crime stories –' and then was disconcerted as he remembered that Lois Keller was a writer of crime stories. He pulled himself together and continued coldly, 'And you're going to tell us that a woman who kills her husband – in a quarrel? –

188

and kills a second time to silence a potential witness, that this cold-blooded killer is so overcome with remorse she walks into the ocean and drowns herself?'

'I'm not saying that. For one thing Andy's murder could have been premeditated, but I think it would be in the form of an execution. If his body wasn't so battered the pathologist might have found a bullet track—'

Laddow was holding up his hand. 'And how did she convince him to go up there in the first place?'

'That man would seize any chance to annoy people. She had only to say that she was going for a hike for him to propose himself as company. He wouldn't need any persuading, merely an indication that she would prefer to be alone. The revolver,' she added, 'if one was used, would have been in her rucksack.'

'And where is it now?'

'Like the Stetson: where you'll never find it. The hat will have been burned; the revolver will be on the bed of a river, or down a deep hole.'

'May one ask' – elaborately polite – 'what the motive was? I mean' – and now the sarcasm was honed – 'for Andy's murder?'

'Didn't you see the bumper sticker that he had put on the Chevrolet?'

'Bumper sticker?'

'You remember,' Hammett prompted. 'The addict – the car thief – rubbed dirt on it because it was conspicuous? It said, "I Love Spotted Owls. Roasted".'

Laddow said nothing but his eyes were furious.

'That could have been the final straw,' she said. 'Not so much the content of the statement but that he should have come here with that sticker on his wife's car. It was showing what he thought of her beliefs – and it was self-destructive. Lois is a wilderness person; she puts animals before people.'

'Was a wilderness person,' Laddow murmured. 'You got the wrong tense.'

'Did I?'

They studied her face. At length Laddow remarked, 'You're not on her side, are you?'

'I'm not on anyone's side. I'm just telling you what happened.'

'You built a whole scenario on one shaky occurrence. You heard voices before the rocks fell so you decided those were the voices of Andy and Lois. You're saying she shot him and knocked down some rocks to finish the job or cover the body, or both. Why didn't you hear the sound of the shot?'

She shrugged. 'She might have pushed him. If she did use the revolver – muffled by the fog – it could have sounded like a branch snapping or the start of a stonefall— '

The men exchanged looks and this had the effect of checking her. She could have gone on to say that Forensics might find one of Lois's hairs inside the red cycling helmet. The Stetson would have been burned but had she thought to destroy the helmet? She could suggest that they might learn a lot from observing the behaviour of Chester and Grace when they returned. She knew now that they would return. She said nothing; she would let events take their course.

The news was on local television that evening. She waited for her telephone to ring but she learned later that it was the Surfbird that Grace called, asking to speak to Laddow. The identity of the owner of the abandoned parka and boots hadn't been named on television but he told Grace what she expected to hear. Chester came on the line then and Laddow said that he had no further information. No body had been found. When might the two of them be expected to return? They were in Eugene, Chester said; they would return tomorrow. All this was relayed to the rest of Sundown as a matter of course by Mabel Sykes.

Chester and Grace returned the next morning, having had a night to get over the first ghastly shock, as Fleur put it to Miss Pink, who had gone down to the gallery in a deliberate attempt to avoid the police and the residents on the loop road.

The fog had rolled away as the sun gained strength, and the air was exquisite: washed and sparkling, the stacks reared above their own shadows on the peacock water. Fleur looked and shuddered.

'Horrible,' she said, 'to think of her out there, drifting on a current. Death is so appallingly sudden.'

'It was for Gayleen too.'

Fleur accepted this in the same vein as anyone else in the community would. Miss Pink had not, and never would, voice her own theories. Whether or not the police laid any credence on these, they would keep quiet too, for obvious reasons. When

190

Lois's parka and boots were found on the sand the case was closed.

'Gayleen was different,' Fleur said. 'She was born prey: with those looks and that immaturity – like Marilyn Monroe when you come to think of it. But Lois was a survivor. How can I say that? It's a contradiction in terms.' And she stared moodily at the sea.

It was quiet in the sitting-room. Miss Pink looked around casually. 'What have you done with Lovejoy?'

'I had to let him out of the shed, he was making such a din. He hadn't touched his food and as soon as I opened the door he streaked round the front of the house and presumably straight back to the Keller place. He adored Lois.'

That Christmas Fleur sent a letter to Cornwall with her greetings card. Miss Pink, ensconced in her cosy drawing-room at ten o'clock one morning, lamps throwing pools of light in the gloom, an opaque wall outside the windows and the fog horn moaning, was transported back to that other barbaric coast on a different ocean, visualising as she read, the stacks and the headlands, the timbered range and the houses clinging to the lower slopes above the cove like nests of migrant birds.

. . . they sold both houses [Fleur wrote]. I guess they couldn't stand the memories. You know they never found the body? How could either of them walk the shore again not knowing what they might come on in a crevice, washed up by the tide?

Grace has to be a very wealthy woman now; the house sold for close on a million, all the land and the cabin up back, and Lois died worth several more millions. Then there's her royalties – all to go to Grace. I was surprised actually. I understood she always meant to expand her business, even start a chain of boutiques, but she hasn't yet and I was in the Portland store and her manageress said there were no plans. Grace herself was somewhere on holiday in the Caribbean so I didn't get to talk to her, and of course she doesn't come to Sundown any more. There's nothing here for her.

When Chester sold up he disappeared. Said he was putting all his possessions in store and just taking off. He bought a pick-up and put one of those camper shells on the back –

you know the kind: only room for one guy – oh yes, and a cat. You remember Lovejoy, Lois's cat I took in the night she drowned? Chester adopted the animal and took him on his travels. That reminds me of an odd coincidence. Jason says Mabel heard a rumour that Chester had been seen in Yucatan or Belize or somewhere – or maybe it was Oliver was down there. Oliver writes to me by the way; he left Sundown and took up with the widow of a Texas oil man. It had to be Oliver; he said there was this guy he glimpsed in a street in some little fishing village, just walked past the café Oliver was in, looked like Chester, but then Chester wasn't remarkable to look at, must be hundreds like him. Anyway it couldn't have been him because he was with a woman. In fact they looked so ordinary that Oliver would never have noticed them at all, just a couple of American tourists, except the woman had a black and white cat draped over her shoulder. It made a pretty story, Oliver writes well . . .

Miss Pink sighed and put down the letter. The fog horn boomed. She wished it had not been necessary to kill Gayleen but then, as Fleur had said, Gayleen was not a survivor; her tragedy was that sooner or later she was going to come up against one, and when she did, it had to be Lois. She suspected that they were quite happy – in Belize or Yucatan – or wherever in the world they established territory.